LIQUID

COMFORT

~A SURF STORY~

By: Cheryl Lee Petro

ISBN-13: 978-1466216310
ISBN-10: 146621631X

Dedicated to Steven St Jean
(AKA: The Real Brady)
for being one of my favorite friends
and reading my novel first.
☺

Author's Note

A "haole" in love with the islands of Hawaii, I visit the island of Oahu regularly, spending most of my time on the North Shore. Only there do I feel truly at home. Although I am not a local, the spirit of Aloha lives in my heart and soul and will remain there forever. After learning to surf at Waikiki when I was eight years old, I developed an infatuation for the sport. It has since become one of my greatest passions.

Acknowledgements

I would like to thank my editor, Jane Haertel, for a book that is shiny and fresh and for teaching me more about the fundamentals of writing. Tammy Selinger-Grant and Chris Rathbun for your time spent visiting and revisiting the pages of this book. And Sarah McPike, for pointing out my bad puns (single-handedly haha).

Sean Tyler Foley, thank you so much for the inexpensive airline tickets that made it possible for me to finish the rest of my research. This book would have never been the same without our grand adventure, walking in Travis's shoes.

For giving Liquid Comfort a taste of authentic Pidgin language, I *absolutely* must thank my friend (Molokai Local) Azariah Pailaka Torres-Umi. I don't pretend to speak Pidgin English, so without his awesome—and promptly returned—translations, Kimo and friends may never have said things like "Shootz" or "Grind". ***MAHALO AZA!***

Also a BIG thank you to:

*Cindy May from ASP International for answering my questions regarding the world championship tour. You were a huge help and I am so very grateful for your time.

*Jerry Balaker (North Shore Lifeguard/Surfer), Neal Miyake (Oahu Surf Photojournalist), Bryce VanDuisen (North Shore Surfer), Casey R Ching (North Shore Surfer) and Andy Tamasese (Hawaii Local/Friend) for your extensive knowledge concerning the North Shore. My frequent trips to the island were not enough to know all there is to know. Therefore, your help regarding O'ahu's surf breaks, local customs, and Hawaiian wave measurements was—and will forever be—very much appreciated.

*Ely (Oahu's best criminal attorney), Nicole, Greg, and Uncle Tim for being open and willing to share your experiences regarding some of the issues I have addressed, such as drug addiction, amputation, legal systems, and criminal consequences.

*Rob McIntyre for taking me to the island in 2005, Dave Mutch, Steve St Jean, and Jayson Shmyrko for putting up with my "Travis talk", and the rest of my friends for all the encouragement.

Above all, *MAHALO* to you for reading my book!

For more information on *Liquid Comfort* or to leave a suggestion/review and check out my other books, please visit: **www.cherylleepetro.com**

A Note on Wave Measurement

In Hawaii, waves are measured from the back. This often causes confusion as most other places measure from the front. "Hawaiian scale" roughly translates to around half of the wave face height. Thus, a three-foot Hawaiian scale wave has a six-foot face. This rule, however, may very well be old style by the time this book is published. I have tried my best to account for this and make my measurements understandable to the reader.

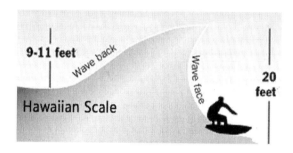

A Note on Pidgin English

Pidgin English is a creole language based in part on English and used by many "local" residents of Hawaii. Also known as a street slang, Pidgin English (or simply Pidgin) is a dialogue evolved from mixing ethnicities on the island. It is influenced by many languages including: Portuguese, Hawaiian, Cantonese, Japanese and more. My good friend and Molokai local, Azariah Torres-Umi, graciously supplied all of my Pidgin dialogue for true, Hawaiian authenticity.

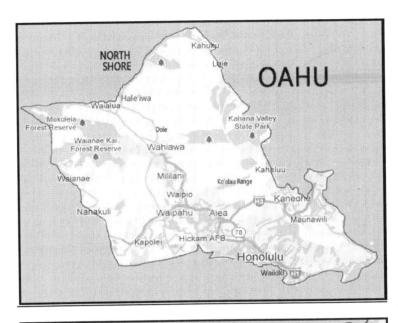

OAHU

NORTH SHORE

Kahuku
Laie
Hale'iwa
Waialua
Mokuleia Forest Reserve
Waianae Kai Forest Reserve
Dole
Kahana Valley State Park
Wahiawa
Waianae
Mililani
Ko'olau Range
Kahaluu
Waipio
Kaneohe
Nanakuli
Waipahu
Aiea
Maunawili
Kapolei
Hickam AFB
78
Honolulu
Waikiki

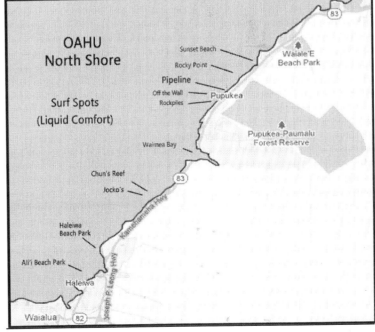

OAHU
North Shore

Surf Spots
(Liquid Comfort)

83
Sunset Beach
Waiale'E Beach Park
Rocky Point
Pipeline
Off the Wall
Pupukea
Rockpiles
Pupukea-Paumalu Forest Reserve
Waimea Bay
Chun's Reef
83
Jocko's
Kamehameha Hwy
Haleiwa Beach Park
Ali'i Beach Park
Joseph P. Leong Hwy
Haleiwa
Waialua
82

Local Hawaiian Surf Slang & Pidgin Terms:

Brah	*Bro, buddy*
Break	*Surf spot (where the waves break)*
Channel	*A channel of deeper water where excess water, piled up by waves, flows out to sea (makes it easier to get out to surf breaks)*
Fo	*To (Pidgin English term)*
For why	*What for?*
Glassy/oil glass	*Smooth surf, no wind, causing the water surface to look like glass*
Grind/s	*To eat/food*
Grom/Grommet	*Young surfer just starting out*
Gun	*Longer/thinner surfboard designed for speed/big waves*
Haole	*White person, foreigner (often meant as an insult)*
Hapai	*Hawaiian for "pregnant"*
Howzit	*How are you?*
In, Inside	*Toward the shore, between the break and the shore*
Kay den	*Okay then*
Kook	*Jerk, idiot*
Lanai	*Porch/patio*
Like Beef?	*Wanna fight?*
Local(s)	*Long-time regulars at a surf spot or area. In Hawaii, the brown skinned native speakers of Pidgin English*

Mahalo	*Hawaiian for "thank you"*
Ohana	*Hawaiian for "family"*
Out, Outside	*Away from the shore, beyond the break*
Pareo	*A sarong or wrapped skirt*
Pau	*Done. Finished.*
Peak	*The spot where a wave first starts to break*
Pro Ho	*Girl that only dates pros*
Pidgin English	*A creole language based in part on English and used by many "locals" and residents of Hawaii*
Pipe-board	*A narrow, fast, custom made surfboard specifically designed for riding at Pipeline.*
Rubber Slippers	*Flip-flops (or rubbah slippahs)*
Shave Ice	*An ice-based dessert, much like a snow-cone, however the ice is finer so it absorbs the syrups*
Shaka	*Hawaiian hand gesture with many meanings: hello, goodbye, thanks, no worries, "hang loose"*
Shoots	*Kay den, All right!*
Sick	*Awesome/cool*
Soup	*White foam of the waves*
Try	*Please (Try wait = please wait)*
Up himself	*Cocky, arrogant (Aussie slang)*
Was da haps	*What's going on?*

~An Unexpected Wave~

An enormous wave spun over his head, a perfect aquamarine barrel. The ocean roared, spitting out a salty spray. Shaking droplets from his face, Travis grabbed the rail of his surfboard and tucked his body as low as he could. As he sliced through the liquid cavern, he caught a glimpse of blue sky, an opening ahead. He pumped his board for speed, but his exit started to shrink.

Muscles tensed, he braced himself, waiting for the inevitable wipeout. The wave trembled and tightened, threatening to collapse right on top of him. Then it spewed him out instead.

"Yeaaah!" Travis flew out of the tube, pumping his fist in the air as cheers rang out from the beach. That'd be a high score for sure!

He spun his board around. He could feel each second passing. Only a few minutes remained in the Hawaiian Bonzai Classic, the last competition on the surfing world tour. It was the final heat. All he needed was a few more points in the ratings and he'd be number one. *The top surfer in the world.*

Taking long, deep strokes, he drove himself back toward the oncoming swell. His lungs burned from the effort and his arms felt like lead, but he smiled, his heart lifting with the challenge.

Pipeline—or better known as Pipe—was his local surf break. He'd grown up on these waves. The shallow water didn't scare him. Nor did the sharp lava or deadly caves. The thrill of sliding down a twenty-foot face, conquering the heaviest surf in the world, was worth any torment the ocean could bring him.

He glanced over and saw his rival, Kane, drop down a massive, blue wall. The reigning champion made a flawless descent, but when he reached the bottom and tried to cut back, his board shot out from underneath him.

Yes! Travis smiled as his adversary got sucked over the falls and locked into the wave. Then he cringed. He knew what it felt like to be dragged under the churning surf and whipped around like a rag doll.

He pressed his fingers over the nasty wound he'd received while practicing for the contest a few days earlier. A jagged scab ran across his right shoulder. Soft from being in the water all day, it oozed a bit of blood.

Pipe had some nasty reef. Travis had the scars to prove it.

He swallowed hard. *No fear.*

When Kane resurfaced, Travis let out a breath and paddled even harder, stopping only when he reached the perfect spot, behind the waves and out of the impact zone. Squinting against the sun, he glanced toward shore to the judges' stand, the sponsors' houses and colorful tents. A sea of spectators covered the sand—all of them waiting to see what he'd do next. Somewhere in that crowd sat his father. Travis couldn't let him down.

He scanned the horizon. A dark swell formed in the distance and moved closer. The wave was beautiful—big and clean, like oiled glass—but he let it pass. The sets had been fairly consistent so far, with the second wave being the better choice, so he got into position and waited for it.

Something slammed into him—a jarring impact. It knocked him off his board and into the water. Sputtering, he broke the surface and spun about, searching the area around him.

Nothing. "What the hell?"

His surfboard popped up next to him and he reached for it. Then came a blur of gray.

A brutal strike hit his right side and dragged him under the water again. A sharp pressure tugged at him.

He struggled to break free and came up choking on salt. A pool of red swirled around him. *Blood.*

He screamed, "Shark!" and ended up with a mouthful of the ocean. Panicked, he scanned the area, seeking the giant fish. Thick, ruby fluid colored the water; confusion clouded his senses. His arms paddled frantically, yet he could barely keep his head above the surface.

Why couldn't he swim?

His board swung toward him and he grabbed hold of it, struggling to pull himself on top. Something was wrong with his right arm. He couldn't feel it. He caught a glimpse of a red fleshy stump, blood gushing from the shredded remains, and he forced his eyes away. It wasn't real. This wasn't happening.

Dizziness overwhelmed him as he swayed back and forth in the surf. He heard the hum of a Jet Ski and a loud shout as someone pulled him onto a rescue board. His vision blurred and the horizon faded. His eyes grew heavy…

"Oh, God!" a voice cried out in the distance.

Sand scratched Travis's back as he lay on the shore. A mask covered his mouth, and as he breathed the oxygen deeply, his mind cleared for a moment. With a raspy voice, he sputtered, "My arm."

He felt a sharp yank and a quick jerk. On his right side,

a paramedic worked fast, applying a tourniquet. Foghorns blasted out shark warnings. The noise made his head spin. He could hear himself groaning, yet he still couldn't feel any pain.

"Hang in there," someone pleaded, as everything faded to black.

~A Load of Crap~

With a jolt, Travis sat up in bed. Beads of sweat covered his forehead, and his heart raced wildly. *Another nightmare.* Images hung at the edge of his mind: black murky water, an ominous gray fin, a giant mouth with blood-stained teeth.

Disoriented, he looked around in the dark. His old bedroom. His father's house. He'd totally forgotten where he was.

With the back of his hand, he wiped the sweat from his brow and a pain shot through his right arm—the arm that wasn't there. Teeth clenched, he turned on his lamp and glared at his stump. Smooth, mended skin stared back at him; the incision scar was still a bit red in places.

Hideous thing. He cast his eyes away.

A cup of water sat on his bedside table. He took a long sip and massaged the stub of his arm.

Eleven months. Had it really been so long? It seemed like only yesterday he'd woken up in recovery, doped up and dazed, strapped to an IV with bandages covering half of his right side. Bouquets of flowers filled the room, the aroma overwhelming.

"What's this?" he'd muttered. "I can still surf, right?" It was all that mattered to him.

A surgeon stood next to the hospital bed. With a grave frown, he bent down to explain, "The shark took your hand at the wrist, but the bone was so badly crushed we needed to amputate at the elbow."

"But it wasn't real. I couldn't feel it."

"Your body went into shock from the trauma. That's why you didn't feel any pain. I'm sorry, but your arm is gone."

Travis could still hear the regret in the doctor's voice. He had let himself cry then. But *only* then.

Another spasm ran across his shoulder. Whimpering softly, he grabbed a bottle of pills from his drawer and snapped the lid off with his teeth. He popped one of the tablets into his mouth and swallowed hard.

"They should've just let me die."

The words echoed through his bedroom, and as he settled back down, he prayed for the painkiller to kick in. Through a gap in his window, he could hear the ocean lapping gently against the rocky beach at the edge of his father's property. It was a sound he hadn't heard in a long time. No wonder his nightmares were back.

Downstairs, someone pounded on the door. Travis lifted his head to listen. His clock read two in the morning, which could only mean one thing. *Devin.*

Feet barely ruffling the carpet, he crept out of bed, crossed the hall, and peered over the second floor railing. In the living room below, his father, Carl, hurried towards the front entrance. Fingers fumbling, he tied up his robe and twisted the deadbolt. The door flew open, and Travis's older brother charged inside. His ex-girlfriend followed him.

Devin whipped around to face the girl. "Damn it, Lea! 'Nuff already. Why can't you jus' leave me alone?"

Lea stopped in the foyer with her hands on her hips, chestnut hair still swinging. "Why should I? She's your daughter too!"

"What's going on?" Carl stepped between them.

"I'm sorry, Carl, but your son is being an *ass.*" Lea hissed the words in Devin's direction.

Leaning further over the railing, Travis watched his brother stumble into the living room. Carl grabbed him by the arm. "Where do you think you're going?" He turned to Lea. "What'd he do now?"

Lea's voice quivered as she replied, "He owes me eight months of child support, and last week Allisa had an infected tooth, but I couldn't afford the dentist bill because *he* won't take care of *his own* daughter."

Devin laughed. "Go home already, you dumb…"

"Devin, that's enough!" Carl's voice bellowed through the house. He put a reassuring hand on Lea's shoulder. "I'll give you the money you need." He disappeared for a minute and came back with a check in his hand.

"Thanks, Carl." Lea took the piece of paper and put it in her pocket. "I really am sorry for all this."

Devin scoffed at her. "Whatever. If you were *so sorry* you wouldn't be taking the money."

Carl smacked him on the side of the head, and Travis clenched his fist. *Money.* That was the reason Devin had come. The thought left a foul taste in his mouth.

The front door clicked shut, and as Lea left sobbing, Travis grabbed the banister, squeezing it tightly. She was his friend, and it sucked to see her so upset. The urge to follow was overwhelming. He wanted to apologize for his brother's behavior. But he held back. If he went down the stairs now, Devin would see him, and that was the last thing he wanted. He pressed his mouth shut and tucked himself behind a tall, potted dracaenas plant.

Downstairs, his father raged on. "You should be taking care of that little girl, Devin. She's your responsibility. And why haven't you come to visit your brother? You haven't seen him since the hospital, and even then he was sleeping."

Devin put his hand on the doorknob. "Ain't my fault you sent him to the mainland."

"I didn't *send* him anywhere. He chose to go to get away from the reporters. He's been home for two weeks now. Two weeks, and you have yet to come see him."

"I'll come tomorrow," Devin mumbled.

As Travis turned away from the scene, every muscle in his body tensed. What a load of crap. Devin wouldn't come.

Back in his room the shadows surrounded him. His father's words rang true. The last time he could remember seeing his brother, was before the shark attack. Before he'd lost his arm. And during the ten months he had stayed with his grandmother in California, Devin had called him once. He'd barely even mentioned the attack.

Travis considered marching downstairs to give his older sibling a piece of his mind, but he slumped back down on the bed instead. *Screw Devin!*

He stared into the pitch-black room; not even the moonlight could find its way in. That's how it had been ever since his return. He made sure his curtains stayed shut. His room had a great view of the North Shore of O'ahu, and if he looked outside, he would see the ocean with its tremendous whitecaps. He much preferred the dark.

The front door slammed and Devin's car fired up.

Travis buried his head under the pillow. "Nice to see you too, bro."

~Worthless~

The morning sun shone through the window, illuminating an old family portrait that hung on the wall. In it, Carl stood by a beautiful petite woman. *Victoria*, his late wife. Reddish blonde hair spilled over her shoulders, light blue eyes sparkled with happiness, and freckles sprinkled her nose.

On her lap sat Travis as a toddler. His blonde curly locks could never be tamed; they stuck out every direction. And next to her, stood Devin at five years old. He had his mother's freckles back then, and was always smiling. They all were. Joyful faces in a happier time.

A shadow of grief touched his heart, and Carl turned away. He clutched the telephone with angry fingers. "Are you coming over today, or not?"

"Can't," Devin answered. "My car's makin' funny noises. I gotta wait till Jonny can look at it. Plus, I got a killer headache."

"Is that because you're hungover? I knew you were going to do this, Dev."

"Whatevahs. I'll come by tomorrow."

Carl tightened his grip on the phone. "Don't say that unless you mean it. I don't want to get his hopes up."

"Travis is a big boy, ya know. He's almost twenty-two."

"He needs his *brother*."

When there was no response, Carl slammed his fist on the counter. "How dare you show up last night, wasted, at two in the morning! Do you know how much money I had to dish out? Well, don't worry about my bank account, Devin, because this time I'm taking it out of yours."

"What? Tha's my money!"

"And she's also *your* daughter. Why should I have to pay because you refuse to take care of your own child?"

"It's my money," Devin stated again. "Mom left it to me."

"Not until you're twenty-five."

"Tha's in six months."

"Yeah, and I dread the day. God only knows what you're going to spend it on. Perhaps I should spend it for you."

The other line clicked as Devin hung up the phone, and Carl paced the kitchen floor, mumbling to himself.

"Too drugged up to care about his daughter, but never too drugged up to care about his finances." He ran a hand through his hair and let out a breath.

Travis stepped into the room and opened one of the cupboards. "I take it Devin's not coming." He took out a mug and poured himself some coffee. "Nice of him to show up last night though."

Carl noted the sarcasm and studied his son. Travis rarely got out of bed, yet it looked as if he hadn't slept in months. Dark bags hovered under his eyes. Long blond hair drooped in his face.

He tried an encouraging smile. "Did you see your truck? I got it back from the auto shop last night. I had a suicide knob installed on the steering wheel and signal controls on the floor. They should help for driving."

Travis shrugged. "Thanks." He took a few sips of his drink and poured the rest in the sink. He turned around. "I'm going back to bed."

"Wait." Carl handed him an envelope. "I need you to mail this and go to Foodland for me. Then you need to go see Brady. I talked to him last night, and he wants you to swing by the shop."

Travis groaned and stood, glaring out the window for a moment. Then he picked up his keys and left the house without saying another word. As the door slammed shut, Carl slumped into a dining room chair. He thought about the loss his youngest son had suffered. Travis had gone from a life of surf and fame, traveling the world and staying in multi-million dollar homes to having to learn how to dress himself again and the probability that he'd never ride another wave. The shark had taken more than his arm that day. It had taken his very soul.

"He just doesn't care about anything anymore."

Travis tried not to look at the ocean that spread to the horizon behind his house, but as he carried the groceries up the driveway, he turned and caught a glimpse of a whitecap in the distance. Winter had arrived. Soon the whole area would be primed for surfing. *Damn it.* He kicked a rock on the ground. Why did he have to live so close to such perfect waves?

Pipeline. Sunset. Waimea. All three were within walking distance, and Travis couldn't help but think about all the times he and his brother had biked to the renowned beaches when they were kids. Back then, Devin would wake him up at six in the morning to go surfing, and afterward they would hang around the surf shops in Hale'iwa, eating shave ice and asking pros for their autographs.

But that was another time.

He pushed the back door open with his foot and found his father sitting at the dining room table reading a newspaper. The old man wasn't even doing anything important. Couldn't he have run the errands by himself?

Without a word, Travis slung the bags onto the counter and headed back up to his room.

"Hey," his dad called out. "Aren't you going to help put stuff away?"

Travis kept going. "He's got two arms. He can do it," he mumbled.

At the top of the stairs, he paused in front of his brother's old room. He could barely remember the days when Devin had lived at home. Housing an old single bed, a desk, and a bunch of surfing memorabilia, the room had sat unused for eight and a half years.

He moved along.

His own room was much the same as his brother's. There were photos of himself as a young grom when he'd first started surfing, posters he'd hung a long time ago, and a couple of old skateboards leaning against the wall. The bed had changed—now a queen, thick and plush—but the room still looked like it belonged to a child.

As Travis crawled under the covers, he wished he was back in California. Nana's house was old, cramped, and smelled of mothballs. She had dragged him to physical therapy four times a week and made sure he ate three meals a day, but at least there he'd had some peace and quiet.

"Don't forget about Brady," his father called out from the bottom of the stairs. "You can't ignore the guy, Trav. He's not just a sponsor. He's your best friend."

Travis forced himself to his feet. Why'd he even come back here?

As he headed back down the stairs, he caught sight of his appearance in the mirror by the door and threw on a baseball cap. He didn't bother to tuck in the strands of hair that stuck out the sides of the hat.

With his foot, Travis hit the signal button on the floor of his truck. He turned the suicide knob on his steering wheel and pulled into the parking lot next to Brady's Surf Shop. It took a bit of getting used to, but the gadgets his father had gotten installed definitely helped with his driving.

In no hurry to see his old friend, he wandered down the Kamehameha Highway, the main street of Hale'iwa. Head hanging, he tried to blend into the shadows, but when he passed a busy tourist shop, a teenage girl glanced over and saw him. She whispered something to her friends, and Travis hissed a sigh of frustration. Did she recognize him from surfing, or was she pointing out his missing limb?

He walked faster.

Halfway across the historic double-arched bridge, Travis stopped to watch a group of boys paddle down the Anahulu River in an outrigger canoe. He glanced toward the boat harbor and could almost see the waves at Ali'i Beach Park beyond. The warm tropical sun pelted his body with heat, and he wiped the sweat off his brow. The long-sleeve shirts he always wore now kept him overly warm, but they also hid his stump.

Finally, he headed back to his friend's store. He entered cautiously and found Brady organizing a rack of rubber slippers—or flip-flops, as the tourists liked to call them.

"Trav! You made it back!" Brady grinned widely; his cheerful voice boomed throughout the store.

For the first time in weeks, Travis smiled. He couldn't help himself. Short in stature, with large tribal tattoos and dreadlocks that stuck out every which way, Brady was one of a kind. Travis clasped his friend's hand, realizing how much he had missed the guy.

Brady paused, his animated grin turning into a frown. "Howz'it, brah?"

The sympathetic expression made Travis wince.

"Okay, I guess." He fought the urge to walk away.

His eyes traveled to the display of surf magazines on the counter and landed on a cover shot of himself tucked deep inside a barrel. The caption beside the photo read: *Travis Kelly: Second Place in the World Tour Ratings After Tragic Shark Attack.* On the bottom right corner, another photo showed him being loaded onto an ambulance. Above it read: *A Vicious End to a Promising Surfing Career.*

He stared at the picture, eyes fixed on the image of his body lying motionless on the stretcher, covered by straps and blankets.

Brady followed his gaze and picked the book up. "Second place. Pretty gnarly, bu. Should'a come in first, if you ask me."

A lump formed in Travis's chest. He knew his friend was trying to make him feel better, but that was an impossible feat. He thought about all the money Brady had invested in him as a sponsor—the free surfboards, the surfing trips—and he cast his eyes to the ground. Such a waste. So what if he was still ranked as one of the top surfers in the world? What did that give him? Money. Fame. His name on the charts. *Worthless.*

Brady studied him for a moment before clearing his throat and tossing the magazine behind the counter. "I got somethin' to ask, bro. Surf season's startin' and I need some extra help. You wanna come work fo' me?"

"Huh?" Travis took a step back. His friend's store, located right in the heart of Hale'iwa, was the most popular surf shop in the area. It was a great place to work, selling surfboards, clothing, and accessories. But a job? He'd still be in bed now if it hadn't been for…

My father. Disgusted, he shook his head. "It's just like him to put you up to this."

"Nah," Brady countered. "This one's all me. I need someone soon, like tomorrow, an' you know more 'bout selling boards than anyone. I been swamped, brah. I only got one otha' person. Help me out, uh? Jus' part time."

Travis ran his fingers through a stack of postcards, trying to think up an excuse. "Uh, yeah … okay." He shrugged.

"Kay den, shootz!" Brady exclaimed. "I'm stoked you're back, Trav-man."

A gorgeous girl came out of the backroom, about the same age as Travis. Beautiful, black hair swished around her shoulders, and at first, he thought she was Hawaiian, until he noticed her eyes. Light green and sparkling like the sea. There had to be some Caucasian in her as well.

"This stuff's tagged and ready to be put out." She dropped some t-shirts on the counter. Then she gasped. Her eyes traveled to the folded sleeve of Travis's shirt, and he watched her turn a bright shade of red.

Brady motioned toward him. "Shayla, this is Trav. He's gonna be workin' here startin' tomorrow."

"*Huh?*" she blurted. "But..." Her eyes focused again on his sleeve.

Travis felt his face heat up. He turned slightly, hiding his arm from her view.

She cleared her throat and shook her head. "I'm sorry... it's nice to meet you."

He mumbled something in return, but he didn't even know what it was. His chest tightened with fury. The way she looked at him—he had seen it before. Strangers always stared, pointed, and whispered behind his back. But this was different. A super-hot girl grossed out by his stump. Perfect. That was just what he needed.

~Dumb Girl~

Shayla fiddled with the clothing on the counter.

Travis Kelly. She couldn't believe it was him. Her cheeks burned as she tried not to look at his pinned up sleeve, his perfect lips, or his powerful jaw. Shaggy, bleached blond hair poked out from under his cap. His blue eyes narrowed slightly as he looked at her.

She turned and started arranging the t-shirts from largest to smallest. The song "Pearly Shells" played on the radio, so she hummed along quietly, trying to hide her humiliation. Why did she have to make such a fool of herself?

As soon as the pro-surfer left, Brady turned to her. "Wha's da haps? How come you freaked?"

Shayla's stomach tied into knots. "I don't know. He startled me. You said a friend was coming by, but I didn't think it was going to be *him*. That was Travis

Kelly! He was attacked by that shark out at Pipe last year."

Brady picked up a shirt and hung it on a rack. "Yeah, tha's right. Were you there?"

"Yeah. I didn't see it up close, but I remember it all. Kane was scared shitless of him."

Kane. That name hadn't crossed her mind in a while. How many times had she listened to her ex-boyfriend complain about the new surfer on tour? Travis had given Kane quite the challenge, a real threat to his two-year reign as champion.

Brady smiled sadly. "Trav ripped. He would'a won fo' sure, if it hadn't been fo' that shark."

"He almost died, huh?"

"He lost a lot of blood. This is the first time I seen him since he got outta the hospital. I guess his arm's all betta', but I dunno 'bout his spirit. His dad says it's been kinda rough, so I'm gonna help him out, yeah? Get him back on his feet, ya know?"

Shayla nodded and turned back to her work, but she couldn't stop her mind from wandering. Eyes closed, she pictured the scene she had witnessed the year before: the ambulance rushing away from the beach, the crowd backing away from the water. She could still hear the foghorns blasting and the concern in everyone's voices.

Everyone except Kane. He had seemed relieved.

Shayla shook her head as she hung the last shirt on the rack. "Travis Kelly," she whispered. What a terrible thing to happen to such a talented guy.

With no destination in mind, Travis cruised down the highway. Outside his windows the coast spun by, dotted with residential homes, beaches, and tourist attractions. He drove past the Foodland grocery store and Shark's Cove—a small rocky bay that was popular for snorkeling. He barely noticed his surroundings.

Thoughts whirled through his mind. He could still see it, the way Shayla had looked at him: her eyes blinking when she spotted his arm, her lips dropping open. She could barely look straight at him. Was he that unappealing? Was that how people saw him now? Like some sort of freak? He ground his teeth together and pushed his foot a little harder on the gas pedal.

Why had he agreed to work for Brady anyway? He didn't want a job. Now he'd have to hang out with that *dumb girl*. And the customers. A bead of sweat dripped down his forehead.

Would they treat him the same way she had?

Gripping the suicide knob on his steering wheel, Travis turned a corner much too sharply and the back end of his truck fishtailed. With a loud yelp, someone leapt out of the way. Travis slammed on his brakes.

A young boy got up from the curb, waving his fist in the air. "Watch where you're goin', douche-bag!"

Travis gasped. He'd almost run the kid over.

Heart pounding, he turned into a parking lot, where he sat for a moment, catching his breath. A group of guys pulled in beside him with surfboards strapped to the roof of their car, and that's when he realized where he was. *Ehukai Beach Park*—home to Pipeline. The last place he wanted to be.

The boys whooped and hollered as they carried their boards down to the beach, and Travis slumped in his seat. His lungs tightened, as his skin grew hot. His hand began to tingle and he shook his fingers, trying to get rid of the numbing feeling.

He reached to turn the ignition and froze.

Standing on the bike path directly in front of him was his ex-girlfriend, Hayley. A bronzed-skinned surfer smiled down at her. She giggled back at him, batting her eyes and tossing her hair over her shoulders. Normally bleached blond, she had died it a bright red color. It looked like crap.

When Hayley turned and made eye contact with Travis, she paused in mid-sentence, her face turning pale despite her overly tanned skin. Travis glared and she took the surfer's arm, pulling him in the opposite direction.

Travis felt sorry for the guy. "He'll find out what she's really like."

Driving much more cautiously this time—and double-checking for pedestrians—he pulled out of the lot and headed home.

With the curtains closed and the lights dimmed, Travis sat on the couch watching television. On the wide screen, a masked wrestler slammed his opponent into the turnbuckle and danced around, pumping both fists in the air. Travis chugged back his third beer and tossed the crunched can on the floor. He leaned forward, grabbed another, and settled in for round two.

His father walked into the room. Lips pressed in a thin line, he looked around, picked up the empty beer cans, and threw them into a trash can. "Brady called to invite you out. He said you weren't answering your cell."

Travis shrugged and glanced over at his phone on the coffee table. The power was turned off. "I ain't going nowhere."

"What happened when you went to see him today?"

Travis rolled his eyes. "I'm sure you already know."

"What are you talking about?"

"My new *job*." He spat the word out viciously.

His dad's face lit up, eyes crinkling at the corners. "Oh, he offered you some work, huh? That's great. It'll be good for you."

"Whatever." Travis turned up the volume on the TV. "Thanks for goin' behind my back like that."

Carl's smile turned into a frown. "I had nothing to do with it, but so what? You can't sit on this couch for the rest of your life. It's been almost a year since your accident, and this is all you do."

Travis ground his teeth together. "I'm fine. I still got money saved up from surfing. I don't need a job right now."

"Then why'd you accept it?"

Without waiting for an answer, his father left the room, and Travis slumped even further into the sofa. His head throbbed with the start of what he knew would be a terrible headache. He glanced over at the mahogany liquor cabinet in the corner and stood up to listen, making sure his dad was gone. Then he reached inside and grabbed a half filled bottle of whiskey. "This'll do," he said and tucked it into his shorts.

The north winds blew stronger than usual, and the clouds blocked the stars and threatened rain. Out of the way, and semi-hidden by the trunk of an ironwood tree, Travis sat on an incline overlooking the beach at Ehukai. He glared at the chaotic waves. The dark, ominous sky made the whole ocean seem so menacing that all he could see were shadows, and all he could think about were sharks.

He swallowed the last swig of whiskey, welcoming the burn as it slid down his throat. The alcohol was strong, and as he stood up, he teetered a bit.

Standing at the edge of the water, he watched the white foam drift up the shoreline. His pulsed raced as he looked out at the spot where it had all happened. Up close the sea seemed even more sinister and the waves even more deadly. Only the frenzied white spray could be seen from the shore—the darkness hid everything else—but Travis knew what lurked in those waters.

"Screw this!" he cried, tossing the empty bottle into the surf. Turning, he staggered, and the moment of vertigo caused him to stumble toward the water. He leapt away from the vile liquid, inhaling deeply, and made his way back toward the parking lot. He had to get away from the beach.

His phone rang. It was Brady. "You comin' to the twins' party, or what?"

"Yeah, okay," Travis slurred. "If they got booze, I'm there."

He jumped into his truck and spun out onto the highway. Dust flew behind him as he raced toward the small central town of Wahiawa. Mika and Ayumi were Brady's friends. Travis didn't know the Japanese twins very well, but he had been to a few of their parties in the past.

As he looked for the house, he swerved onto the wrong side of the street. Another driver honked her horn. He veered away and almost drove right past his destination. Tires squealing, he hit the brakes, and one tire went up on the curb. He left his truck where it stopped, got out, and stumbled toward the house.

Music blared in his face as the door opened. His vision blurred; he had no idea who answered it.

A handful of people swarmed him at the entrance, asking questions about his return and patting him on the back. He tried to focus on what they were saying, but their faces were foggy and so was his brain. Shaking his head, he pushed his way inside the house.

Brady spotted him as he entered. "Whoa, Trav. You buss already? How much you had to drink, bu?"

Travis answered with a chuckle and followed his friend into the living room.

A large, Samoan guy handed him a beer, and as Travis chugged it down, he grabbed the back of the sofa to steady himself. One of Devin's friends waved from the kitchen. Travis stepped forward and looked around. Did that mean his brother was here too?

He blinked his eyes trying to see through the haze, but the room started to spin and suddenly everything faded. The party swirled around him. His legs faltered. Someone caught him and helped him into another room. Through fuzzy eyes, he recognized one of the twins. She pointed to a bed. "Don't puke on it, okay?"

"Sure," he muttered, and the lights went out.

~Wasted~

Devin looked at his watch. It was half past midnight. Pleasantly intoxicated, he stood on his father's front lawn, wavering slightly as he chugged the rest of the beer in his hand. His best friend, Jonny, stood next to him, smoking a cigarette. Red hair stuck out from his hat, and freckles splattered his cheeks. His crooked smile looked goofy in the light of the street lamp, and Devin couldn't help but laugh at him. "You're such a dork, bro." He threw the empty beer can into the bushes

Jonny snickered. "Litterbug."

"Whatevers, it's jus' my dad's house." Devin waved him onward.

The two young men snuck up the driveway. Devin tried the front door, but it was locked. Most of the house was dark, but he could see a bit of light reflecting off the trees in the backyard. He headed toward it. A lamp was on in Travis's bedroom. "He's home," he whispered to his friend.

He paused for a moment, nerves tickling his stomach. His fingers clamped around the small bag of cocaine in his pocket. He pulled it out and took a bump off his fingernail, sniffing up the drug, inhaling specks of courage.

"Come on."

He snuck up to the back door. It was unlocked, and he pushed it open quietly. Voices hushed, he and Jonny came in through the kitchen. The floor squeaked and Devin jumped backward. He bumped into a stool at the breakfast nook and it crashed to the floor. Jonny gave him a buck-toothed grin.

Devin punched him in the shoulder. "*Shhh!* You're gonna wake my dad."

"*Me*?" Jonny chuckled. "You da one bangin' shit over."

Somehow, they snuck through the living room without making any more noise, but as they started up the stairs, Devin tripped, and Jonny fell over him, snorting with laughter.

The lights came on.

"What the hell?" Carl stood in his bathrobe, rubbing sleep from his eyes. "Devin, what are you doing here?"

Devin stopped laughing and got to his feet. Eyes

blurred, he saw two of his father. "I'm lookin' for Trav."

Carl looked him up and down. "I thought I told you not to come here wasted."

Devin shook his head. "I'm not."

When Jonny snickered again, Devin punched him in the arm, but it was too late. His father was already seething.

"You finally want to see your brother, huh? Why the sudden change?"

Devin stammered, "I dunno... I jus' been thinkin'...."

"Well, he isn't here," Carl raged.

"Where is he?"

"Some party with Brady, probably getting messed up like you."

"So that's my fault?"

No longer smiling, Jonny backed down the stairs.

Devin glanced at the mantle above the fireplace. On it sat a row of trophies and a framed picture of himself holding one of the awards in the air. His jaw clenched as he looked at the photo. His father kept it there on purpose. Just to piss him off.

Whatever.

His hand clamped around the cocaine in his pocket. He pushed a craving aside. "I thought you wanted me to come see Trav."

"Not in the middle of the night. Do you really think

he'd want to see you like this? Drunk and stoned out of your mind."

"I'm *not!*" Devin grabbed the stair railing to steady himself.

"Go." His father pointed to the front door. Jonny was already holding it open. "And if you find your brother, tell him he's supposed to work in the morning."

Devin took one last look at his old man and whirled around. He threw his car keys to Jonny and hopped in the passenger side. "Let's get outta here. I think I know what party Trav's at."

There were people everywhere, on the lawn and in the house. Music blared from inside, pumping through the windows, and as he walked across the yard, Devin could see some girls dancing in the living room. Practically naked, they wore nothing but bikinis.

He flung the front door open and marched into the party like he owned the place. Greeting people with high fives and handclaps, he made his way through the living room. Jonny followed him.

"Move it, punk," Devin snapped to a teenage boy who was standing in his way. He snickered when the kid fled the room and stood even taller.

He noticed his friends in the kitchen and let out a loud, "Hui!"

"Ho, cuz!" One of the guys pounded Devin's fist and handed him a beer. "I saw your braddah, brah."

Devin's eyes darted around the room. "Trav's here? Where's he at?"

"Passed out or somethin'. Check the bedroom, down the hall."

Devin cracked open his beverage, took a long sip, and headed in the direction his friend had pointed. He peeked into the first room and saw Travis passed out on the bed, face half hidden by a mess of blond hair. Instantly, his heart started pounding. He rushed over and shook his brother's shoulder. "Trav!" He shook him again. "Bro, wake up."

Travis mumbled something and rolled toward the wall. A lump formed in Devin's throat, and he chased it down with some booze. It was a good thing Travis was sleeping, because Devin couldn't take his eyes off his arm—or the stump that had once been his arm.

Travis almost died.

Suddenly his knees grew weak and he had to clutch the edge of the dresser to keep from falling. The sleeve of Travis's shirt was pinned up, hiding the limb. But Devin wondered what it looked like. And what would he say when he saw it?

Shame washed through him like a rip current forcing him into a frantic state. He had always been one to get tongue-tied over other people's misfortunes, but this was his brother. He couldn't keep hiding. Sooner or later, he was going to have to face him.

The idea made his body tremble, and he stepped back toward the door. There was no point in waking Travis now. There was always tomorrow, or the next day, and then he would play it off like nothing ever happened.

Yeah. He nodded slightly. That's what he'd do.

As his heart rate slowed, Devin listened to his brother snoring. Travis wasn't dead. He was just fine. The past was the past, and this was a party. It was time to have some fun.

The rest of his beer went down smoothly. Devin tossed the empty into the garbage and left the room in search of his friends. In the kitchen, Jonny grabbed a can of whipped cream from the refrigerator and sprayed it at some of the girls. A playful fight ensued, white foam flying everywhere. Devin scooped up a handful and joined in, throwing it back at his friend.

"Can you please stop that?" somebody whined. It was Mika, one of the twins. She flinched when she saw Devin, her cheeks growing pale. Calling for her sister, she rushed from the room, waist-length black hair swishing behind her. Pretending to grab her ass, Devin flexed his fingers and gave a lewd wolf-whistle. Jonny laughed.

Moving outside, Devin and his group took over the patio, where no one made a fuss about giving up their chairs. Devin took a bag of cocaine from his pocket and chopped up a few lines on the table. He rolled up a twenty dollar bill and snorted the coke through the tube. The powder hit his senses and buzzed through his veins, bringing confidence with it and instant relief.

"What the hell are you doing?" Ayumi's voice shrilled loudly as she marched out onto the lanai. She looked identical to her sister, except her hair was pixie short. She pointed at the cocaine. "Get that stuff outta here or I'll call the cops."

Arms crossed, Mika stood behind her.

Devin leaned forward, snorted the last rail, and rubbed the excess powder on his gums. Flicking his tongue against the numbing sensation, he flashed Ayumi a bold grin. "Easy, sleazy," he hissed, stuffing the rest of the drugs into his pocket. He stood up, sniffed once, and wiped his nose with his fingers. "This is a junk party. We were jus' leavin' anyhow."

"Good." The girl put her hands on her hips. "You weren't invited."

With his friends in tow, Devin started toward the door. As he passed Ayumi, he gave her an awful sneer.

Then he slipped an arm around Mika's waist and tried to pull her in for a kiss. Tiny fists pounded his chest as she struggled to shove him away. "Get off me," she cried. "And don't ever come back!"

Devin released the girl. Laughing, he shook his head and turned back to the partygoers. "We outta here, suckers!" He and his gang charged out of the house causing a drunken ruckus all the way down the driveway. Devin looked back and saw the twins watching from the living room window. Ayumi gave him the finger. He smiled and threw her a shaka.

~Gross!~

Shayla drove into the town of Wahiawa and pulled up to a small, yellow bungalow. *Mika's house.* Sun glinted off the red metal roof, and shadows danced on the wraparound porch. In the side yard, a rope-swing still dangled from an old wooden tree-house. Shayla had helped paint it pink. No boys allowed.

Her heart pained as the memory struck her, and she was tempted to drive away. Then she shifted into park. She couldn't chicken out now. She needed her surfboard back. It was brand new and one of her favorites. "I shouldn't have left it here to begin with," she muttered, as she unfastened her seat belt.

Stomach tied in knots, she smoothed down the front of her sundress and stepped out onto the lawn. The front door of the house stood ajar and swung open a bit further as she approached.

"Hello?" She peered inside.

The stench of stale alcohol hit her and she had to refrain from covering her nose. A girl in a slinky bikini was sprawled out on the living room sofa, and someone else had passed out in the middle of the floor. His legs blocked the entrance. Shayla had to step over them to enter the house.

A huge and heavily pierced Hawaiian guy, wearing nothing but a sarong, stood at the refrigerator, drinking juice straight from the carton. He nodded a greeting.

"Is Mika home?" Shayla asked, hoping the answer was *no*.

"She stay in da spare room." His voice came out hoarse, and he swigged down another gulp of juice. "Brah, dis' w'at I call one party." He extended the carton toward her. "You like some?"

Shayla recoiled. "Thanks … but no."

Her feet rustled the soft shag carpet as she tiptoed down the narrow hallway. She peeked into the first bedroom and found Mika sleeping soundly, curled up next to some guy.

Disgusted, Shayla rolled her eyes. When had Mika become such a sleaze? She had never been the type to randomly hook up with men.

Until she started going after mine.

With a strong shudder, Shayla pushed the thought from her mind. Mika's latest victim lay facing the wall, pillow covering his face. For a brief moment, Shayla wondered who he was. Then she decided she didn't care.

In the far corner, her longboard stood propped against the wall. It was proof the two girls had once been friends.

But not anymore.

As she crept into the room, the person on the bed moaned in his sleep and rolled over. It was Travis.

Stunned, Shayla stood there, staring. Then she glared at the back of Mika's head. With an angry huff, she snatched her board and fled the room, moving swiftly back toward the front door.

The guy who had been drinking the juice was now cooking up some Spam and eggs. "Eh, wait," he called, as she left the house. "You no like eat breakfast?"

Something caused Travis to stir. He opened his eyes and sat up, only to be pierced by a blinding headache. He put his hand to his forehead and leaned back against the pillow as a wave of nausea hit him.

He wasn't alone.

Mika sat up beside him and rubbed her bloodshot eyes. She glanced around and gave him a puzzled expression. "What the hell?"

Travis shrugged, and the pounding in his temples intensified. His mind whirled as he stared at the girl. Her face was flushed, her long hair tangled.

He noticed a condom wrapper on the bedside table.

"Oh, no. We didn't … you know … did we?"

Mika gaped at him and shrugged.

"I … I'm sorry." Travis shuddered as he looked away. The last thing he remembered was arriving at the party and talking to Brady. What had happened after that?

Embarrassed, he pushed back the covers. The Velcro on his shorts was undone, so he pressed it back together. He refused to look at the girl. He barely knew her.

A blast of regret hit him. The last time he had blacked out his brother had pressured him into playing a drinking game. Luckily, that time, he had woken up on the floor of the bathroom and not in someone's bed.

This was something Devin would do.

The thought turned his stomach, and he swallowed repeatedly to keep from throwing up.

What if she had seen his arm?

Murmuring another apology, Travis forced himself upright. His head spun as he stood, and he could no longer take the nausea. That—combined with the remorse he felt—forced him into the bathroom.

Mika's temples throbbed as she watched Travis run from the room. She pressed her eyes shut, and as she massaged her eyelids, she kicked herself for being so irresponsible. She hadn't planned on drinking so much. At least not to the point of passing out.

Frowning, she looked around, and as she tossed the blankets aside, she tried to recall the events of the night before. What had happened? Why wasn't she in her own bed? She was pretty sure nothing had happened with Travis. She barely knew the guy and couldn't even remember seeing him at the party.

Looking at the condom wrapper on the bedside table, she chewed on her lower lip. The package was open, but the latex was still inside, rolled up and unused.

And she was fully clothed.

"Well, that proves it," she whispered. But just to be sure, she wandered down the hall and knocked on her sister's door.

A wave of dizziness ran through her as she waited for Ayumi to answer. She steadied herself and rubbed her queasy stomach.

She knocked again and took a peek inside the room.

"Hey, Mikki," Ayumi lifted her head and blinked the sleep from her eyes. "How you feelin'?"

"Not sure," she replied, "Why was I in bed with Travis Kelly?"

Her sister burst out laughing and propped herself up on her pillow. "Sorry, Mik. You drank too much. Mark carried you in there."

"Why didn't he put me in my own room?"

Ayumi's boyfriend poked his head above the covers. "Someone was using it. I had no other choice."

Mika wrinkled her nose. "Someone was *using* my room? That's disgusting!"

Any thoughts she'd had about waking up next to Travis were quickly replaced with plans for washing her sheets. *Gross!*

As she stormed down the hall to investigate her room, Travis came out of the bathroom. She didn't bother saying goodbye, and neither did he.

~Rough Morning~

"**I** told you, he doesn't want any interviews."

That damned reporter from the local news was on the other line again. Knuckles white, Carl clutched the phone to his ear. "My son doesn't want to talk about the attack or his arm. If he changes his mind, I'll get him to call you, but until then, please stop bothering us."

He clicked the phone onto the charger, and Travis walked into the house. His face was a pale shade of green and he reeked of booze. Without a word, he headed straight for his bedroom.

Carl followed and stood in the hallway for a moment, wondering if he should impose. Travis was a grown man. He didn't have a curfew. At the same time, he had never been big into partying, and his behavior was starting to remind Carl of someone else.

He knocked on the door and pushed it open with his foot. "So you stay out all night and don't even call? That's not like you."

Travis lay face down on the mattress. Carl glanced around the disaster of a bedroom. He kicked some clothing out of his way and ran his hand over the papers that littered the desk. An unpacked suitcase sat against the wall; a glass of milk had turned sour on the bedside table.

"Your brother came by to see you last night, but you weren't here." He left out the fact that Devin was wasted.

Travis replied with a sick moan.

"Come on, Trav. Out of bed. You can't party all night and expect the world to wait. Brady's expecting you to show up for work." Carl walked to the window and swung the drapes apart. Rays of sunlight poured into the room.

Travis groaned again, louder this time. "Dad, it's too bright. My head is killing me." He pulled the blanket over his eyes.

"That's your own damn fault." Carl whipped the covers aside. "I'm sorry, but I'm not about to let you turn into a drunk. *Now get up!*" It was the first time he had yelled at his son since the accident.

Travis sat up, grabbed his pillow, and threw it across the room. It hit a lamp, which crashed to the floor and shattered. Carl shook his head and headed back down the stairs.

In the living room, he moved over to the mantle and

picked up one of Travis's trophies. He held it for a moment, wiping away a layer of dust with his finger, remembering the day his son had won the award. It was the very first contest after joining the world tour. Since he was a rookie, no one had expected him to pass the third round.

"He sure proved them wrong," Carl whispered, a sad smile crossing his lips.

Hearing footsteps, he gave a startled jump and stashed the trophy in a chest underneath the mantel. Travis took no notice of him as he came down the steps. Nor did he say anything as he passed through the room. He kicked on his rubber slippers, threw on a hat, and shut the front door behind him.

When Travis arrived at work, his head was still pounding, and the bells on the door caused a sharp pain behind his eyes as he entered.

"*Aloha.*" Shayla looked over. Then she frowned, her cheeks growing red when she saw it was him.

He grimaced as well, gave her a slight nod, and headed toward Brady.

"Trav, you made it!"

He put his hand to his head.

"Rough morning?" Brady snickered.

Travis nodded. "You could say that."

Beside him, he could've sworn he saw Shayla roll her eyes, but when he looked over at her, she quickly turned away.

"New t-shirts and baggies." Brady patted the top of a box on the counter. "They're all tagged but need to be folded. I gotta cruise to the bank, so Shayla can show ya what to do, and when I get back, I'll teach ya the till."

"Sure." Travis glanced at his coworker.

She cleared her throat and took a stack of surf-trunks out of the box. "Um…you can just help customers if you want. I can fold this stuff."

Travis narrowed his eyes. "I can do it."

Before she could respond, he snatched the box and carried it over to a folding table. He could feel his blood pressure rising as he pulled out some bright colored t-shirts and laid them on the table. Sometimes, he wondered if adjusting to life without his right hand was worse than the pain he'd suffered losing it. Simple things like bathing or eating had suddenly become complicated. He'd had to learn to do them all over again, and it had taken a while to get used to. But he wasn't helpless.

Using a small plastic board, he tried to fold one of the t-shirts but messed up and had to start all over again.

Shayla walked by slowly. "If you want help, just let me know."

Damn it. He rolled his eyes. How was he supposed to do anything with that stupid girl watching? He looked at the exit. There was no turning back. He tried again and mumbled, "I can fold a fricking t-shirt."

Shayla heard the comment, but she pretended not to. Her stomach wrenched. What had she done wrong? Had she upset him when she'd offered to fold the clothing? Having never known anyone who was missing an arm, she didn't know what his abilities were. What if she had asked him to do something he couldn't do? Wouldn't that have embarrassed him more?

With a sigh, she moved to the front of the store, where she helped an old lady pick out a pair of sunglasses. After that, she made an attempt to rearrange the sun hats, but her fingers fumbled and she knocked over the entire rack. Embarrassed, she picked it up and glanced at Travis. He hadn't even looked her way. He had given up folding clothes and had gone to help a man who had come in asking about surfboards.

"This one's a gun," Travis explained, pulling out a tall white board with a stripe down the middle. "Big wave board. Narrow nose and tail, tons of rocker, really shoots down the face." He pulled out a longboard with a rounded nose. "This Malibu is pretty sweet, double concave for speed, trims like no other."

As he spoke, he ran his fingers over the face of each board, and Shayla could hear the underlying passion in his voice. His eyes flickered to life as he described the different styles, shapes and uses, and in the end, the customer left with the Malibu tucked under his arm.

Brady came back to the store, passing the man on his way in. "T-man! You sold that guy a board? Tha's sick! He's been comin' in here every day for a month."

Shayla turned to congratulate Travis as well, but as soon as they made eye contact, he frowned and walked away. As he disappeared into the back room, she looked at Brady. "What's his problem?"

Brady shrugged and threw a questioning glance in his friend's direction. "Dunno. Never seen him act like that before."

It was almost closing time, and the stub of Travis's right arm ached. He hadn't used it half this much since the accident. During the time he had stayed with his grandmother, he had exercised and strengthened his muscles at physical therapy, but since coming home, he hadn't bothered to keep any of that up.

As he massaged his arm, a strange feeling shot through it. Sometimes, the nerves in his stump sent signals to his brain making it feel as if his hand were still there. It was called phantom pain, and he didn't like it at all. It was weird to feel sensation in a body part that was no longer there. But at least it didn't happen as often as it used to.

He propped a skim-board against a rack, stretched, and took a deep breath. Other than some stiffness and the occasional wave of nausea, his first day had gone better than he'd expected. He hadn't had to talk to many customers or to Shayla, and he'd managed to avoid anyone who'd recognized him by ducking into the back room. He'd rearranged the quivers of boards and refolded half the store's clothing. Plus he'd made it through his whole shift without getting sick.

He rubbed his forehead, trying to remember a time when he had felt so hungover. Again, he berated himself for getting so drunk—*and stupid.*

An image battered his mind—Mika sitting up in bed beside him—and his hand automatically went up to cover his missing limb. As he massaged the stump, he wondered again if she had seen it. He forced the thought away, pulled his painkillers from his pocket and stared down at them, turning the tiny bottle over in his hand. *Do not mix with alcohol.* The warning was written clearly on the label.

Was that the reason he'd blacked out? Because he'd mixed the pills with booze? A wave of disgust traveled through him. There was no excuse for his behavior. If he couldn't control himself and take the pills responsibly, then he deserved every bit of pain he felt. He tossed the container into the garbage. That's it, he thought. No more pills and no more drinking.

~Huge Druggie~

As the following week went by, it grew more and more difficult for Travis to avoid people at work. By his fourth shift, it seemed as if everyone from the island knew where he worked and had come in to catch a glimpse of him. "Can't people mind their own business?" he complained to Brady after ducking into the back room for the tenth time that day.

"No worries, brah, they jus' curious. Try to ignore 'em. You'll be old news soon. And look, at least you're bringin' in customers."

Brady laughed at his own joke, but Travis didn't find it funny. For the next two hours, he refused to go back up to the front of the store. Brady gave him some boxes to sort through and they spent time marking down sale items.

By noon, it started to rain quite heavily, and the crowd thinned out considerably. A few tourists came in, to get away from the downpour, but no one Travis recognized. He finished the inventory he was working on and went back up front again.

His brother walked into the shop. "Eh, Trav!"

Travis stepped back and had to stop himself from covering his nose. Devin's face was thin and pale. His clothing reeked of marijuana and body odor, and his eyelids were sunken, heavy, and bloodshot.

"Was' da haps, little braddah?" Devin gave him an awkward slap on the shoulder. He flipped his fingers through a rack of board shorts, acting as if they had seen each other yesterday.

Well, if that was the game he wanted to play, Travis could play it too. He gave a nonchalant shrug and leaned against the counter. "Not much, bro. You ditching work again?"

"Nah, man, I got fired. I was jus' on my way to see Dad, to see if he can help me out."

Money. It always came down that.

Travis hid a frown. "What happened now?"

Devin opened the display case next to the cash register and took out a thick, silver watch. "Nothin' really. Rent's up in a week and the landlord's bein' a dick. Says he's gonna evict me if I'm late again."

Acting a bit jumpy, he admired the expensive accessory and put it back.

Travis locked the cabinet and tucked the key in a drawer. He wondered about his brother. Going to their dad for help was normally a last resort. Were things really that bad now? Was Devin getting desperate?

A lump formed in the pit of his stomach as he pictured his coke-crazed sibling, homeless and living in a tent on the beach—or worse.

"I doubt you'll get anything from Dad," he muttered.

"For why? He bein' a hard-ass lately? Don't take dat, bro. You can always come party wit' me." Devin slapped him on the shoulder again, and Travis realized why it felt so awkward. Devin had aimed high to avoid touching his stump.

Turning the limb in his brother's direction, Travis purposely played with his pinned-up sleeve. Devin wouldn't even look at it. Did it bother him that much?

Irritated, Travis glared at his brother, but Devin didn't seem to notice. Instead, he raised his eyebrows and nodded toward Shayla, who had just come up front to collect a stack of skateboards. "Who *dat*?" he whispered, as she made her retreat.

Travis hissed, "Don't look at her, man."

"For why? You got somethin' goin'?"

Travis shook his head. "Me and her, brah? No way."

"Yeah, okay, whatevers."

When Devin gave him a sly grin, Travis turned

around and sighed. There was no point in arguing. With her hair up in braids and pink polka dots painted on her fingernails, she looked so incredibly hot. There was no way his brother would believe he wasn't attracted to her. Glowering, he dug his fingers into his stump again. The last person he liked was Shayla.

Shayla sat on the floor in the back room helping Brady mark down the sales prices on a stack of last season's skateboards. "Who's that guy out there with Travis?"

Brady glanced up front and leaned forward. "Tha's Devin," he whispered. "Trav's brother. He used to surf pro too but now he's a huge druggie."

Peering around the door, Shayla took another look. Devin was shorter than Travis, with tousled brown hair, tattooed arms, and baggy, worn-out clothing. At least a few years older than his brother, he had the same striking blue eyes, but he was scrawny and not nearly as good looking.

"Is he on ice?" She kept her voice low. Crystal meth was a problem on the island. She'd seen a lot of people lost to the drug, and they were always skinny like that.

"Nah, cocaine," Brady answered. "Dev's a cokehead to da max. Started hangin' out with some older guys when he was younger, an' they messed him up good. That was right after their mom passed away."

Shayla paused, holding the sales gun in her lap. "Their mom died?"

"Yeah." Brady frowned. "That whole family, *ohana*, they got some crappy luck."

He handed her a stack of boards—now adorned with bright orange tags—and as she put them into a large sales bin out front, she heard Devin ask Travis if he wanted to come over later to play video games.

Travis answered with a grin, and it startled her.

Oh, so he does know how to smile.

Over the last week, Shayla had worked three full shifts with Travis, and in that time, he had barely spoken to her once. She couldn't figure it out. Why did he dislike her so much?

With a tired sigh, she moved over to the cash register, and as she stood behind the counter, she couldn't help but notice the adorable way Travis's hat sat a bit crooked on his head. He was so tall, his shoulders so broad. *Probably from all the surfing.* She bit her lip and stared out the window, trying to focus on something—anything— else.

Humid air drifted in from the coast, taunting her nostrils with the salty smell of the ocean. Occasionally, when the surf was good, Brady would close up early so they could catch a few waves. If only it were one of those days.

Travis said goodbye to his brother, and Shayla realized they were alone. She tried to busy herself, sorting receipts on the counter, but it wasn't long before she glanced over at him again. He caught her staring and turned away with a scowl. *Damn it.*

~What a Dick~

Devin entered the house through the backdoor and found his father cleaning the kitchen. It seemed the man had aged ten years over the last few months. His hair, once a dark copper, had grayed from root to tip, and the wrinkles around his eyes had grown deeper.

"What do you want now?" His dad gave him the once-over, wiped up some crumbs from the countertop, and shook them into the sink.

Ignoring the question, Devin grabbed a mug from the cupboard and poured himself some coffee. A few drops spilled onto the counter, but he made no move to clean them up. He sipped his drink quietly, trying not to look at his father. The liquid hit his empty stomach, warming him from the inside.

Carl handed him a bagel. "You look terrible. Don't you ever eat?"

Devin took a small bite, but as usual after a coke

binge, the food just didn't appeal to him. It was dry and moved slowly, scraping as it slid down his throat. He took another sip of coffee. "I went to see Travis today."

"Good. Your brother needs you."

Devin rolled his eyes. "He's fine."

"No, he's not. He's depressed and angry, drinking and staying out all night."

"Scared he'll turn out like me, huh?"

His father's forehead furrowed. "Travis needs a brother right now ... a *sober* one."

Devin tossed the bagel into the garbage and dumped his coffee into the sink. His chest grew tight, as a lump formed in his throat. "I didn't come here for no speech."

"Then why *are* you here?"

Devin turned and stared out the window. He could barely force the words from his lips. "I need to borrow mo' money."

The kitchen drawer slammed shut. "No way! I'm not giving you any. All you're going to do is buy drugs."

Devin whirled back around. "No, I'm not. It's for rent."

Carl threw the dishrag in the sink and gripped the ledge of the counter. Age spots covered the skin on the back of his hands—the same hands that had held storybooks, and fishing poles, and swung Devin around when he was little.

Devin blinked twice, pushing the memories away.

His dad sighed. "If it isn't child support, it's rent. It's not my fault you quit surfing and wasted away all your money. Maybe if you hadn't gotten involved with those *kooks* you call friends, you'd still have some left."

Devin snarled. "Why do you always bring that up?"

"I could give you the money, Dev, but it's not going to help. It never does. If anything, it supports a habit I want nothing to do with. You need to start being more responsible. You have a daughter. You should be taking care of her."

As his father lectured, all Devin heard was *blah, blah, blah.* What surprised him, however, was the no-nonsense tone.

Devin crossed his arms. "So, you'll give Lea money, but you won't help your own son?"

"That *was* helping you."

"Please, Dad? There's nothing I can do right now."

"You can get a job and straighten yourself out. You know I'll help you with that."

"I don't have time. I need rent by the end of the week."

Carl shrugged. "You should've thought about that before you got into this mess. I'm sorry, but I've had enough. I'm done bailing you out."

Devin glared at him. "You're serious?"

His dad nodded.

"Fuck this! I'm outta here then." Devin whirled around and headed back out the door.

"And don't even think about asking your brother for money either," his father called out behind him.

As Travis walked up the driveway, he heard yelling. Seconds later his brother came storming out of the house. "What a dick!" Devin strode past. He jumped into his rusty old beater and slammed the door. Dust filled the air as he peeled away.

Travis stared after him. He had a good idea what had happened, and when he entered the house, the look on his father's face confirmed it. Devin had asked for money.

"Hey, Dad."

Carl looked up. "Hi, Trav. How was work?"

"Super." His sarcasm hung in the air. "I can't do anything right, and people keep coming in to stare at me, like everyone in the world knows what happened."

His father gave him a sympathetic frown. "It'll get easier, and you know whenever you're ready we can get you that prosthetic."

Travis nodded and groaned inwardly. Was that the

best he was ever going to get—a prosthetic arm? People were still going to notice, and it wouldn't make him feel any better. As realistic as they made them these days, he just didn't want an artificial hand. He wanted his real one back.

From the fridge, he grabbed a soda, wedged it against the side of the counter with his hip, and popped the lid. As he took a sip, he glanced toward the fireplace. He stopped drinking and swallowed hard. "Where's my trophy?"

His father stammered. "I ... I ..."

Travis asked again, "Where's my trophy?" He put his drink down and went over to the mantle. It didn't take him long to find the award, stuffed in an old wooden trunk. He took it out and stood there, fuming. "What the hell?" He could feel his blood pressure rising.

"Trav ... I just didn't want you to see..."

"No. Whatever." Travis's eyes narrowed as he looked at the man. He saw the truth—the disappointment in his father's eyes, the regret on the older man's lips. Fingers gripping his trophy firmly, he whirled around and fled the house, slamming the door behind him.

Travis's truck spun out of the driveway, spitting a long stream of rocks behind it. Carl watched it go. Sadness pressed in on all sides as he slumped down on the front steps. He put his head in his hands. Why had he hidden Travis's trophy? What a stupid thing to do.

Tall coconut palms rustled in the breeze as he sat there massaging the stress from his forehead. If only his wife were still alive. Life was so much easier then.

He glanced toward the tire swing that hung from the branches of a large bo tree in the front yard. He remembered pushing Travis and Devin in it when they were kids. Laughing, they had spun around until they were dizzy causing such a ruckus the boys' mother had run outside. "You just ate," she'd scolded all three of them. "You're going to make yourselves sick."

Carl smiled at the memory. Once, he'd had the ideal family—a loving wife and two sons who adored him. *Hell*, he thought, as he patted his dog, Jasper, on the head. *We even had the golden retriever.*

Jasper licked his face as he sat there brooding. Gone were the days of sleeping next to his wife. The days of sharing supper with his family at the kitchen table while laughing over the day's events. Now, he was left with one son who was wrecking his life snorting cocaine and another who was suffering and shutting him out.

Carl got up and settled down on the porch swing. It was old and the paint was starting to peel. Victoria had bought it a few months before she died, and sometimes rocking in it made him feel better. He ran his hand over the faded purple cushion. Tonight, the swing creaked on its hinges. It wasn't any comfort at all.

~Another Life~

Tires squealing, Travis pulled into the parking lot at Hale'iwa Ali'i Beach Park. He got out of his truck and slammed the door. "It's not like I gave up surfing on purpose," he grumbled, as he stormed across the mowed lawn and over the thick, brown sand. At the water's edge, he took one last look at his trophy and chucked it into the surf.

As it sank out of sight, he dug his nails into the palm of his hand. If only he had never gone on tour or surfed in the Bonzai Classic. It wasn't his desire to compete in the first place. He never would have if it weren't for his family and friends. Especially Brady and his father. He could still hear their voices, pleading. "You're better than your brother was, Trav. You could win it all."

His eyes narrowed as he stared across the water. If only he hadn't listened to them. Sure, it was fun at first, partying at the sponsor houses, traveling around the world, making new friends, surfing the different breaks.

Until he got lost in it all.

His stomach turned as he thought about that last competition, the day of the attack. If only he hadn't waited for that second wave. If he had taken the first the shark would've missed him, but no, he'd wanted to score more points. "I wanted to stomp Kane."

He could still see the champion surfer sneering as they'd entered the water. "Dumb Haole. I goin' smoke your ass." The words rang through Travis's head as if he'd heard them only yesterday.

Kane Walker. That fucking kook.

A sandcastle lay in Travis's path. He kicked it over and moved down to the shoreline, where he stopped and let the ocean touch his feet for the first time since he'd come back to Hawaii. He wanted to run, but he wouldn't let himself, and as his toes sunk into the sand, he forced himself to look out at the surf and all he was missing.

He watched a surfer carve a sweet cutback. Ali'i was another popular surf spot on the island. Bigger swells had a habit of sneaking up on a person and some days the current was relentless, but the waves more than made up for it. They had a lot of juice, with hollow sections and workable walls, not to mention a nice steep takeoff.

Travis frowned. The waves were ideal. It would have been a good day for practice, perfecting maneuvers and trying out new tricks.

But that was another life.

Hearing laughter, he glanced toward a small group of kids who were playing in the reform. Behind them, someone took off on a longboard. Her stance was good, but as she walked the deck, her board cut into the wave and sent her flying into the foam. She came up for air and rested only a moment before heading back out again.

Travis lost sight of the girl in the lineup, but she caught his attention once more when she popped up and cross-stepped her board. She placed five toes over the nose as it planed across the liquid face.

Not bad.

Travis shaded his eyes as he watched her come out of the surf. She flipped her hair out of her face and pulled off her rash guard, and as the water glistened off her tanned skin, he couldn't help but stare.

It was Shayla.

Travis cringed as she spun toward him. He tried to turn away, but he wasn't fast enough. She saw him and started making her way over. *Shit.* He kicked some sand with his foot and tried to think of something to say.

He remembered her wipeout. "You shouldn't be surfing alone, you know."

She stopped in front of him and shrugged, her fingers playing with the cord of her leash. "I guess you're right." One side of her mouth tilted up. "Good thing you were here then."

Fiddling with his pinned-up sleeve, Travis pursed his lips. "Yeah, right." He twisted sideways.

She frowned. "Are you okay?"

He felt the blood rush to his cheeks. He was definitely not *okay*, but who was she to ask? All she seemed to do was make him feel worse. "I'm fine!" he snapped, and when he saw her wince, he spun around and sprinted down the sand.

Digging her toes into the speckled earth, Shayla watched Travis disappear around a bend. Above her, the sun dipped low, setting the heavens ablaze with a fire that matched her confusion. She debated going after him, but held back. Why should she care what he was going through? He was always so mean to her. And besides, he had slept with Mika. It was an image she couldn't seem to get rid of.

She snatched her longboard and splashed along shore. A large wave swept up the beach, threatening to knock her over. As it recoiled, something flickered in the water. Another rush of foam brought the object even closer.

Shayla reached into the shallow surf and picked the treasure up. It was a surfing trophy. It belonged to Travis. Had he thrown it away?

She glanced in the direction he had gone but could no longer see him, so she took the object with her. In the parking lot, she leaned against her bright yellow hatchback and took a closer look. *First Place,* she read, tracing his name with her finger. So tragic. Losing an arm must have put a stop to his entire life.

She couldn't fathom having to give up surfing. Catching a wave was so powerful, so liberating—like you could fly if you just reached out your arms. Maybe Travis found it impossible to fly now. How difficult his new life must be.

Shayla slid into her car and put the trophy on the passenger seat. As she drove away, she saw Travis once more, sitting on a picnic table, watching the sun take its last breath before it dove into the ocean. Again, her heart went out to him, but she didn't stop.

~Trippin'~

Devin snorted the powder in a long, deep line and waited. The drug charged through his body, filling him with much needed bliss. It didn't last long, so he turned to needles instead. Injected straight into his bloodstream, the cocaine buzzed through his veins. Brief satisfaction. A rapid euphoric rush. Then, the intensity faded along with his patience, and he threw the paraphernalia across the room.

Exhausted, he fell back on the couch and looked at the empty plastic bag on the coffee table. He'd spent the last of his money on that little bit of dope, and he'd been trying to get high all day. Evening had come. Why wasn't it working?

"Ho, braddah!" Jonny entered the house with a grin on his face. "Try look." He opened his hand; in it sat some small off-white nuggets.

Devin hesitated. Usually he refrained from smoking

crack. The chemically altered cocaine was more potent and unstable, the toxicity levels much higher. It was considered a poor man's drug. Devin was from a rich family. He was no crack head. Those people had problems.

Shaking his head, he almost turned his friend down. Then he thought twice. Cocaine wasn't working, and he needed a good high. Besides, no one would know.

He patted his friend on the back. "You're a good man, Jonny."

Devin pulled out a glass pipe and loaded up the bowl. He sprinkled some cigarette ash inside and added one of the chunks. With his lighter, he heated the powerful drug, rolling the pipe over. The rock sizzled and melted quickly. He placed the rod to his lips, inhaled, and held the white smoke in his lungs. Within seconds he could feel it, the release he had been looking for.

Thank God for Jonny.

Eyes closed, he found himself lost in an elevated void. He opened them again and leapt backward. He could've sworn he saw his coke dealer, Vince, staring in through the living room window, but when he got up to check, no one was there. And even worse were the bugs under his skin. They itched and crawled, biting and pinching. He picked at his arms, trying to get them off.

"Eh," Jonny asked. "You okay or w'at?"

Devin barely heard the question. He had to get rid of his skin. He pulled a switchblade from a drawer and rubbed the blade across his arms, scratching. He cut his arm. Blood dripped down his elbow.

"Whoa, brah, gimme dat."

Jonny grabbed the blade, and Devin backed into the corner. "Get away from me!" he shouted.

With a frown, Jonny set the knife on the coffee table. He shook his head and pointed to the sofa. "Brah, you trippin'. Just go sleep already."

Crawling onto the couch, Devin watched his friend leave. He grabbed the knife and clutched it to his chest.

Still staring at the window, he found it hard to swallow and even harder to relax, but at least the bugs under his skin were gone. His mouth grew dry. Thirst overwhelmed him, but he was too lazy to go get a drink. He wanted more drugs, but there was none left. His body felt heavy; he couldn't move. Legs curled to his body, he twitched and trembled, and finally, he crashed.

Darkness hovered and stars splattered the night sky. No one was around, the roads were quiet, and as he walked, Travis could hear the wind whistling through the branches of the tattered palm trees that grew between the houses on his brother's street. Devin lived on O'ahu's west coast in a rundown community on the outskirts of Wai'anae. Travis had driven over an hour to get there.

Kicking beer cans out of the way, he walked across the dry grass and climbed the creaky steps of the house. The outside motion detector came on, blinding him for a moment, and he knocked over a jar with his foot. A thick liquid spilled out. He leaned over. Was that chewing tobacco? He wrinkled his nose.

"Dev?" He stuck his head inside. The door was open and the lights were on. "Hello?" His call went unanswered.

He stepped into the living room and found Devin lying on the sofa, passed out cold with a knife in his hand.

His heart slammed into his stomach as he rushed to his brother's side. He shook Devin hard. "Wake up!"

Devin stammered some incoherent words. He rolled over, twitched, and started to snore. His breathing seemed steady enough.

Travis picked up the knife and tucked it inside a drawer. He inspected the room. On the coffee table sat a syringe and a glass pipe; crack residue filled the bottom. The sight of the needle caused a lump in his throat. It was bad enough his brother was wrecking his sinuses snorting the stuff, but now he was injecting it too?

Travis headed down the hall and found Devin's bedroom filled with garbage, boxes, and grimy clothes. He gathered a blanket from the floor, shook it out, and brought it back to the living room. "Sleep it off," he murmured, gently covering the wheezing addict. He barely recognized his brother anymore.

From the cooler beside the sofa, Travis grabbed a beer. Then, he glanced at his brother, put it back, and popped open a soda instead. He took a long swig.

"So much for hanging out."

Looking around, he shook his head. The living room was worse than the yard. He kicked an empty beer can out of the way and it landed in a moldy box of half-eaten pizza.

A lamp was tipped over, so he set it upright. He grabbed a garbage bag from under the sink and got to work. The floors, the counters, the dishes—he scrubbed them all until his body ached, his temples throbbing with irritation. Why had he started this? Here he was— with only one arm—cleaning a house that wasn't even his.

He kept going.

At four in the morning, he glanced around. Finally, it looked like a normal person lived there.

After checking on his brother once more, Travis turned off the lights and locked the door as he left.

Back at home, he walked up to a quiet house and fumbled with his keys in the darkness, trying to find the hole in the knob. Leaving his shoes on the back deck, he went in and passed his dad's room on the way to his own. He peeked inside.

Even in sleep his father looked troubled. He lay snoring on the bed, his mouth curved into a frown.

Travis shut the door.

In his own room, he fell exhausted into bed, yet sleep eluded him. Awful thoughts swirled in his mind. Devin on the streets. Devin in the morgue.

He pulled the blankets over his head, trying to block the light that crept through a gap in his curtains. Outside, a wild rooster crowed. In the next room, the shower dripped, beating out a maddening rhythm. The sounds were deafening. Unable to lie there any longer, Travis pulled on a hoodie and slipped down the back stairs, leaving the house before his dad was even aware he'd come home.

~Done~

Sobbing madly, Mika sat on her fuzzy, pink day bed, clutching a feather pillow to her chest. She looked down at the pregnancy test in her hand. The stick read positive. A stream of tears ran down her cheeks. She couldn't have a baby. Not like this. She sat up straighter. It couldn't be right. But she knew it was. Her period was late, and the test had two blue lines.

She grabbed a tissue from her bedside table and blew her nose. Her cheeks stung raw from crying, and her head throbbed as she swallowed back her nausea. She'd been feeling sick for days. She'd hoped—prayed—it was just the flu, but clearly no one had answered.

A cloud of misery hung over her now, as she muttered softly into the pillow, "Only I would get pregnant from a one-night stand."

She jammed the stick deep in the trash. She couldn't chance her sister finding it. Ayumi would be so disappointed.

That made her cry even harder. Never had she kept a secret from her twin. "How could I be so stupid?"

Mika thought about calling her parents, but they had just moved back to Japan, and with the time difference they would still be asleep. Besides, this wasn't exactly something she could tell them. They were extremely traditional. Her mother would yell at her for having premarital sex, and her father would demand to know who the father was.

If only she had someone else to talk to. Unfortunately, her only close female friend had stopped speaking to her over a month ago.

Mika touched her eye. It had healed since her fight with Shayla. The puffiness had disappeared, and the blood blister had faded. Only regret remained.

Moving into the next room, she ran a bath, and in the time it took to fill the tub, she figured out a solution to her problem. She would have an abortion. Simple as that.

Squeezing her eyes shut, she sank into the claw-footed tub and let the aromatic water soothe her soul. Her conscience called to her, but she pushed her convictions aside. There was no way she could raise a child alone, with no help at all. "Yes." She exhaled deeply. "It's definitely the right decision."

Smooth brush strokes hit the canvas as Shayla applied more crimson to her painting. She stood at her bedroom window, recreating the view from her room—the sun rising above the ocean, casting shades of red and yellow onto the clean, glassy surface.

So far so good, she thought, as she stepped back to inspect her work. The piece would fit in nicely with her collection. She would add it to her portfolio, and come springtime, she was certain to get into the summer art program at the university. Something she'd always wanted to do.

A myna bird landed on the windowsill and sat chirping as Shayla took her blender brush and swept it over the top portion of her work. When he flew away, she looked outside again and couldn't help but smile.

Every day, the beauty of her backyard moved her. The house she and her mom had moved into only four months earlier sat inside a tiny cove on the North Shore of Oʻahu. It was a small home—barely big enough for the two of them—but the location more than made up for the size, and she and her mother were more than willing to give up a little space so they could live a stone's throw from the ocean.

At the end of her yard, scattered, choppy surf broke gently onto a secluded beach that extended into a forest of palm trees to her left. To the right, a lush gulch lay between her home and another, as well as a short peninsula that cut off any view of the coast to the east. The land jutted outward, rising twelve feet above the water.

Something caught Shayla's eye. A solitary figure stood on top of the cliff, holding a surfboard and staring out to sea. Was it one of her neighbors? His profile contrasted perfectly with the brightening sky.

She reached for a different brush, dipped it in black, and started to outline the shape of the man. Then she noticed something oddly familiar. Her eyes moved at once to the trophy on her desk—Travis's trophy—and flicked back to the person on the cliff.

That silhouette! It was unmistakable.

Quickly, she grabbed a pair of binoculars and darted out onto the lanai. "It *is* him!"

She stood there for a moment, studying Travis's form. Even from that distance he looked sad—the stillness of his body, the way his shoulders slouched. Maybe she should try talking to him. Just one more time. He was her neighbor after all.

With nervous fingers, she tore off her apron and ran a brush through her tangled hair. Still in her paint-stained overalls, she ran through her back yard and cut across the ravine between the two homes.

Travis stood on the tall cliff at the end of his father's property, running his fingers along the deck of a bright blue custom-made 'pipe-board'. One of his sponsors had given it to him to ride in the Bonzai Classic Surf Competition. The day he'd lost his arm. The day he'd lost his *life*.

The surfboard was still in perfect condition—not even a single ding marred its surface—and as he traced the logo on the nose, he wondered if it would ever touch the ocean again. Three times already he had lugged it up to the top of the rocks, intent on throwing it over the edge and into the sea. But each time he'd stopped.

"It's an unlucky board," he told himself. "I'll never use it again." Yet he just couldn't bring himself to ruin such a beautiful piece of work.

Travis heard someone approaching. Expecting another lecture from his father, he rolled his eyes and turned. His jaw dropped when he saw Shayla there instead.

She gave him an awkward smile. "I was painting you."

"Huh?"

"From my bedroom window." She pointed toward her house. "I didn't know it was you though."

Travis swallowed hard. He hadn't been aware anyone could see him out here. Before he'd left to stay with his grandmother, the little house across the gulch was vacant. Even before then, when it was occupied, no one had ever come up to the cliff before. At least not while he was there. He debated finding a new spot to think.

"I didn't know we were neighbors."

"Me neither, but I don't know anyone around here yet."

Travis shifted from one foot to the other and cleared his throat. Shayla always seemed to appear when he was in no mood for company.

She looked out at the ocean. "I love this view."

He didn't respond. His fingers tightened on his surfboard. Now he wished he hadn't brought it. His ears grew hot with shame as he tried to focus on his surroundings. The morning air blew crisp and clean and carried in the sound of the surf. A large frigatebird, with a bright red throat pouch, soared across the sky. It dipped low, snatched something from the surface of the water, and flew away with it in its beak.

Smiling, Shayla watched it with him. "I think this is the most beautiful spot on the island. Do you come out here a lot?"

Travis shrugged. "I guess."

"But you don't go out there anymore, do you?" She pointed out at the waves.

"No."

Travis clenched his jaw. *That* was none of her business. Why had she come? What did she want? Covered in paint, with her hair blowing in the wind, she looked so sweet and innocent, but he knew from experience looks could be deceiving.

She reached out and brushed her hand over his board. "You must really miss it. So why don't you just try it sometime? Brady and I go surfing after work. You could come with us. You could do it. You'd just have to relearn some things and...."

Rage boiled inside him, and the look on his face must have shown it. Shayla backed away, stammering, "I ... I'm sorry. It wasn't my place to say."

"No ... it wasn't."

Travis's breathing grew shallow; his pulse echoed in his head. She was right. Every day he missed surfing. Whenever he saw the ocean, he ached, desperate for the exhilaration and freedom he felt while ripping down an enormous wave. He'd never feel that again. And he didn't need *her* to point that out to him.

He intensified his glare.

Shayla stood her ground. Travis was mad at her ... *again*. What had she done this time? She held his gaze, determined not to break contact first. The light reflected in his deep-set eyes, giving off a hint of turquoise blue. She followed the sun's path along his strong, square jaw and lingered on his lips. Oh, how she wished he would smile. She'd only seen him smile once, but the memory nearly drove her insane. She just wanted one smile directed at her.

Suddenly, she realized that by looking at his mouth, she was no longer staring him in the eye. She took a step back. Travis cleared his throat and flicked his eyes away. Had he noticed her scrutiny?

He let out a heavy sigh. "Please, just go away."

"Fine, but I only wanted to help."

"Help with what? You know what would help? If *you* left me *alone*."

The words were a vicious slap. Shayla whirled around and cut back through the trees, flinging branches out of her way. Through her yard and up the steps, she rushed back into her room. Her painting sat on the easel unfinished, but she was in no mood to complete it now.

Fingers fumbling, she put her paint away and took her brushes into the bathroom. As she rinsed them clean, she looked at her reflection in the mirror. Exasperation flashed in her eyes. "That's it! I'm done with him."

~Delicious Elevation~

Arriving early for work, Travis helped Brady pull the sliding doors open, exposing the front of the store to the street. Shayla got there just in time to help bring out the beach rental equipment. Travis turned his back when she entered the shop. Days had passed since he'd last seen her, and the fire in his veins blazed again as he recalled their last conversation.

Avoiding eye contact, he stared outside feigning interested in some kids riding by on skateboards. Then he realized she wasn't even looking.

Well, that was fine with him.

From his peripheral view, he studied the girl. A white tank top clung to her figure, highlighting her bronzed skin, and she had pinned her hair up on one side with a flower. There was an angry tilt to her lips as she picked up a stack of boogie boards, and when she brushed past him, she knocked them into his shoulder. He knew it wasn't an accident. He glowered as she set them out on the sidewalk.

Brady stepped in between them. He placed his hands on his hips. "A bunch'a new stuff came in today. Everythin's gotta be checked off an' tagged. It goes quicker with two people, so that'll fill up most'a your mornin', yeah?"

Travis gaped at his friend.

Shayla coughed. "Huh?"

With a devious smirk, Brady shooed them both toward the rear of the store and rushed over to assist the first customer.

In the back room, Travis surveyed the boxes of inventory. There had to be at least twenty of them.

Shayla glanced at him. "He did that on purpose."

Travis tried not to look at her. "Yeah." It took all he had not to run out the door.

"Let's get this over with then," she said.

With a utility knife, Shayla cut open the first box and pulled out some plaid sundresses. She sorted them by style and size, while Travis checked them off on a list.

Working so close to the girl made his stomach queasy. But why? What was it about her that got him so riled up? She was always asking questions, constantly butting in. Like the other day on the cliff. What was that all about? And why had she come out there to begin with?

"Travis?" Shayla interrupted his thoughts. "Did you write down what I said?"

The question startled him, and he almost dropped the clipboard that was balanced on the stump of his arm. He wedged it tighter against his chest, hoping she hadn't noticed. "Sorry," he mumbled, and tried to focus once again on the list.

An hour later, they had completed all but three of the boxes. Shayla opened the next one and let out a tiny squeal. "Yes!" she exclaimed, pulling out a handful of multicolored bikinis. She divided them into two different groups.

Travis pointed with the pen. "What's that pile for?"

She leaned over the next box and paused before cutting it open. "Oh," she replied. "Those are the ones I'm trying on."

Her excitement amused him. He couldn't help it. He shook his head and smiled slightly.

With a startled look, she smiled back and sliced the knife over her thumb. "Shit!"

Travis dropped the clipboard and rushed to her side. "You okay?"

Blood poured from the wound. He jumped up, hurried into the bathroom, and came back with a bandage. "That looks deep," he said, as he knelt beside her.

Her skin paled. "I hate blood."

Travis ripped the package open with his teeth. Then he paused, looking at the adhesive strip. With only one hand, he wasn't sure how to apply it to her thumb. Shayla had only one free hand herself.

He let out a chuckle, and she broke into a grin. Combining forces, they pulled the bandage open together and applied it to her wound. "Thanks," she said, still giggling as she inspected their work.

Travis nodded. His mouth had grown dry. As he stepped backward, an uneasy silence surrounded them. It was strange. For once they were getting along, and he was less sure how to deal with that than when they were at each other's throats.

Shayla gave him a smile and turned her attention back to the boxes. "Only a couple more." She picked up the knife.

Travis snatched it from her. "I'll take that."

"Oh, so now you're worried, yeah? One little cut and you think I'm useless."

Travis snickered. "Nah, I just don't want you to cut me next."

All awkwardness left as he sliced open the box, and as he laid some board shorts on the floor, her words ran through his head. *You think I'm useless.*

At once, he understood. By offering his assistance, he

hadn't meant she was useless. So perhaps whenever she had offered help in the past, she wasn't suggesting his incompetence either. If his missing arm had bothered her before, it didn't seem to now. Maybe—just maybe—she wasn't so bad.

"I'm sorry I've been such a jerk," he said quickly, before he could change his mind.

Shayla's hand paused over the list. She sat back on her heels. "It's okay. I gotta learn to mind my own business sometimes."

"Nah. It's not your fault. I've just been having a tough time lately." He pressed his lips together, unsure of how much he wanted to share.

She shook her head. "I never should've asked you to go to the beach. I just thought you wanted to surf and..." She stopped. "There I go again."

Travis swallowed hard. There was a moment of silence, until he whispered, "Of course I want to. It was my life."

He turned and cut open the last box. Neither of them spoke as they focused on their work, but as soon as they finished, Shayla turned to him. "Want to hang out with me and Brady after work? I'm doing a show at one of the resorts. You could come too."

"What kind of show?"

"Hula," she answered. "I've been dancing since I was six."

Travis paused. He was still a little unsure, but the look on her face was so hopeful, he felt himself weaken. He nodded slightly. "Kay den."

"For real?" She beamed up at him. "Sweet!" With an armful of bikinis, she bounced up to the front of the store, soft curls dancing around her shoulders.

Brady poked his head into the back room. "Eh? You guys make up?"

Travis scoffed. "Your little plan worked."

Brady laughed. "Das right, cuz. Why even doubt me?"

Eyes sparkling, Shayla stuck her head back through the door. "Hey, Brade. Don't make plans after work, okay? You're coming to hang out with us."

The distinct smell of marijuana filled the air as the intoxicating vapors swirled lazily through the living room. Devin sat on the floor playing video games with three of his friends and taking hits off a homemade bong. Coughing and grunting, he held the smoke in his lungs and passed the contraption to Jonny.

As he leaned against the side of the couch, a sea of beer cans and dirty ashtrays covered the carpet around him. Only a few nights before, someone had cleaned the entire room. *Well, whatever.* Devin puffed on a cigarette. Houses were meant for living in, and he had yet to figure out who had cleaned up in the first place.

From the mini fridge, he grabbed a beer and popped the tab. There was a knock on the door, and a local boy stuck his head inside. "Ho, wazz'up braddah? You get some buds for sell or w'at?"

"Yeah, brah." Devin waved him in.

Two young girls followed the boy and lingered by the doorway. Neither of them made eye contact. *Must be their first time buying dope,* Devin thought as he retrieved his stash from under the sofa and reached inside the coffee table for his scale. He pulled out some good-sized buds, weighed a few grams, and put them inside a baggie. The boy handed him some money.

"You bettah' be lightin' one up," Devin ordered.

"Yeah, okay." The boy sat on the couch, took out a rolling paper, and crumbled a large pinch of green stuff into the middle. He rolled it expertly, licked the edge, and sealed the joint.

Devin threw the kid his lighter. "Try sit," he said to the girls, who were still standing by the entrance. He motioned them over to some chairs, and fifteen minutes later, they were giggling up a storm. One of the girls gave Devin a flirtatious smile and playfully touched his arm. She was just his type: tiny, young, and brunette. He smiled back.

The door opened again, and a heavy-set Samoan man walked in. It was Vince, Devin's coke dealer.

Coughing out smoke, Devin jumped up to his feet and hurried forward. Although he had known the guy for years, he was always impressed by how intimidating Vince looked—razored-bald with a tattoo on the side of his head and metal piercings through his bottom lip.

"Eh, Vince. Howz'it?"

Vince's eyes darkened as he appraised the group. "You like come outside?"

Devin hurried forward.

As the door closed behind them, Vince frowned. "Brah, I rather come when nobody stay."

"Sorry, Vin. They just showed up."

"Whatevahs." The darker man's eyes narrowed. "Jus' hurry den."

Devin pulled out his wallet and hesitated before flipping it open. He knew he shouldn't be buying cocaine—he had spent all day selling pot for rent money—but it seemed like ages since his last good high.

A craving hit him hard. Glancing around first, he passed his dealer a wad of bills. Vince handed him an eight ball, stuffed the money in his pocket, and left without saying another word.

Devin watched the sleek, black sedan pull away from the curb and slumped down on the porch sofa. A dented-up vehicle sat in his own driveway. He thought about the shiny, white sports car he had bought when he was still surfing. If it weren't for the drugs, he'd still have it.

As he fingered the small bag in the palm of his hand, he considered selling cocaine. Dealing marijuana had always kept him from hitting rock bottom, but the money he made selling weed was nothing compared to what he could bring in selling the white powder.

As usual, he shook the idea from his head. Selling coke didn't sit right with him. It never had. And he didn't know why either, since he liked the stuff so much.

Quickly, before he could do any more thinking, he scooped up some snow and snorted it off his fingernail. Finally relief hit his bloodstream, and he lingered in delicious elevation.

The young brunette stuck her head out the door. "Why you sitting here all by yourself?"

He hid the cocaine in his pocket. "I was waiting for you." He patted the sofa and some dust rose in the air. He waved it away and smiled.

She smiled back and sat beside him. Taking that as his cue, Devin leaned toward her and gently kissed her lips. "Let's go for a walk."

Hand in hand they strolled down the street, making small talk. Devin found out the girl's name was Bobbie, and that she had just moved to the island from California. She told him about her plans to go to nursing school and about her family back home, and all the while he pretended to care.

He didn't really. He had no intentions of seeing her again, after he got what he wanted. And from the way she kissed him, as he pressed her up against a fence, he was pretty sure he would get it.

~Possession~

Travis sat at a dining table in a draped tent, eyes glued to the stage as Shayla danced, moving her hands and hips to the music. At the side of the stage, a man in a flowered shirt plucked the strings on a slack key guitar. Travis didn't understand the lyrics of the song or the meaning behind Shayla's hand gestures, but he felt the raw emotion of her movements. The Hawaiian dance had never affected him like this. Up on the platform, Shayla looked like an island goddess. Her colorful muumuu clung to her body and bracelets made of ti-leaves circled her wrists. Their eyes made contact and she smiled.

More dancers moved onto the platform. It was the last song of the evening so they encouraged the audience to join in. Shayla managed to coax Brady onstage. She dressed him in a grass skirt and coconut bra, and he shook his hips provocatively at a rowdy girl who was hooting at him from the audience. A goofy grin plastered his face. Travis laughed until his sides hurt. He had to admit he was having a good time. And it was nice to be surrounded by strangers for once. No one seemed to notice him, or his arm.

When the show ended, Travis, Shayla and Brady hung around for a bit, talking to tourists and feasting on macadamia nut cream pie and shave ice. Travis smiled slightly as he scraped the last of the sugary remnants out of his cup. Shave ice was his absolute favorite treat. The fluffy ice topped with flavored syrups was a tradition on the island—one he was more than happy to partake in.

It was after midnight by the time they got back to the surf shop. Brady straddled his motorcycle and pulled his helmet onto his head. "I gotta jet," he said through the visor. "Gettin' up early tomorrow."

Engine screaming, he took off down the highway leaving Travis and Shayla alone.

Travis cleared his throat. "You need a ride home?"

"Nah, it's okay. I got my car."

There was an awkward moment as they stared at each other. The wind blew Shayla's hair to the side, and Travis caught a whiff of her perfume. The flowery fragrance made his pulse quicken, and he had a strong urge to ask if he could see her again, alone, on a date.

He covered his stump with his fingers. 'You looked great tonight. I really liked your dancing."

She gave him a bashful smile. "Thanks."

He opened his mouth, about to ask if she had plans the next night, when a car squealed around the corner. Muffler roaring, it tore up the highway, crossed the bridge, and disappeared around another bend.

Travis straightened. "That's my brother's car."

Sirens blasting, two police cars came barreling around the corner in pursuit.

"Shit! What's he done now?" He fished his keys from his pocket and glanced at Shayla.

She nodded. "Go. I'll see you tomorrow."

Devin held a large bag of weed in his hands, ready to toss the green stuff out the window the first chance he got. Jonny stepped on the gas and the car skidded around a corner. Behind them, the police cars vanished for a moment. Devin seized the opportunity and flung the package into some bushes at the side of the road.

"We're good!" he called out. "I tossed the shit!" His hands shook visibly. He sat on them.

The sirens grew louder as Jonny slowed down and

pulled to the side of the road. "Fuck, brah. This is junk!" he hissed.

Devin turned to Bobbie in the back seat. The girl's eyes were wide with fright. "Don't say nothin' about no drugs," he whispered.

She nodded.

Lights surrounded them, blue and red beams flashing. One police car squealed to a stop behind them. Another pulled up in front.

Gun drawn, an officer jumped from the vehicle in the back. "Driver, exit the vehicle! Keep your hands where I can see them."

Jonny complied, slowly stepping outside. Holding his hands in the air, he backed toward the cop, who re-holstered the gun, shoved him up against the side of the car, and handcuffed him quickly.

Devin tried to listen. Their voices were muffled and he couldn't hear what they were saying, but he could tell Jonny was being mouthy. Red hair spilled from his cap, matching the fire in his eyes. He struggled while the officer held him.

Out of habit, Devin's hand reached inside his pocket and gripped the small packet of cocaine within. *Shit!* He hadn't had time to toss it.

He was about to hide the stuff under the seat when a second officer came to his side of the vehicle. "Step outside." His voice rang with authority. A thick mustache hid his upper lip.

Devin cursed silently and shoved the drugs into his waistband as he unfastened his seatbelt. He opened the door and got out slowly; the eight ball felt as if it was burning a hole in his side. *Fuck!* Why was he so stupid?

The officer turned him around and cuffed him. Cold steel dug into his wrists.

"What's your name?"

"Devin Kelly."

"What did you hide in your pants? You got any weapons on you? Drugs?"

Devin shook his head. "No."

The officer patted him down, reached inside his waistband, and brought out the package of powder.

"This looks like drugs to me." The cop put the bag of weed along with Devin's wallet on the top of the car. He turned Devin around. "You high right now?"

Devin shrugged.

"Not much of a talker, huh?"

"No, sir," Devin answered. He squirmed in his cuffs, trying to loosen them a little. His last hit was fading, and he tried to avoid the cop's penetrating eyes. His stomach churned, and he had to fight to keep his knees from buckling underneath him.

"Looks like we're gonna have to charge you," the cop stated. "Anything else in the car?"

Devin shook his head.

"You have the right to remain silent. Anything you say can be used against you in a court of law. You have the right to speak to an attorney and have an attorney present during questioning. If you cannot afford a lawyer, one will be provided for you at government expense. Do you understand your rights?"

"Yah."

The cop put Devin into the back of the nearest police car and went to talk to Bobbie. Devin watched the girl get out of the car. Her hands trembled at her sides, but they remained free. Why didn't the cops cuff her too? That wasn't fair.

The policeman asked her name, and Devin heard her answer through the open window.

A female officer came forward. Devin hadn't noticed her before. She went through Bobbie's purse and frisked the girl, patting down her clothes and checking through her pockets. When she didn't find anything, she asked, "Are you high too?"

Bobbie shook her head. "I smoked some pot." Her voice sounded squeaky. "I don't even know these guys. I just met them tonight. I've never been in trouble before. I swear. We were just going for a ride."

The cop frowned. "Well, now you know what a ride can get you."

Bobbie nodded, and Devin could see her shoulders shaking. He frowned. This wasn't how the night was supposed to end.

Gripping his steering wheel, Travis watched the cops snap Devin and Jonny into handcuffs and load them into separate vehicles. A young girl stood next to Devin's car, clutching her arms to her chest.

Travis got out of his truck, but when he tried to approach, one of the officers told him to stay back. "I'm family," he explained, pointing at Devin. "I'm his brother."

"Have you been partying too? Let me see your ID."

Travis pulled out his wallet and handed over his driver's license. "I wasn't with them," he replied. "I just saw the chase. What's he done? Can I do anything to help?"

The cop simply shook his head and handed Travis back his license. Travis didn't move any closer, but he stood nearby, listening while the female officer asked the girl questions.

"Did you know he had cocaine on him?"

Tears streamed down her cheeks. "No, and I promise I won't talk to them again."

"Good," the officer said. "These aren't the type of guys you want to hang out with."

The girl nodded, and the policeman that had arrested Jonny interrupted. "Tow truck's here. We're good to go."

Travis stepped forward again and motioned toward the girl. "She's my friend. I can take her home." He had never met her before, but he couldn't stand to see the terror in her eyes. He didn't want her to have to pay for his brother's stupidity.

The cop looked at her. "You know him? You're okay with that?"

She glanced at Travis warily and nodded.

"She can go," the other officer agreed.

Without hesitating, the girl hurried toward Travis, who directed her back to his truck. "What's your name?" he whispered as he opened her door.

"Bobbie," she replied, voice quivering.

"I'm Travis," he said. "In case they ask." But when he turned around again, the police cars were already leaving. Devin locked eyes with him as they drove by. He knocked his head against the window and mouthed a single word. With a quick nod, Travis understood. He pulled his cell phone from his pocket and dialed their father's number.

~First Offense~

Carl spent the entire morning and half the day talking to policemen and bailing his oldest son out of jail. Devin had been caught with cocaine. Only a small amount, but nevertheless, he was up for charges of possession.

Rain poured from the sky as Carl stomped down the steps of the correctional center. Droplets stung his face and splattered his clothing, yet the storm's fury was nothing compared to his own. "You're lucky you had a good judge," he snarled. "Bail could have been set way higher. You know you could end up in jail for this?"

Devin scoffed at him. "They won't lock me up for that lil' bit."

"You don't know that."

"At least I wasn't selling it."

"This time!" Carl's voice bellowed across the parking lot. He lowered it. "Don't think I'm blind to what goes on in your life, Devin. Even if you don't get jail time, this'll be your first offense, and who knows how many more if you don't straighten yourself out."

Devin dragged his feet, scuffing them through puddles as they walked. "It ain't my fault Jonny was speedin'."

Ignoring the drops of rain trickling down the back of his shirt, Carl stopped beside his vehicle. "Jonny's license is suspended. He's got fines and community service. And it serves him right too. Do you even realize how many lives you endanger with the shit you do, including your own?"

"Whatever."

Carl threw him a fierce stare. "This is serious, Dev. You don't even care, do you?"

Devin glared back at his father. Yes, he cared. He had just spent the entire night locked in a holding cell with nothing but a thin mattress to curl up on and three guys who looked like they'd stepped out of an asylum. He had tried not to look at anyone, but even so, he had felt the hostility oozing from the others. The largest of the three, a creepy looking bald guy, had wanted Devin's mattress. With nothing but a grunt, he had picked Devin up by his clothing and thrown him into a wall. Devin hadn't slept after that, and every hour had seemed like an eternity. Did his dad seriously think he wanted to be locked up in a place like that for months … or years?

Forcing back a shiver, he got into the vehicle and shrugged. "No worries, Dad. We'll get your friend, Paul to help. He's the best defense lawyer on the island. They'll let me off with probation. I know guys who've been in this same situation and…."

"Yeah, that's the problem."

Devin shut his mouth and leaned against the headrest. In the backseat, his brother sat motionless. Travis hadn't come into the station, and he looked away when Devin glanced back at him.

His father backed out of the parking spot. Devin could see him grinding his teeth as he drove.

Leaving the city behind, they cruised down the H-3, heading east toward Kaneohe. Dark clouds rumbled overhead, and a flash of lightning streaked across the sky. As they entered the Tetsuo Harano tunnels that passed though the Ko'olau Range, Devin thought about the game he and his brother used to play when they were younger. They would try to hold their breath until they reached the other side. Usually they ended up laughing and no one would win.

Did Travis remember that too?

His father glanced at him. "Dev, you need help. There's a clinic in Honolulu. Maybe they'll let you off if we can get you in."

"I ain't goin' to rehab." Devin gripped the door handle.

Carl let out an aggravated sigh. "Then you're coming to stay with me until we figure this out."

Devin shook his head, and his dad nodded. "Yes, you are. I want you where I can see you. I wanna know you're going to show up for your hearings. And if you don't, you can pay for your own damn lawyer."

The threat caused a rush of fear down Devin's spine. His hands began to tremble, so he clenched them in his lap. "How long you gonna lecture me?"

"As long as it takes," his father replied. "You're supposed to be a good role model for your brother, not some coke-head getting arrested."

"Dad, don't bring me into this. I'm not a fricking child," Travis said from the back.

Devin broke into a cold sweat, and it took all he had not to leap from the moving vehicle. The lights in the tunnel made him dizzy, so he shut his eyes and pretended to sleep for the rest of the way home.

When they finally pulled up to the house, both he and his brother jumped out of the vehicle. Travis hurried over to his truck. Devin headed inside the house. Two different doors slammed shut behind them.

~Could've Been~

Due to heavy rains, no one was around. Travis entered the surf shop and found Shayla sitting behind the register, watching a surfing documentary. A small lizard scurried across the carpet beside her foot but she took no notice of it.

"No customers?" He leaned over the counter.

She jumped. "Trav! You scared me. Howz'it? I was worried when you didn't come in today."

With a shrug, he pulled up a stool beside her and sat watching the surfers on TV. At first he didn't say anything. He didn't really want to talk about his brother's arrest, but his lips seemed to loosen and before he knew it, the words spilled out on their own. "Devin's always getting into trouble," he concluded. "He's had it pretty rough."

"So have you," Shayla said quietly.

Silence lingered for a moment. Then he spoke again.

"My dad thinks I'm going to turn out like him. First Devin, and now me."

Shayla frowned. "But it's not the same."

"Yeah? Dev was pro too. He won nearly every competition in his division from the time he was nine years old. When he was sixteen, he almost won the world title. Then he gave it all up. I don't think he even cares about surfing anymore.

"When mom died, Dev got real quiet. He'd talk to me and his friends some, but not to Dad. He started failing school and getting in trouble. Dad would yell at him, and I'd stay outta the way. But it just got worse. He started partying hardcore, doing drugs. That's when Dad really flipped out. Kicked him out of the house. They barely spoke for years." He paused. "Devin could've been great."

Shayla shook her head. "Still, it's not the same. You're nothing like your brother."

Travis turned to her. "I was my father's last hope. Every time I look at him, I can see it. And the other day, he hid one of my trophies. Guess it reminded him too much of what I could've been."

She put her hand on his. "I wish there was something I could do."

Glancing down at her fingers, Travis shrugged. They pulled apart.

"So, Brady told me your brother has a kid."

"Yeah," Travis sneered. "But you'd never know it. He has nothing to do with her. He's such a deadbeat. Wrecked his whole life if you ask me."

"It doesn't have to be that way for you."

Again, Travis shrugged. "At least I have better friends."

Shayla gave him a sheepish grin, and his heart raced.

"Tell me about your accident," she spoke softly.

On the television, a Jet Ski towed a surfer into a massive wave. As the guy charged down the sixty-foot face, white water closed around him, hiding him from sight. Travis looked away and cleared his throat. "It happened during the final heat. A tiger shark came outta nowhere."

"Did it hurt?"

"I don't remember feeling anything until I woke up in the hospital. It's all kind of a blur. I just remember getting tugged real bad and holding onto my board."

"Did they catch the shark?"

"Nah, but sharks don't usually attack on purpose. It probably thought I was a turtle."

Shayla grinned. "Yeah, you look pretty turtle-like to me."

Feigning offence, Travis punched her lightly on the shoulder. "Gee, thanks."

She smiled.

Suddenly, he had to ask. "Does my arm gross you out?"

Shayla gaped. "No, of course not."

He stood up and shrugged. "Seemed like it did."

"What do you mean?"

"The first time you saw me ... you freaked."

Shayla's brow furrowed. She burst out laughing. "Is that what you thought? That I was *grossed out*? Is that why you didn't like me?"

When he didn't answer, she laughed again. "No wonder. I couldn't figure out what I did wrong." Amusement flickered in her eyes as she looked at him. She slid her hand toward his. "I wasn't grossed out. Quite the opposite really."

As their fingers entwined, Travis studied her carefully. Did she mean it? Had she liked him all along?

Although her words surprised him, the look on her face was so genuine it drew him in. He leaned forward and kissed her lips gently. They were soft against his and sweet, tasting of cherry lip-gloss. He kissed her again and a warm rush traveled through him.

The front door chimed, and they pulled apart.

"Customers," Travis stated. "That's awesome."

Shayla smiled. "Rain must have cleared."

"Damn. I think I'll cruise over to Ali'i. You want to

meet up there when you're done?"

"Sure," she answered. "And Trav?"

"Yeah?"

"You can still be great, you know."

The ocean was still a bit choppy from the storm that had passed. The setting sun peeked out from the clouds, splashing the last of its warmth on the quiet beach, and gulls cried overhead, anxious to find treasures that had washed ashore.

Sitting on the damp ground, Travis buried his feet in the sand and watched a young grommet surfing alone. The kid was Hawaiian with bleached hair, and his style reminded Travis of himself at a young age. At one with the water, the grom played with the waves, trying out new tricks and working on turns. He was good, Travis thought. If he got a bit better at setting himself up, he could be quite the threat one day.

It wasn't long before the boy's mother signaled him back to shore. The kid grumbled as he came out of the ocean and carried his board toward the showers. Travis couldn't help but smile. He knew all too well the hunger to stay in the surf forever.

He rose and moved over to the water's edge, and as

the warm foam crashed onto his feet, an image of Shayla flashed in his mind. He felt the touch of her lips on his and thought about their conversation. It had been a long time since he had talked about his feelings, and although she hadn't said much, she had listened. He appreciated that more than anything else.

A tremendous longing came over him, and before he could think about what he was doing, he tossed his shirt on the ground, stepped out of his shoes, and waded chest deep into the ocean. Travis closed his eyes, letting the waves crash over his body. The smell of salt invaded his senses as the water caressed him. Wrapping around him in a fluid embrace, it cleansed his soul and swept the anger from his heart.

He paused, and as he peered into the murky liquid, a blast of terror hit him. What was he doing in the ocean after a storm? And at dusk! Sharks were night feeders. The cloudy water would make him look like food.

Elation turned to panic. He had to get back to dry land. He tried to run, but the backwash slowed him down, and the sharp reef cut his feet. He imagined the blood seeping into the water and that made him fight even harder. The current pushed him back again and again, but finally he reached the shore. Breathing hard, he grabbed his t-shirt, wiped his face with the fabric, and sat there for a few minutes, trying to calm himself down.

A young couple walked by. His whole body tensed. Had they seen him in the water? Had they seen his fear?

Then he realized he was naked from the waist up. No one but his family had seen his arm uncovered. Quickly, he pulled his shirt over his head, but his skin was wet and the fabric clung to his body. Humiliated, he fought to finish dressing, and when he finally succeeded, he saw that the couple had moved on, oblivious to his discomfort.

~No Choice~

Mika sat on the examining table, while her family doctor explained the abortion procedure, the health risks, and her options. He leaned forward and put his hand on her shoulder. "Are you sure this is what you want? The choice is yours, and I'm not saying it's a bad one. I just want to know you've considered everything and this is right for you."

Mika nodded. "It's right."

"Okay. I can set up an appointment now if you like. You should be at least seven weeks along before they do the surgery, so you'll only have to wait a couple weeks."

Again she nodded, hands clutching the arms of the table. "Yes, please," she whispered.

The doctor gave her a reassuring smile. "The clinic will call within the next few days. Do you have any other questions? Any worries?"

When Mika shook her head, he took her chart and left the room. It was done. She had made her decision, and in a few weeks, her life would be back to normal.

The sun had set by the time she left the doctor's office, but instead of going home, she wandered down the street, past the Ali'i boat harbor and onto the beach park beyond.

Once again, she told herself she was doing the right thing. How could she raise a child on such a small income? She only had a part time job at the flower shop her parents had left to her and Ayumi before they moved back to Japan. And she had never liked working there. That was more Ayumi's thing. Mika had no idea what she was going to do with her life.

She clutched her arms to her chest and tried to push the worries aside. It was all going to be okay. No longer would she have to worry about her pregnancy. The abortion would solve that.

She kicked the grass as she walked. It all sounded so convincing, yet when she thought about the upcoming appointment, she ached. Tears formed in her eyes, and she blinked them away.

Stopping beside a vending machine, she dropped some quarters into the slot and retrieved a bottle of ginger-ale. She took a small sip, sat down at a picnic table, and glanced around the nearly deserted beach. The sky had darkened to navy, casting little light, but she could see someone sitting by himself on the sand, slumped forward with his head in his hand. She looked closer. It was Travis Kelly.

He looked so upset that for a moment she was tempted to go to him. Then she paused. What did she really know about him?

The shark attack. Everyone knew that. But what else?

His mother had died when he was younger, and his girlfriend had left him right after his accident. Those were all stories she had heard from her sister. And the latest news: his brother had just been arrested. Mika shook her head. Devin's charges didn't surprise her. The guy was a moron. He deserved to end up in jail. Still, her heart wrenched. The Kelly family had been through so much. Especially Travis.

"Poor guy," she whispered. "He must be so lonely."

She glanced over again, and couldn't help but recall the look on his face when they'd woken up together after her party. He'd left angry because he had seen the condom...

Mika froze. An idea struck her—an ingenious one. More than two weeks had passed since the night of her birthday. Was that was enough time? Just barely.

Gently she rubbed her hand over her stomach, and for

the first time in days, she felt hopeful. It could work, she thought. But first she'd have to find out for sure. Did Travis still think they'd had sex?

It was getting late. Brushing the sand off his shorts, Travis made his way to the parking lot, where he noticed Mika sitting on the grass by his truck. A street lamp illuminated her like a spotlight, reflecting down her straight, black hair. Her arms were crossed over her legs. Tears streamed down her cheeks.

He walked slower, uncertain if he should pass by. Then he stopped. He barely knew the girl, but he couldn't just leave her crying on the beach.

"Mika?" He knelt down. "What's the matter?"

Placing a hand over her throat, she stopped sobbing and sniffled. Eyes filled with despair, she looked up at him. "I'm pregnant," she said. "*Hapai!* And all because of one night of stupidity."

He leaned back on his heels. "Huh?"

"It's true. I tried to get an abortion. I made the appointment and everything, but I can't go through with it. I just can't." Her weeping started again.

Travis's head whirled. He had to be hearing her wrong. He blinked. *One night of stupidity?*

He gripped the girl's shoulders. "Is it mine? Was it the night of the party? The night we...." He couldn't finish.

She jerked away and studied his face for a moment. "Well...I..." She leaned forward, light shining in her pupils. "You don't remember, do you?"

Travis shuddered. "I'm sorry." He tried to bring the memory back, but all he could see was darkness. The next morning, however, was extremely vivid.

"The wrapper on the nightstand," he blurted. "We used a condom. I saw it."

She shook her head. "It was still in the package. I guess we were too drunk to use it."

Humiliation crept into his cheeks as the images flashed in his mind: Mika in bed next to him, her ruffled hair, his untied shorts. And what about his arm? Had she seen it? Had she touched it? The thought sent him spiraling. He couldn't think about it. He didn't want to remember. He swallowed hard. "Is this for real?"

Mika rubbed her eyes with the back of her hand "I'm sorry," she whispered. "Please don't tell anyone, okay?"

Shit! He cursed inwardly. One night of drunken stupor and now he was going to have a baby? He trembled. He couldn't have knocked up some girl. What would his father say?

He felt like running. He could deny it. He could turn her away. Then he thought about Lea, the mother of

Devin's child. He had seen firsthand how difficult it was for her, raising her child alone. What Devin had done just wasn't fair.

Travis couldn't move. He could barely breathe. Mika's sniffling, combined with the image of his niece, finally forced him to break his silence. "I have no choice. I'm not like him."

"Huh?" Mika looked up.

"Nothing."

In as comforting a manner as he could manage, he put his arm around her. "It'll be all right. I'll take care of you." The words cut him like the reef.

Their kiss, their conversation, the way Travis's skin smelled like coconut oil—all of it kept running through Shayla's mind as she finished the rest of her shift. Time dragged, every minute felt like ten.

She looked outside. The sun was down. Would he still be at the beach waiting for her? With a quick glance around, she pulled her bag from under the counter. There were no customers. Surely Brady wouldn't mind if she closed a few minutes early.

Humming cheerfully, she pulled the sliding doors shut, counted the till, and left through the side door, locking it behind her. As she walked through the harbor, her legs felt like skipping, but she forced herself to slow down.

In the window of a minivan, she checked her reflection, scrunched her curls with her fingers, and added a touch of gloss to her lips. Then she looked up and saw Travis sitting under a streetlight. With Mika.

Her breath caught in her throat. She blinked a few times, hoping her eyes had deceived her, but nope, there they were. Holding each other.

She leaned against the side of the van, steadying herself, her legs growing weak. She hadn't forgotten about the morning she had seen Travis and Mika in bed together, but Travis had never mentioned it. She had figured it had meant nothing.

Or was that just what she wanted to believe?

Shayla's heart sank. Had Travis and Mika been dating this whole time? Through clenched teeth, she cursed. "Why can't she find her own frickin' men?"

Without taking another look, she whipped around and ran back to her car. Ten minutes later, she burst through her bedroom door. Moonlight shone through the open window, illuminating her painting of Travis on the cliff. She tore it off the easel, tossed it under her bed, and replaced it with a different painting. One she had made before she'd ever met him.

With a single sob, she threw herself down on the mattress. Her phone rang. It was her father calling.

She hit the reject button. Kane, Travis, and even her own dad. *Why are all men such jerks*? Squeezing her eyes shut, she forced away the tears and crunched her blanket in her fists. Crying over boys was stupid. So she turned all her hurt into anger and dwelled on that instead.

~Worse~

Devin wanted to pack up his house by himself, but his father wouldn't let him. Together, they shoved boxes into Carl's SUV, loading up anything important and tossing the rest into the trash.

Sweat ran down the back of Devin's neck. Every moment brought them closer to his drugs. Could he get rid of the stuff without his dad seeing? He looked outside to the darkness beyond. Maybe he could throw it out the window and come back for it later.

He stood in front of the bedroom door. "This room's done. Nothin' else I need."

Carl stopped and studied him. Then he pushed his way inside. He searched the room and pulled a large paper bag from the closet. Devin tried to snatch it away, but he wasn't quick enough. His father opened the bag and sifted his fingers through dried green buds. Holding one up to his nose, he took a sniff and frowned.

Devin felt his face flush. Why did he even care? His dad already knew he sold weed.

"Is there any more? You may as well tell me now."

Devin looked at the ground.

"Where is it?"

"Under the sofa."

As his father headed into the living room, bile rose in the back of Devin's throat. "What are you gonna do with it?"

Without answering, his old man reached under the couch, retrieved the smaller bag of pot, walked outside, and dumped them both into the dimly lit stream that flowed behind the house.

As his skunkweed floated away on the water, Devin dug his nails into his palms. *Gone.* All the money he would've made and the joints he could've smoked. He looked up at the stars, silently naming them every foul word he could think of. At that moment, he hated his father.

"There's nothing else?"

Devin shook his head. "No."

An hour later, he sat on his old bed in his childhood room in his father's home. Stacks of trophies lined the top of his dresser, and surfing posters hung on the wall along with a cartoon he had drawn when he was twelve.

His father hadn't touched a thing. He could have turned the room into an office or a den, but he had kept it exactly as Devin had left it eight years earlier.

Devin opened the drawer of his bedside table and peered inside. Some old school supplies, a faded pack of chewing gum, and a picture of his mother. It was the same photograph that sat next to Travis's bed, gifts from their father the day after her funeral. Travis had always kept his nearby, but Devin—apart from sticking it in the drawer so long ago—had never touched his.

He picked it up, blew off the dust and stared at his mother's freckled cheeks, her smiling blue eyes.

He put it back.

There was a scratch on the door, and Jasper pushed his way inside the room. He bounded forward and licked Devin's face.

"Did'cha miss me, boy?" Devin scratched the dog behind the ears and leaned against him.

It was eerily quiet in his room—in the whole house for that matter. He got up and pulled open the drawer to his old desk where it seemed someone had been poking around after all. Scattered inside was a bunch of magazine clippings from back when he still surfed. His dad must have put them there.

As he flipped through the articles, they seemed surreal—as if they weren't even about him. Winning the title at only sixteen would've been quite the feat for someone so young. Unfortunately that was the year he'd met Vince.

At first, the dealer's cocaine had given Devin a confident edge, a sense of power. He had won a few contests and thought the drug was helping him. Until things started to backfire. Surfing competitively took a lot of dedication, and it was hard to be victorious when he was doped up on drugs and sleeping through events.

Devin picked up a more recent magazine and read the front cover. *Where's Devin Kelly Now?* He flipped to the middle and skimmed the article. *No one has seen Devin enter the water in years. I don't think he surfs anymore.* He scrunched up the page and shoved the magazine back inside the drawer.

He stared outside. Clouds hid the moon; it was too dark to see the ocean. He never saw it anymore. He tried to remember the last time he'd felt a wave underneath him, but he couldn't.

Whatever.

Next to his bed sat a large box waiting to be unpacked. Aside from a case of clothing, it was all he'd been allowed to bring into the house. His father had checked through it twice, in an attempt to keep drugs out of the house, but he didn't know all of Devin's tricks.

Devin pulled a small desk lamp from the box, unscrewed the base, and extracted a small package of cocaine. He turned on his television, chose a channel, and settled in for the night.

A little past midnight, Travis drove through Waialua. The whole world seemed to be asleep. He pulled into Brady's driveway, rushed up to the house, and pounded on the front door, praying his friend would answer.

A light turned on, and the door opened. "Wha's up, brah?" Brady asked. "You look hurtin'."

Travis pressed his way into the house. "I can't go home. Dev's going to jail and Mika's pregnant."

Brady hurried after him. "Whoa, slow down. Who's pregnant? Was da haps?"

In the kitchen, Travis stopped. "*Mika's* pregnant." He ran his hand through his hair and plopped himself down at the dining room table. "My life keeps getting worse."

Brady grabbed a six-pack from the fridge and slid one across the table. "Prego? By who?"

Travis chugged the beer, slammed the can down, and threw his friend a grave expression.

Brady frowned. "Oh. No way, brah."

Travis sunk further into the chair. "For real."

"What you goin' do?"

"I don't know, man. I just don't want to go home."

He glanced around. Brady had decorated his place with Tiki statues, and at the moment, they were all staring at him, judging him. He looked away.

Head propped in his hand, he told his friend about Devin's arrest. "That's why I couldn't come in to work today."

"Wha's gonna happen?"

"I don't know. He might get fined, might get thrown in jail. He's got a hearing in a few weeks and he's staying with us until then."

"Unreal." Brady shook his head. "Is he gonna try for a plea? He got a good attorney?"

"Yeah," Travis nodded. "One of my dad's friends. He thinks we can get the sentence reduced." He gripped the arm of his chair. "Why'd she have to get pregnant, Brade? How am I gonna tell my Dad? It's Devin all over again." Eyes glued to the table, he cracked open another beer and drank it down, wallowing deep in self-pity.

At a loss for words, Brady took a bottle of vodka out of the cupboard and mixed them both something stronger. Travis paused before accepting the drink. Ever since he'd discovered his brother passed out in the living room, he'd been trying not to get drunk. He shrugged. What did it matter anyway? He guzzled the beverage and asked for another.

Brady slid the whole bottle toward him. "I always forget Devin has a kid." He sat down.

Travis snorted. "Yeah, most people do."

"How is Lea? You still go see her?"

"Not since I got back. I probably should though."

Two hours and many slurred words later, the bottle of booze was empty. Travis stumbled over to the living room sofa, where Brady handed him a pillow and a blanket.

"So what about Shayla? She seems pretty into you."

Travis rubbed his blurry eyes. A million years had passed since he had kissed the girl at the shop. The room began to spin. "All gone to shit." He put his head on the pillow. "Thanks for letting me crash here."

Brady nodded. "No worries."

~Deception~

Mika couldn't believe it. Her plan had worked. She'd said she was pregnant, and Travis said he'd take care of her. Simple as that. He hadn't even asked any questions.

She smiled. It was perfect really. Travis was the ideal father. He rarely left the island, had lots of money, and was willing to raise the child with her. Not only that, but this would give him the opportunity to be loved and have a family. If anything, she was helping him, giving his life purpose now that he could no longer surf.

Any lingering doubts fled. Everything would be all right. If the baby couldn't have its real father, she would give it the next best thing.

Sitting cross-legged on her bed, Mika flipped through the pages of a fashion magazine, but she was barely able to concentrate on the pictures. She jumped when her sister entered the room and scattered the book across the bed.

Ayumi gave her an odd look. "You okay? You've been acting weird lately."

"No, I haven't. You scared me, that's all." Mika patted the blanket beside her. "Guess who I'm dating," she said with a grin. "Travis Kelly!"

"Really?" Her sister sat down. "That's awesome, Mik. He seems nice. Maybe this one'll work out for you."

Mika's smile grew as her twin gave her a hug. The seed of deception was planted. In a few weeks, she could tell Ayumi she was pregnant and pass Travis off as the father. She wouldn't have to go through with the abortion, and no one would ever have to know the truth.

All through the night, Mika tossed and turned. Unable to sleep, she finally gave up trying and went outside to watch the sunrise instead. Blanket tucked around her legs, she sat out on her lanai, listening to the morning birds and watching the sky turn a light shade of purple. The scent of ginger hung in the air. She breathed deeply, but it did little to soothe her mood or her stomach.

What if her plan failed? What if Travis found out the truth? She had no real claim on him. They hadn't even slept together, and not only that, but she had lied to her sister.

"I had no choice," she whispered. "It's too late to back down now."

Trying to be strong, she swallowed the lump in her throat, tossed her blanket aside, and shuffled back into the house. Perhaps some tea would calm her queasiness. She placed the kettle on the stove, turned on the burner, and waited.

Her cell phone rang; the vibration on the counter startled her. "Hello?" she answered.

"How come you neva' call back?"

Mika recognized the voice and groaned beneath her breath. It was Kane Walker, calling from Brazil where he was on tour waiting to compete in one of the final events of the season.

"I'm busy," she answered. "Shouldn't you be out surfing, winning your stupid title?"

"So w'at, you still mad at me?"

Mika tried to control her breathing. "You made it pretty clear what you wanted."

"Sistah, I said I sorry. Shit, I knew I shouldn't of made dat bet. Was stupid. We was both drunk, das all. I promise."

"Whatever." Mika's fingers tightened around the phone. "Just stop calling me, okay?"

She hung up and paced back and forth in her living

room. She pictured Kane's dark skin and magnetic eyes, his body rippling with muscles. At one point, she had found it all hard to resist. But not anymore.

She hugged her arms to her chest and ran a hand over her belly. *If only he knew,* she thought. *He wouldn't want me then.*

The tea kettle whistled, shrill and sharp; the noise pierced her ears. Mika hurried over to stop it and poured herself a cup of hot water. She dipped a teabag into the steaming liquid and stirred it lightly, breathing in the fragrance of rose and lavender. She took a long sip, determined to push the champion surfer out of her mind. She wouldn't let Kane's phone call ruin her day. It was already messed up enough.

~Loser~

A gray fin broke the black, murky surface and headed straight toward him. The mouth of the beast opened, blood glistening along its snout. Travis tried to grab hold of his surfboard, but he didn't have any arms. He screamed, and his voice came out muffled.

Then it was gone. The shark disappeared, and he sat in the lineup at Pipe. An enormous wave formed in the distance. Closer it came, rising taller and taller, until it towered over him like a mountain. Row upon row of giant teeth materialized from the lip. The mouth slammed shut on him...

Travis woke in a hot sweat and threw his blanket on the floor. Blinking sleep from his eyes, he glanced around and found himself in Brady's living room. The events of the past evening came back to him, and he sat up slowly. His head throbbed. Rays of sunlight spilled through the living room curtains. It was well past noon.

Brady had left a note on the coffee table telling him to

stay as long as he liked, so he turned on the television and settled back down, but he couldn't concentrate on the screen. All he could see were the images in his mind—the shark coming for him, his surfboard taunting him. He ran his hand through his hair and let out a breath. At least it wasn't the other dream—the one where he had his arm back and was surfing with all of his friends. That was the real nightmare.

After a quick shower, Travis left Brady's and drove back home. Expecting to walk into a war zone, he opened the front door cautiously, but the house was peaceful as he entered. The only sound came from the TV in the den, where he found his brother, lying on the couch, doing absolutely nothing as usual.

"Is Dad up yet?"

Devin didn't budge. "I think so. He's been in his room all mornin' though."

"Awesome." Travis snarled as he walked by and pushed his brother's feet off the coffee table.

"Was' da haps?" Devin put them back up. A puzzled expression crossed his face.

Travis shook his head and suddenly he couldn't hold back. "Why can't you stop being such a loser?"

Devin's mouth dropped open. He looked stunned. Or confused. Or was that just plain stupidity?

Travis was about to say more, but he didn't get the

chance. His dad came into the room. "Where were you all night?" he inquired, placing his hands on his hips.

Head still pounding, Travis threw his brother an accusatory glare. He turned to his father. "Don't worry, I wasn't out selling drugs." With that, he pulled his keys from his pocket, spun around, and headed back outside.

Expecting another lecture, Devin stiffened and stared at the television screen with unseeing eyes, but his father didn't say anything to him. He marched back into his bedroom and slammed the door. *Whatever.* Devin folded his arms across his chest. If his dad wanted to give him the silent treatment, that was fine with him. But what was up with Travis? It'd been years since he'd scrapped with his brother.

Leaving the comfort of the couch, he wandered up the stairs. Near the top hung a photograph taken when the boys were much younger. Standing next to Devin in the picture, Travis looked so happy. A mass of golden locks covered his head as he laughed. In the background, waves crashed against the gleaming shore. Their surfboards lay on the sand.

Devin remembered that day. He had shown Travis how to hit the lip of the wave and had watched him wipe out so many times he thought the kid would give up. But Travis refused to quit. He bet five bucks he could do it and was laughing in the picture because he had won.

Devin pushed open the door to Travis's room and went inside. Clothing littered the floor, and blankets were tossed haphazardly on the bed. He pushed a pillow aside and sat down. Things just weren't the same anymore. Travis had grown up. Devin barely knew him at all.

A strong urge for cocaine hit him, and as he clenched his teeth against it, his eyes traveled around the room. Maybe Travis had some pain medication. A couple of those might do the trick.

He pulled open the drawer to the nightstand and poked around inside. He didn't find any pills, but he found his brother's wallet and cell phone. His heartbeat quickened. With his father watching his every move, he hadn't been able to get any drugs. Now he hardly hesitated. He picked up the phone and dialed Vince's number. "Hey, brah," he whispered hastily. "Meet me in an hour…yeah, the basketball courts."

He hung up, flipped the wallet open, and pulled out a couple of bills. He wasn't worried about the money. He'd pay his brother back.

As soon as Travis entered the surf shop, he spotted Shayla over by the shoe rack. Black hair flowed down her back in loose ringlets, contrasting sharply with her pale blue sundress. He lingered in the doorway, remembering the way she had kissed him so sweetly less than twenty-four hours ago.

Now everything was ruined.

He started forward, but when Shayla saw him, she gave him stink-eye and whirled away.

He turned to Brady. "Does she know anything?"

His friend shrugged. "I didn't tell her."

At the back of the shop, Travis found her again. "Are you mad at me?"

Her hands shook as she fiddled with a shelving unit. "You should've told me about Mika."

Shit.

"Yeah, I know all about it."

Dazed, Travis stood there, with a lump in his throat. How had she found out? "I'm sorry, Shay."

"Whatever." Tugging a little too hard, she pulled the shelf off the wall and it clattered loudly to the floor. She picked it up and changed her tune. "No worries. It's fine. You and I are just friends anyway."

"*Shayla...*" Travis leaned against a rack and ran his

hand through his hair. "What else could I do? You're the one who told me I didn't have to be like my brother."

"Huh?"

His voice rose defensively. "I didn't even know she was pregnant until last night, and that was after I kissed you..."

Shayla gasped. "Mika's *pregnant*?" She backed up. The word seemed to echo in the air.

"I thought you knew."

She stood silently looking at him. Then, she shook her head. "Figures."

"I'm sorry," Travis said again. "I didn't mean for this to happen."

"It's all good. You're doing the honorable thing. You don't want to be like your brother. I get it. Like I said, we're just friends." She turned around and propped the shelf against the wall.

Friends? Travis didn't like the sound of that, but before he had a chance to say anything further, an older woman approached, wearing an *Aloha* shirt. A camera dangled from her neck. "Excuse me? I told my son I'd bring him home something from the islands, but I have no idea what to get him."

Shayla turned swiftly to the woman. "No worries. What kind of stuff does he like?"

"T-shirts, hats." The lady laughed. "I just don't know what's hip these days."

With an overly cheerful smile, Shayla led her customer to a different section of the store, leaving Travis standing alone. Hoping to continue their conversation, he waited, but she didn't return.

Time passed slowly as he worked. Customers came and went, but he avoided talking to any of them, and when a couple of old surfing buddies showed up, Brady intercepted. He spoke to the guys in hushed tones and swiftly turned them away. Grateful, Travis nodded. He finished fixing the shelves, and when it finally came time to close the store, he hurried out the door.

Brady caught up to him in the parking lot. "You need somewhere to stay tonight?"

Travis's truck beeped as he turned off the alarm. "Thanks, but I'll be okay."

Brady pulled his helmet onto his head. "Kay den. If you change your mind, jus' come by."

As the motorcycle sped across the double arched bridge, Travis watched it go, frowning. His own bike sat collecting dust in his father's garage—just one more thing he'd had to give up since the accident.

He started his truck, and a light mist hit the windshield. The drizzle matched his mood, and for some reason, he thought about his mother. She had died of lung cancer when he was eleven, which seemed such a long time ago now. Would things have been different if she were still alive? Could she see him now? Did she know how badly he'd ruined his whole life?

The questions ran through his mind until he could no longer take it. Foot pressed to the ground, he spun his truck out of the parking lot and took off, driving way too fast. Shayla, his mother, his brother, his arm—what else could he possibly lose?

~Reckless Abandon~

Standing in front of the television, Carl blocked his son's view and cleared his throat. "Is this what you're going to do now? Nothing?"

Feet propped on the coffee table, Devin rolled his eyes. He put down his beer and stretched his arms above his head. "What else am I s'posed to do?"

"You could help around the house. The dishes need to be done. Or you could come in and work for me at the office. There's tons of stuff you could help with there."

"Whatevahs. Tomorrow I will." Devin waved him away and turned the volume up with the remote control.

Carl's blood pressure soared. He pulled the power cord from the wall. "You're not going to just sit here all day."

"Fine." Devin picked up his keys. "Then can I get an advance? I wanna go out."

The request was so ludicrous it almost made Carl

laugh. But instead, he frowned and shook his head. "I'm not giving you drug money. How about working off some of your rent?"

"What? Travis doesn't pay rent. You can't make me. It ain't my choice to live here."

"Travis didn't get caught selling coke."

"I wasn't selling it!"

"Oh, so you were just going to snort it all? That's so much better, Dev."

Carl studied his son. Dilated pupils, glossy eyes, twitchy jaw—it was obvious the young man was stoned. How did he keep getting drugs into the house?

Aggravation turned to grief, so he said the only thing he could think of to say, "What would your mother say about this?"

Something flickered behind Devin's eyes. "I gotta go."

Carl stepped in front of the door. "Dev, please, stop this. You're going to get yourself killed."

"Dad, I'm fine. I'm jus' goin' out for a bit."

"I'm talking to the drugs right now, aren't I? If you get caught doing that stuff you're going straight to jail. You know that, right?"

Devin growled. "I ain't gonna get caught."

"I won't let you go." Carl crossed his arms.

Devin shoved past him, knocking him into the front door as it opened. "I'm not in jail yet. You can't stop me."

Carl winced as the doorknob jabbed into him; a jolt of pain shot up his spine. "Get back here!" he shouted. But it was pointless. Devin was already getting into his vehicle.

As he watched the car disappear, Carl rubbed his back. It was the first time Devin had ever gotten physical with him. Had he actually struck a chord by mentioning the boy's mother? *Nah.* Carl shook his head. Devin didn't care about anything.

He let out a breath of frustration. If only he could force Devin into rehab and keep him locked there until he was better. But that wasn't how it worked and Carl knew it. The fact was he had three choices. He could enable Devin, watch him wreck himself, and wait for him to reach a turning point. He could kick Devin out, refuse to watch him demolish his life, and hope he would hit rock bottom. Or he could stop caring.

The last one wasn't an option.

All of the choices sucked.

Back with his regular crowd, Devin partied with reckless abandon. His dad's words still echoed in his head, and as usual, he knew only one way to cope. Much to his relief, he found what he was looking for, and as he sat in the parking lot of a gas station snorting lines in the back of his car, the snow hit his senses in an ecstatic release, a mind-numbing joy. He opened the door and rejoined his gang. The stereo blasted, music pumping from stolen speakers.

People pulled up to the station and away again, taking no notice of the boys who regularly hung around there. As long as they stayed at the far end of the lot, no one paid them any mind. Anyone could have been watching—his dad or the cops—Devin didn't care. He was stoned, and right now, that was all he wanted.

Closing his eyes, he thought about the first time he'd ever tried cocaine. It was at a victory party at one of the luxurious sponsor houses that backed onto the beach in front of Pipe. He had just won a major surf competition, however he wasn't in the mood for celebration for it was also the anniversary of his mother's death.

He couldn't recall who had introduced him to Vince, but he remembered how he'd felt the first time he tried the dealer's drug. He could still feel it—the excitement, the energy, the power. And the more he wanted, the more Vince gave him. After that, he couldn't get enough of the stuff. Nothing had ever rid him of his grief like coke. Not pot, or alcohol, or sex.

It was good then, and it was good still.

Lost in the memory, Devin leaned against his car. The drugs he had snorted, mixed with a few beers, had put his head in such a fog he hoped he'd never come back down.

Through the clouds, he thought he heard someone say, "Daddy". He shook his head and took a drag of his cigarette. Next came a persistent tap on his arm, and when he looked down, a pair of small blue eyes stared up at him.

His daughter. What the hell was she doing there?

Lea ran toward him from a car parked at the gas pumps. *Shit.* He tried to clear away the mist.

The child babbled something. What did she want?

He bent down to listen just as Lea reached them, out of breath and angry. "Come on, Allisa. We have to go!"

She took their daughter's hand and shot a glare in Devin's direction. Some of his friends snickered, which seemed to aggravate her further. She started shouting—accusing him of being irresponsible—but his vision blurred and so did his brain. He tried to react, but for all the confidence the drugs usually gave him, he couldn't find any now.

He said nothing. Normally, he would've yelled back or called her names. Tonight, however, he felt a strange pressure in the middle of his chest. He looked down at his daughter. Her cheeks were flushed, rosy, and streaked with tears.

Those eyes … they looked just like his mother's.

Devin took a step back, and when Lea's boyfriend, Duke, came out of the station, his head began to clear. The last thing he needed was a fight—not while he was stoned and waiting for his trial. He looked at his friends and readied himself. At least it was five against one.

Duke barely glanced his way. Tight-lipped, he picked Allisa up and headed back toward their vehicle.

Allisa kicked at him, screaming, "Put me down. I'm six years old! I'm talking to Daddy!"

"Duke is your father." Lea's voice was firm. "You listen to him."

All the way back to the car, Allisa cried and called out for her *real daddy*. Devin watched in silence, his mind twisting around the whole thing. *Duke? Allisa's father?*

"Did I miss something?" he muttered.

Duke returned alone. "Lea and I are getting married. Allisa's my daughter now, so if you're smart, you'll stay away from my family."

Devin clenched his fists, but before he had time to make a move, a couple of his friends pushed their way to the front, forcing Duke to back down. There was a lot of shouting, but Devin only heard one thing. *Married?*

He shook his head. Lea was the only woman he'd ever loved. She couldn't get married. The parking lot spun as he tried to erase the fog from his brain, and he tried not to hear Allisa crying as the vehicle drove away. He hadn't seen his daughter in over a year, yet she had recognized him right away. What had she been trying to tell him?

Quickly, before he could do anymore thinking, he reached into his pocket for another hit.

~Humiliation~

The young grom stomped his foot. "Mama, I don't want a foamie! It's gotta be something cool!"

Travis searched through a quiver and pulled a bright orange surfboard he thought the kid would like. "If you don't want a foam board, I'd go with this fish. It's thicker and wider, so paddling isn't as hard, and it's good for smaller waves. Makes them easier to catch and doesn't scream beginner."

Visibly pleased with the selection, the boy took it and ran his fingers over the logo on the nose.

"Yeah, yeah. This one! Please, Ma?"

When the mother nodded her consent, a huge grin lit up the grom's face. Intent on carrying the surfboard himself, he dragged it up to the cash register and bounced up and down as Travis rang up the sale.

As the two customers left, Travis heard a short squeal. He turned around and saw Shayla rushing toward the side door. A tall, lanky Hawaiian guy had just come into the store. She leapt into his arms and he spun her around in a circle.

Travis stiffened when he saw the embrace. It was Kimo Kalena, one of his old surfing buddies, home for the Bonzai Classic Surf Competition.

Travis frowned as he thought about the upcoming event. It was that time of year again, when surfers from all around the world came to Hawaii to get in on the action on the North Shore, some vying for the world title, others trying to get themselves noticed by the cameras on the beach.

The whole thing made him sick.

Hoping to go unnoticed, he ducked behind a display case. He had competed against Kimo many times. The guy ripped, and before the shark attack, the two of them had struck up a friendship. Now, his scowl deepened as he watched Kimo put his arm around Shayla's shoulder.

Brady rushed out of the backroom. "Kimo! You're back!"

"Yeah, brah, look what I get." Kimo pulled out a magazine and tossed it into Brady's hand. His picture was on the front cover.

"And he has a new sponsor." Shayla patted Kimo's arm, giggling. "You look like a walking billboard."

Dressed from head to toe in his sponsor's clothing,

Kimo ruffled her hair. "Good fo' see you too," he teased.

Pride covered the surfer's face as he told Brady about his latest big win.

"That's sick." Brady flipped the book over in his hand. "Big name now, huh? You should sign some boards fo' me."

The surfer grinned from ear to ear. "Shootz! Just grab me one pen."

While Kimo signed the boards, a small crowd gathered, all of them anxious to talk to the pro. Travis struggled to keep his envy at bay. He hadn't been following the ratings in the surf magazines, or watching the contests on television, so it surprised him to hear Kimo was doing so well. His old friend was living the life he was supposed to be living. It wasn't fair.

As Brady hung one of the boards on the wall—with Kimo's name inked on the front—Travis turned his back on the whole thing. He tried to rearrange the accessories in the display case, but he ended up making a mess. He closed the cabinet a bit too hard, and that was when Kimo noticed him.

"Travis!" The surfer's eyes widened. "Howz'it, braddah?" Then it came—the all too familiar look of pity. "Man, sorry 'bout your arm. It must suck. Too bad you no surf dis season, brah."

"Yeah," Travis huffed. "Guess it worked out for you though."

As soon as he said it, he clamped his mouth shut. He saw the way Shayla looked at him. It was the same way he used to look at people who couldn't handle defeat—especially when it came to surfing. Avoiding the stares of anyone else, he rushed out of the store.

"Can I have a shot of tequila?"

Travis swigged it down. Then he asked for another.

As he sat in the small bar down the street from Brady's Surf Shop, he brooded quietly to himself. The liquor cut straight to his stomach, but it barely took the edge off his humiliation. Why had he acted like such a kook? He was supposed to be Kimo's friend.

Two more shots later, Travis left the bar and headed straight for his truck, but when he got there, he patted his pockets and cursed. He'd left his keys behind the counter at the surf shop. He had to go back.

Still surrounded by people, Kimo stood outside the shop, writing his name on various items. Travis snuck past him quickly and watched his old friend from an inconspicuous spot. Kimo was living every surfer's dream. Not all surfers wanted to go pro, mind you—not all of them believed in competition—but most, if not all, appreciated the respect and admiration of others. It felt good to be acknowledged for your talent.

At that moment, one of Kimo's fans looked inside, and

when he made eye contact with Travis, his mouth dropped open. *Shit.* Travis darted toward the back of the store, but he wasn't quick enough. The kid followed him.

"Wow, brah! You Travis Kelly, yeah?"

Travis cursed under his breath. Then he realized he had seen the boy before. It was the same young grom he'd watched surfing the other day.

"That's me."

"Right on, you my favorite surfah! I wish I could surf like you."

Travis felt the blood rush to his cheeks, and he took another step toward the backroom.

The kid pointed at his arm. "Trippy what happened to you, brah, but when you goin' come back?"

The question took Travis by surprise. "I ... I don't surf anymore," he stammered.

"What? How come? My cousin from Brazil only got one arm, but that neva' stop him. He still launchin' huge waves."

Yeah, right. Travis shook his head. "Look kid, I'm not your cousin, and I don't feel like it, okay?"

When the boy pouted, Travis bit his tongue. "Sorry lil' man, it's just not my life any more. He's the big star now." He pointed at Kimo, who was still chatting with his fans.

The youngster kicked at a rip in the carpet. "Well, brah, if you ever surf again, no forget to teach me some tips, okay? Promise?"

Travis's mood softened. "Sure." *Like that'll ever happen.*

The boy smiled and hurried off to join his friends. Pointing at Travis, he whispered something to the group. They gawked, and Travis turned away.

Standing behind a large rack of sunglasses, Shayla held her breath, hoping to go unnoticed. She had seen the entire thing—Travis talking to his star struck fan, the look of adoration in the boy's eyes. She had heard the kid's comment about his one-armed cousin and witnessed Travis's snappy reaction along with his regret afterwards. The kindness he had shown, the softness in his voice. That was the real Travis. She just knew it. The thought tore her in two.

Ever since she had found out about Mika, Shayla hadn't spoken to Travis at all. First it was out of anger, but now that she'd had some time to reflect, she just didn't know what to say. Travis had told her he was sorry, that he just wanted to do the right thing. And maybe that was true. But none of it mattered. He belonged to Mika now. For the next eighteen years at least.

Hugging her arms tightly across her chest, Shayla watched Travis walk to the back of the store. She could tell he was upset by the heaviness in his shoulders, the sour slant on his lips. Over the last two days, he'd gone back to being his moody self, acting distant and cold. And not just towards her, but with Kimo as well.

As she cleaned up the mess in the display case, she thought about his reaction to her cousin. Kimo was traveling the world, surfing, and getting paid for it. Plus, he was doing better in the ratings than he ever had before. In the past, he had never finished higher than sixteenth place, but this year, he had won one of the events and had totally ripped in several others. He was in fifth place overall, and it made sense for Travis to be jealous. It had to be hard watching the pros come back, the excitement building in town.

The Bonzai Classic was rapidly approaching. The waiting period would soon begin—a two-week time slot that allowed the participants to wait for perfect surf and compete in optimum conditions. Once the waves were ideal, the contest would last a few days, starting with trials and ending with the main event. Shayla knew her cousin didn't have enough points to win the world title, but he could still win the final competition, and she couldn't wait to watch him compete.

The thought lightened her heart a bit, and she smiled

at Kimo who was still outside the store. He flashed her a grin and poked his head inside. "Eh, Shay, you like go eat some grindz?"

She nodded. "Yeah, I'm starving, and after that let's go to Chun's. I want to see all your new moves."

"Shootz!"

Shayla shouted goodbye to Brady and grabbed her bag from under the counter. She headed for the door and laughed when her cousin picked her up and carried her out in his arms. She gave Travis a small wave, but he sent her a dirty look.

As Shayla and Kimo left the store, Travis turned back to his work. Life sucked. He glanced up at the surfboards Kimo had signed and again felt the cold sting of resentment. He tried to push the negative feelings aside, but he couldn't. Not when Shayla seemed so smitten.

"Hey, Trav." Brady poked his head out of his office. "You wanna go too? I can handle the rest tonight."

Letting out a tired breath, Travis rubbed the tension from the back of his neck. The stub of his arm ached.

He gave his friend an appreciative nod. "Thanks, Brade."

Out in the parking lot, he crawled inside his truck. The

interior was hot from sitting all day in the sun, and as the heat seeped into his back, he laid his head against the headrest, wondering why he'd accepted the job in the first place. He wasn't ready to deal with people, he didn't like being recognized all the time, and he was tired of putting on a fake smile, trying to avoid any mention of his arm.

He thought about quitting. He considered telling Brady he couldn't do it anymore, but then he remembered the chaos waiting for him at home, and his head started to throb. Working for his friend seemed like the better of two evils.

Grunting in frustration, Travis fidgeted with the seatbelt. It was far too constricting. His heart beat fast and his breath came in shallow gasps. He wasn't getting enough air. As he sat up straight, he began to feel tingly—first his legs, and then his neck and throat and cheeks.

What the hell was wrong with him?

He turned the air conditioner on full blast and let it rush over his face. Slowly, the feeling started to pass as his lungs filled with cool air. Was he going insane? Never in his whole life had he felt like this. A total fucking failure.

~Score~

Sitting at the computer in the dimly lit den, Devin browsed through pictures of tattoos on the Internet. Not that he could afford one. He didn't have a dollar to his name. Or twenty-five cents for that matter.

He rocked back and forth on his chair, tapping his foot on the edge of the desk. The night called to him, but he refused to answer. Ever since his run in with Lea at the gas station, he hadn't left the house. And he had yet to sober up. Every time he thought about his ex, he went outside and smoked a joint, and whenever he pictured his daughter's face, he drank another beer.

Unfortunately, it was getting harder and harder to score any drugs. He'd stolen all the money he could from his family, and his friends were sick of giving him hits for free. He had no cocaine left, and he had just smoked the last of his weed. He was going to have to try something else.

Devin switched off the computer and stood by the window where he came to a quick decision. He sprinted up to his room, changed into some darker clothes, and stepped outside just as his brother pulled up in the driveway. The truck door slammed, and Travis shuffled up the sidewalk, green faced and pale.

"Wha's up, man?"

"Nothing." Travis pushed past him and headed up the steps.

Devin followed. "Nah, for real. Was' da haps? You look like hell, bro."

Travis stopped in the doorway. "Oh, so now that you live here, you give a shit?"

Devin paused.

"Don't worry about me. I'm fine!" Travis snapped. "And by the way... that money you stole from me, I want it back." He slammed the door and it rattled on its hinges.

Biting on his bottom lip, Devin stood there for a moment. Then he snuck away from the house, stopping briefly to get a screwdriver from the shed. Creeping carefully, he crossed the property and headed down the highway, scanning for parked cars and watchful eyes.

Tucking himself deep into the shadows of a red-stemmed snowbush, Devin watched as some tourists parked their SUV Tracker next to a path that led down to a darkened beach. Hand in hand, the elderly couple walked down to the sand, and as they disappeared around a bend, Devin slipped up next to the vehicle and peered inside. The woman had left her purse on the seat.

Gripping the screwdriver tightly, he glanced around again to make sure no one was watching. Hopefully there was a lot of money in that bag, he thought, because now he had to pay Travis back as well.

Travis stared at the ceiling. Underneath him, the pillow felt lumpy, the mattress uncomfortable, and no matter how much he tossed and turned, he couldn't seem to find a position he liked.

He reached under the bed, groping for the bottle he'd hidden there earlier. When he found it, he propped it between his knees, twisted off the top, and brought it to his lips. The liquid burned as it slid down his throat. He took another swig, and another. The stump of his arm began to throb. He wished he hadn't thrown his pain pills away.

An hour later, the bottle was empty and Travis was drunk. The alcohol helped soothe the pain in his arm, but it did nothing for his mood. He looked around his room, glaring at the skateboard in the corner and the trophy on his dresser. Above him, a poster hung—a picture of himself catching a perfect wave out at Pipe. He ripped it off the wall. Then he forced himself to close his eyes and drifted into an uneasy sleep.

The nightmare began: *He sat on his surfboard, blood gushing from the shredded remains of his stump. The thick warm fluid turned the entire ocean red. Unable to move, he watched in horror as a school of sharks surrounded him...*

"Dude, you okay?"

Travis bolted upright. He took a gasp of breath and scooted backwards. A bead of sweat rolled down his forehead and he wiped it away with the back of his hand.

Devin stood beside the bed. "You were thrashin' in your sleep."

Travis blinked and looked at his clock. It was three o'clock in the morning; he could still feel the effects of the booze.

"I'm fine." He laid his head back down. "What are you doing in my room?"

Shamefaced, Devin pulled a couple of bills from his back pocket and dropped them on the nightstand. "This should cover what I owe ya." He turned around and left.

Travis reached for the money. He knew where it had come from. Devin had been breaking into vehicles and stealing money for years. He stared at the bills for a second. Then he tore them into tiny pieces and dumped them in the trash.

~Nice Guy~

For once, her stomach wasn't rejecting food. Mika took a bite of her pizza, the first thing she had eaten all day. When she'd tried earlier, morning sickness had engulfed her, and she'd ended up throwing her entire breakfast in the garbage. Now the food tasted wonderful.

Another slice later, she noticed Travis had barely touched his. "Are you worried about your brother?" She took a small sip of iced tea and patted her lips with a napkin.

"A little." He offered nothing further.

"When's his trial? Is he going to jail?"

Travis picked an onion from his food and placed it on the side of his plate. "He's got a hearing in a week or so … and I don't know. Can we talk about something else?"

Mika frowned and scrutinized his appearance. Travis looked pale; dark bags gathered under his normally gorgeous eyes and the worry wrinkles on his forehead never ceased.

Over the last week, they'd hung out almost every evening, and today he had picked her up for a late lunch. Yet still, he seemed like a stranger. She hadn't been able to break through his tough exterior at all. Sure, he'd accepted the baby as his, but they barely seemed friends. Did he enjoy her company even a little?

Pushing away her empty plate, Mika looked at the couple sitting at the table next to them. They seemed so happy, she thought with a sigh. If only she were in the other woman's shoes. Being in love in a fresh, new relationship would be so much better than being pregnant in a fake one.

Well, whatever. She was just going to have to try harder.

Reaching over the table, she put her hand on Travis's. "Maybe you could stay over tonight."

She felt him tense and bit her lip. Why had she said that? She didn't want him to sleep over. And by the look on his face, he didn't want to either.

She released his hand, and he pulled it onto his lap. Taking another sip of her drink, she decided it was best just to keep her mouth shut.

Travis cringed inside. Stay at Mika's house? No way in hell. Sure, she was having his baby, but he couldn't even remember being with her. And he didn't want to.

All week he'd been hanging out with the girl, trying to give her the support she needed, and until now, she hadn't asked for anything further. He was glad. He didn't think he could handle that.

Dark brown eyes looked into his, and as she pushed a piece of hair from her cheek, her lips pouted slightly. She was pretty, no question about that, and she seemed nice enough, but he had no desire to date her.

Shoulders slumped, he sighed. "Sorry, Mika, but I just think we should take things slow, okay?"

She exhaled rapidly, and Travis could've sworn she looked relieved. "Sure." She nodded. "But thanks for being okay with all this. Most guys would run."

There was a commotion at the front entrance as Devin and his gang charged into the restaurant making far too much noise. The hostess tried to direct them to a booth in the far corner, but Devin ignored her. He waved at Travis, and staggered over. "Howz'it, little braddah? I saw your truck out front."

Travis pushed his plate away. It was mid-afternoon

and his brother was already wasted. "Aren't you supposed to be at home?" he asked.

Devin shrugged. "It's all good." He noticed Mika and gave Travis a smirk. "Bro, wha's up? What you doin' with this lil' hootchie?"

Mika slid further into the booth.

Travis sat straighter. "Watch it, man."

"For why?" Devin wrinkled his nose. "You can date all the skanks you want, brah. I got no say in that."

Travis stood up and slammed his fist on the table. "What the fuck, Dev? Why do you have to be such an ass?"

"Hey, now." Devin slipped an arm around him. "I don't wanna scrap, bu."

"Get off me!" Travis pushed his brother backward and he crashed into a table almost knocking it over.

"Whoa, brah." Jonny helped Devin up. "He jus' drunk, cuz'. Relax."

Travis snarled. "He should be at home, not out getting loaded, insulting my friends. You of all people should know that."

Jonny took a step back. "Yeah, yeah, we was jus' leavin'. We goin' take him home."

"Good. Go do it then."

By this time, the restaurant manager and some of the

staff had come over, hoping to break things up. Too late to make much of a difference, they supervised Devin's exit.

Lip quivering, Mika still sat, scrunched in the booth.

Travis slid in beside her. "Sorry about Dev. He doesn't know what he's saying. He gets like that when he's high, disrespectful, especially to girls. But he can be a nice guy too … when he's sober."

Though the words were true, Travis could barely remember the *nice* Devin anymore. He hadn't seen that side of his brother in a long time—not since his family was all together and would get up on Sunday morning to go to church, or sit together on a Friday night in the backyard, roasting marshmallows in their fire pit. Back when he and Devin would spend sunup to sundown fishing or catching waves, acting like real brothers.

"He had no right to call me a skank." A tear threatened to roll down her cheek. She blinked it away and put her hand on her stomach. "He doesn't know, does he? About the baby?"

"No, and I'm not going to tell him."

"Good." She looked around. "I don't want anyone to know, yet."

"Me neither," Travis agreed.

Tired and frustrated, he picked up the bill and pulled

out his wallet. "Come on, I'll take you home." He put some money on the table, leaving an extra large tip to make up for the disturbance his brother had caused.

~Stupid Fish~

A rising swell fluctuated between the north and west peak at Chun's Reef, Shayla's favorite surf break. Mostly known as a longboarding spot, Chun's had a safe channel and long walls, perfect for practicing all kinds of tricks. Every morning for the last week, she and Kimo had hit the waves, so he could try out some new boards for the upcoming contest.

Shayla floated on her longboard while Kimo charged a nice wave. He launched off the crest, spun his board in the air, and landed back on the face. "That was sick!" she exclaimed, giving him a high five when he returned. "You're landing aerials now? No wonder you're doing so well."

Kimo smiled, as he straddled his shortboard. Then his expression turned solemn. "Know who use to bust out some mean airs?"

"Who?"

"Travis Kelly."

Shayla leaned forward and her board dipped down on one side.

"Da bugga was good. Too good. He wen push himself to da max. Nuttin' wen scare him. Brah, unreal all da perfect scores he could get."

She nodded. "It's sad what happened to him."

"Yeah." Kimo splashed some water on his deck and trailed his fingers through it.

Out in the waves, a surfer wiped out. Shayla held her breath as he got sucked under the falls. He broke the surface and rested for only a few seconds before paddling out again.

She smiled wistfully. Surfing had a way of making people forget about the danger and ignore their fears. The feeling of racing down the face of a wave with breakneck speed or getting spit out of a perfect barrel was simply worth any kind of torture the ocean could dish out.

Or was it?

She thought about Travis. Would he feel the same? Was it no longer worth it to him? Kimo had said he used to be fearless. Now he wouldn't even enter the ocean.

Peering into the watery depths, Shayla frowned and wondered if anything was swimming around beneath her.

"You like him, hah?"

Her cousin's question made her jump. "It doesn't matter," she answered. "He's with Mika now." She decided not to mention the baby.

Kimo gave her a sympathetic frown. "I no see how he can like dat girl when he can get you."

Shayla huffed. "He's not the first. Typical guy, I guess."

Kimo grabbed his heart. "Hey! I'm a guy. I not li' dat."

She splashed him. "Yeah, and if you weren't my cousin, I'd snatch you up. You're the only decent one left."

Laughing, he leaned over and gave her a hug. "No worry, cuz'. You goin' find somebody."

"I don't need to." She pointed to the ocean. "I got all this."

When he saw Kimo's car parked alongside of the highway, Travis stopped to take a look. What a stupid idea. Sitting in his truck, he could see Shayla and Kimo out in the water, hugging each other and looking so happy.

He growled inwardly. Never in his life had he felt so bitter. Spinning away from the scene, he headed straight to the nearest liquor store, where he purchased a bottle of whiskey. Then he drove to an empty tourist spot.

Below a small overhang, he spotted a large sea turtle swimming in the water. The sun's rays lit up the sand, promising a beautiful day, yet the beach remained vacant. He was alone with his alcohol.

An image of Shayla flashed in his mind, forcing him to close his eyes. Holding the bottle between his knees, he twisted off the lid, took a throat-burning swallow, and clenched his jaw as the liquor cut its way down into his stomach. He waited for the turmoil in his mind to go away. It didn't, so he took another swig.

A lump formed in his throat and he glared at the bottle, a sick feeling rising in his stomach. Jealousy. Anger. He wasn't used to the feelings. And burying his emotions in booze. That wasn't like him either.

Would getting drunk even solve anything? It was stupid. A cowards way out.

If he'd let himself, he could have cried, but instead, he stifled a moan. With all his strength, he wound up his arm and hurled the bottle into the ocean. Could anything rid him of his anguish?

Travis stood for what felt like hours, and at first, the only answer he could think of was to throw himself into the ocean as well. He thought about the boy from the surf shop, and the kid's voice rang in his head. *"My cousin only got one arm, but that neva' stop him."*

Teeth clenched, Travis nodded, and suddenly he knew what he needed to do. With his mind set, he drove home and headed straight for the shed in the backyard where he rummaged through a quiver of surfboards. His hand landed on an old favorite—his white squash tail. He almost pulled it out, but he changed his mind. A longer board with a wider nose would be far more stable. He grabbed a nine-foot board instead and headed back to his truck.

Leaving a trail of dust behind, he hammered on the gas pedal, but he wasn't quite sure where to go. The first beach he came to was far too crowded, and the second was no better. Surfers were at every break, and the waves were far too big.

Cursing his luck, he sat, until he remembered another spot—a place that was much more private. Half an hour later, he approached the huge banyan tree that marked the beginning of a small path. He parked his truck in an inconspicuous spot, grabbed his surfboard, and hiked through the rainforest until he came to a small secluded beach.

He remembered his first visit to the place. Devin had shown it to him on his seventh birthday. "It's a secret spot, just for us," his brother had said as they walked, but when they got there, Travis learned he had ulterior motives. A cute girl with curly brown hair waited for them.

Devin went off with her, leaving Travis alone. At first, he was angry, but once he got in the water with the new surfboard his mother had given him, he forgot all about his brother. It was the perfect spot for learning with some great beginner waves.

In the end, Devin tried to kiss the girl, only to get smacked in the face, and Travis—who had just taught himself to surf—laughed at him all the way home.

Shaking off the memory, he looked out at the lagoon. It had been a long time.

Thigh-high waves rolled up to the rocky shoreline surrounded by trees and tall cliffs. No one could walk to the beach except by taking the path he had just came down and there were no footprints in the sand. A good sign.

Travis walked to the edge of the sea and stripped down to his surf trunks. He knew he wasn't heading out into heavy surf, but he strapped a leash to his leg anyways. He was unlikely to get up on his first try, and he didn't feel like scrambling around after his board.

Satisfied, he looked out at the surf. The waves were small, yet a spark of fear raced through him as he looked into the swirling water. A large piece of seaweed rolled toward him, and further out there were shadows.

"Get a hold of yourself. It's only the reef."

But the more he scanned the ocean, the more sinister it became. He clamped his teeth together and tried to control his shaking. What the hell was wrong with him? He'd never seen any sharks here before, and so what if there were any?

Cursing himself for being such a wuss, he took a deep breath and held it. Back when he'd surfed professionally, he'd earned a reputation for taking waves other surfers turned down. He took off late on purpose, astonishing the crowds and pulling off gnarly tricks. He seemed to know what the wave would do before it did. He was fearless.

"Now I'm scared of a stupid fish."

Shaking his head, he squared his shoulders and waded out—first up to his ankles, and then up to his calves. The water crept up his legs, splashing him with terror and dread, but he forced himself to keep going.

"Come on," he spoke aloud. "It can't possibly happen again."

All his life he had swam in the ocean, and some of those times, he'd seen sharks swimming beside him. They didn't attack him then, so what were the chances they'd do so now? Twice in one lifetime?

The water reached his knees, and it took all the courage he possessed not to run back to shore. Waist deep, he started to panic. Recurring nightmares flashed in his mind, and for a second, he was living them. *Sharks were all around him, swimming toward him...*

His breaths came in wheezing gasps, and where the salty liquid touched him, his body grew numb. Still, he wouldn't let himself flee. He looked at the horizon, not at the ocean, and forced himself to breath deeper. Finally, when nothing bad happened, his pulse slowed and his wheezing stopped. "I can do this," he whispered.

As soon as Travis climbed onto his surfboard, the familiar feeling overtook him. Eyes closed, he relished the sway of the sea underneath him and the heat of the sun on his back. He started to paddle and found it awkward. With only one arm, it took longer to gain distance, and his board kept tipping to the side. But at least the waves were small, so he didn't have to dive underneath them.

When he got beyond the breaking waves, he sat up and waited. Eyes flicking left and right, he scanned the water around him, searching for shadows. There were none.

A little wave headed toward him and all fear fled from his mind. Paddling as hard as he could, he pushed himself forward. The wave began to lift him. His board hovered on the lip, the first half gaining air, but when he tried to pop up, he put too much pressure on one side of his board. After a quick twirl under the water, he came back up, spitting salt from his mouth.

He tried again. This time, he put the palm of his hand on the center of his board. Down he went again, but it was better. It could work. It had to.

Four more times he tried before he started getting discouraged. He stopped for a moment, looking out at the miniature white caps. Surely he could do this. He'd ridden waves ten times this size.

He thought about the brutal surf at Pipe and Waimea. Those heavy waves had pummeled him so many times he should have been dead, yet he hadn't given up then. He got into position and waited. If it killed him, he would surf again.

On the next wave, he pushed himself up and landed perfectly in the middle of his board. It surprised him so much, however, that he fell right away. The board kicked out from underneath him and he landed with a plop in the ocean, swallowing a bit of water as it rolled over his face.

He came up, laughing. With his board in his hand, he jumped up and down, giggling like a child. It took him two more tries to do it again, but once he was up the riding was easy. It was only a short ride and he couldn't do much on such a small wave, but it didn't matter. He had surfed. He may have only ridden in the soup, but as far as he was concerned, he had just caught the best wave of his life.

~Surf Stoke~

Early the next morning, Travis woke up to the sun shining through his bedroom window. Spread out across his mattress, he yawned, stretched, and sat up. Glancing out at the view, he saw the bright blue sky smiling at him, and for the first time since he'd returned to Hawaii, he smiled back.

He hadn't told anyone what had happened the day before. As soon as he'd ridden a few waves, convinced it could be done, he had gone straight home, said goodnight to his family, and hopped into bed. Too tired to think, he had covered his head and fallen into a dreamless slumber.

Now, faced with a brand new day, his surf-stoke hit him hard. Moving over to the window, he stared out at the sea. Yesterday he had gotten up in the soup, so surely with a bit of practice he could get up on some real waves as well.

A thrill of anticipation rushed through him as he picked a towel off the floor and looked around his messy room.

Disgusting. He would have to clean it up. But first, a shower.

Hot steam filled his bathroom as the water rushed over his body, draining any remaining tension from his shoulders and neck. It had been a long time since he had felt this good. He decided not to let the feeling end. Dripping water, he stepped out of the shower, picked up his cell phone, and dialed Brady's number.

"Hey, brah," he said, when his friend picked up. "Can you do without me for the week?"

"For why?" Brady sounded concerned. "Wha's up?"

"There's something I gotta do," Travis answered. He offered no further explanation.

There was a brief pause on the other end. "Okay, no worries. Shayla and I can cover the shop. Take all the time ya need."

Travis was certain his sigh of relief traveled right through the phone. "Thanks, bud. I appreciate it."

He dialed another number.

"Hi, Aunt Kendra, it's Travis. Do you mind if I come stay with you for a bit?"

Bacon sizzled in the pan and the sweet smell of coffee wafted through the house as Carl cooked, intent on making a real breakfast for his sons. It had been a long time since they had all lived together, and he wanted to sit down and enjoy a meal like a real family.

"Smells awesome." Travis smiled as he walked into

the room. His exuberance nearly knocked Carl out. Was there magic in his cooking?

Travis grabbed a slice of bacon from the plate beside the stove and popped it in his mouth, licking his fingers ravenously. He grabbed a plate and served himself a huge serving of French toast, bacon, and eggs. He sat down at the table, poured some coconut syrup over the whole dish, and proceeded to stuff his face.

Carl watched. He hadn't seen Travis eat so much in a long time. What had happened to bring about such a change?

Before he could comment, Travis looked up. "Hey, Dad, do you mind if I borrow the camping gear? I want to go to Aunt Kendra's for a few days ... to get away for awhile."

Carl pondered the request. His sister lived alone on the small island of Kaua'i, and in the past, Travis had only ever gone there to train for surfing competitions. Clearly, he wasn't doing that now, and since Kendra wasn't the most sociable person, it couldn't be her company the boy was after.

"You've talked to her already?"

"Yeah, I got a plane ticket, and I'm gonna sleep in the tent so I don't bother her."

"All the stuff's packed in the mudroom," Carl answered.

Travis nodded. "Thanks, Dad."

Seeing his son so full of spirit, Carl couldn't help but wonder what he was up to. He had a hunch, but he didn't ask. "Be good for you to get away. I wish I could."

Travis gave him a sympathetic look just as Devin entered the room. Wearing nothing but boxer shorts, he grabbed a cup of coffee—black—and sat down at the table.

Carl frowned. Nine years of partying had taken its toll on his older son's body. Growing up, Devin had always been the stockier one, and back when he used to surf he was in such good shape. Now he looked thin, weak and pale.

Well, that could change. Carl filled a plate and set it on the table. "Eat," he ordered.

Devin poked his fork into a small piece of pineapple and slowly put it in his mouth. He appeared to have trouble swallowing. Carl sat down with his own dish and nibbled on some toast. "Are you coming to work with me today?" He fully expected a quarrel.

"Yeah, whatevahs," Devin mumbled and continued to pick at his food.

"Really?" Carl gaped. "Well, good. We leave in ten minutes, so hurry and get ready. It's going to be a busy day, loads of stuff to sort though."

He grimaced as he thought about his workplace. As an architect, designing large custom homes, he'd found success, but he lacked in his organizational skills. Since his assistant had left for maternity leave, he'd had no time to replace her, and his office was starting to look as chaotic as Travis's room.

He took another bite of his toast and added, "I appreciate the help."

Travis, who still hadn't acknowledged his brother, got up to rinse his empty plate. He hurried into the mudroom and came back out with a tent and a tarp.

As he left the house with the belongings, Devin whined, "How come he gets to go camping?"

Carl answered the question with a glare.

Leaving his breakfast uneaten, Devin headed back up to his room, and Carl scraped the remainder of the food into the trash. From the kitchen window, he watched Travis pull three surfboards from the shed, all of them different sizes and shapes. He fumbled a bit, as he tried to lift more than he could handle. Lightening the load, he carried the boards to his truck, one at a time.

"Where's he going anyways?" Devin asked as he came back into the kitchen, pulling a t-shirt over his head.

"To Aunt Kendra's."

"For why?"

Carl gave a proud smile. "It was his favorite place to surf."

~Screw the Sharks~

After landing on the island of Kaua'i, Travis rented a four-wheel drive and took off toward the property where his aunt lived. As he drove, he gazed out at the lush taro fields and rugged mountains, impressed by the beauty of it all. He had always loved this place. He could see why it was called the Garden Isle.

Growing closer to his destination, he watched for the sign that told him where he needed to turn. Finally he saw it, half covered in vines. As he turned in, mud covered his tires and branches reached inside his windows. His aunt worked at a research station on protected land, and the road he traveled in on was windy and rough.

Holding the steering wheel tightly, he bumped around several sharp turns until he came out into a small clearing and pulled up beside his aunt's tiny wooden shack. The blinds were drawn, some of the windows boarded up, and aside from an abundance of fat, healthy chickens, the place had a creepy, abandoned feel.

He didn't go inside. Instead, he pulled a shortboard from the back of the truck, tucked it under his arm, and hurried down a long path to the white sand beach at the end of the property.

Smiling, he looked out at the clean, deserted waves and was just about to rush into the water when he saw it—a dark outline, a fearsome, shark-like shape in the waves. His smile faded.

For an hour, he stood on the shore, studying the spot. His body trembled, his heart pounding. He shook his head. This was ridiculous. He'd gone surfing the day before and nothing had happened. He wasn't supposed to be scared anymore, and definitely not of this place.

These were some of his favorite waves—consistent surf with several points where the reef offered long lefts and hollow rights. And best of all, because very few people had access to the place, he usually had them all to himself. It was not a place for fear.

As he stared out at the horizon, he remembered himself as a child, surfing with his brother. He had just taken a nasty spill and was crying because he'd swallowed a bunch of seawater. He didn't want to get back on his board, and Devin had scoffed, *"Stop being such a sissy. Fear is what'cha make of it. It's somethin' ya gotta face, and surfing ain't gonna come without it. So do ya want it or not?"*

Travis wanted it then, just like he wanted it now, and to this day, his brother's words rang true. If he didn't face his fear, he would never get over it. Surfing was all he had known for so long, and now that his surf-stoke was back, he wasn't about to give it up again.

Board tucked under his arm, he plunged into the water. Screw the sharks. If they wanted him, they could take him.

The waves were smaller than usual—barely four feet on the face—yet they battled him. With gritted teeth, Travis drove his board forward, trying to force his way over the oncoming peaks. Again and again, they pushed him back toward shore. If he was ever going to get out to the surf, he needed to duck dive. With only one arm, it was difficult to push his board far enough so he could travel under and through the back of the waves.

If only he had something to hold on to.

He left the ocean and headed for his aunt's tool shed, where he invented a new method by attaching a rubber strap to his board. It made a difference. Back in the water, he held on tightly, and when a wave rolled toward him, he dove the nose of his board as deep as he could. With his back foot, he pressed on the tail, leveling out and angling upward as the wave passed over top of him. He broke the surface and paddled as hard as he could before the next one came.

With every oncoming wave, he repeated the process, until finally he made it out beyond the breakers. There he sat, catching his breath, and as the sun seeped into his shoulders, he inhaled the salty air and let the tension out through his lips. He could do this. He pushed a lock of hair from his eyes.

Water rose in the distance as a dark blue wall built up. He got into position and started stroking, thrusting his hand through the speeding liquid. His surfboard lifted, his fingers found the center, his feet leapt to fiberglass, and he tumbled over the side.

After a quick spin under the swirling currents, he came back up with a grin. He crawled back on his board. It had almost worked. He tried again.

The next wave snatched him up and flung him over the peak. He twirled under the water, instinctively bringing his arm up to protect his head, yet the side of his face found the reef and a piece of coral scraped along his cheek. He tried to relax, letting the energy of the wave pass him by, but when he opened his eyes, he saw blood in the water and his first thought was *sharks.*

Scanning the murky underworld, he searched for any. He fought for the surface and choked down a mouthful of ocean. Finally he came up and gulped a breath of air.

He hobbled out of the sea and collapsed on the sand, sputtering and coughing.

He heard someone clapping.

He looked up and saw his aunt, Kendra, peeking out from the jungle. A grubby orange *pareo* with pink hibiscus flowers flapped around her legs as she pressed through some shrubs and came out onto the beach. Her feet were bare, her long brown hair tangled. She slapped her thighs and gave him a tilted smile. "A valiant effort." Her voice was gruff. She helped him up and handed him a black rubber glove. "Try this for paddling. Might speed up the process a little."

Travis turned the glove over in his hand. It was thick and webbed, and when he tried it on, it fit perfectly. It was the first gift his aunt had ever given him. Grateful, he nodded, but she was already shuffling back into the trees. She disappeared from sight and Travis smiled. His aunt had never been one for conversation. At least he could count on her to keep his surfing a secret.

Gathering his courage, he headed back into the surf, and as soon as he tried the glove, he could feel the improvement. With it, he sliced through the water, faster and stronger. In just the right spot, he jumped to his feet and caught his first wave. It was small and didn't take him very far, but he laughed anyway, splashing the water and hooting loudly.

He caught another after that. And another.

Once he was on his feet, he found that he still had his style and could pull off most of his old tricks. As long as he paddled hard enough and didn't fall off trying to get up, he ripped.

For the rest of the afternoon, Travis worked on his pop-ups and perfecting his timing. More than ever before, he had to be in the right position at exactly the right time in order to catch the wave, but eventually it got easier, and when he finally retired to his tent that evening, his muscles were raw and torn. He crawled into his sleeping bag and rubbed the stiffness from his legs.

If he was going to ride in heavier surf, he knew he needed to back get in shape, so the next day he surfed and trained too. Whenever he took a break or the waves closed out, he jogged on the beach or went swimming. He held his breath for minutes at a time, practiced on a balance board, and did enough one-armed push-ups for an entire boot camp. It became routine. Every evening, he worked out, and each day, he paddled further out into bigger and steeper waves.

On the sixth day, the late afternoon sun beat down on the shimmering surface; the entire ocean glistened like glass. Travis sat on his board. His body ached, but it was a good ache. He stretched his neck and smiled. On the horizon, he saw a dark rise forming, and he got into position. This would be it—his biggest wave yet.

Taking deep strokes, he pressed his board through the rising water. The wave shot up steep and fast, picking him up with little effort. He leapt to his feet, made a quick bottom turn, and found himself crouched in a blue-green barrel. He shot out of the tube and flew up the face, launching off the shoulder and into the air. He did a small somersault just for fun, and when he resurfaced, he smacked the water with his gloved hand. "I did it!"

Without looking back, Travis raced out of the ocean and toward his rental vehicle. He didn't need to stay any longer. He could surf again, and now, he just wanted to go home.

As he sat on the charter plane, flying back to Oahu, he stared out the window at the ocean below. His hand gripped the edge of his seat. He couldn't wait to tell Shayla and show her what he'd done.

Back on land, he headed straight for the surf shop, but when he pulled into the parking lot, he saw Kimo's bright, red low-rider sitting next to Shayla's hatchback, and his heart took a plunge. He had forgotten about her man.

Jealousy came flooding back. A violent pain thumped in his chest. He dialed Brady's number. "Hey, Brade, I'm back in town. You want to go for a drink?"

~A Good Day~

There was money in his father's desk. The drawer was open a crack; inside lay a stack of hundred-dollar bills. Devin stared at them hungrily. It seemed like forever since his last real fix. His bank account was drained and so were his pockets, yet the drug called to him constantly.

His dad came back into the office and Devin averted his eyes. He pointed at the filing cabinet in the corner. "I put all the current files at the top, old ones I stuck in the bottom. Receipts are in the middle drawer." He stood up and flipped his father's laptop around. "I put 'em in your computer too."

His father smiled—a real smile. "You're doing a great job."

Devin's hand paused over the last box of papers. He cleared his throat and nodded. It was strange to hear a compliment from his dad. Several times in the last week, he had come in to help out at the office, and he had to admit he was actually enjoying his father's company. Instead of talking about drugs or his arrest, they'd been having pleasant, almost friendly, conversations about architecture, cars, and sports.

It was nice for a change.

As his father left the room, Devin's eyes fell once more on the money. Only two days remained until his next court appearance, so this was his last chance to enjoy himself. Things were going so well lately. Surely his dad wouldn't notice. He moved closer, slid some bills from the drawer, and stuck them in his back pocket.

What a good day.

Arms folded behind his head, Carl relaxed on the living room sofa. Not only had he managed to finalize a deal at the office, but he was pleased with the work his son had done on the filing cabinets. It had taken Devin only three days to sort a stack of papers that would've taken his previous assistant a week to finish.

The boy had more potential than he let on.

Feet propped on the coffee table, he picked up the remote control and flicked through the channels on the television searching for the late evening news. Jasper jumped up beside him and stared at him with eager eyes.

Carl patted the golden retriever's head. "Okay. Let's go for a walk." He stood up and the dog jumped around his legs, letting out a few loud woofs.

As Carl grabbed Jasper's leash, Devin came down the stairs. It was obvious he had raided Travis's closet, because he was dressed quite nicely for a change.

Carl eyed him. "Where are you going?"

"Out."

"No, you're not. It's late, and Paul's coming to talk to you in the morning. He's doing us a favor, you know. If you want him to tell the judge you've been staying out of trouble, it's not going to be very convincing if you're hungover."

"Fine." Devin moved toward the door. "Then I won't drink."

That was ridiculous, and Carl knew it. "I mean it, Dev. You've managed to get past me almost every night this week. This time, I'm putting my foot down."

"Dad, come on. I worked all day. You can't expect me to stay home."

Carl didn't budge. "Walk out that door, and I'll call the cops myself."

His son glared at him. "For what? It ain't no crime to go hang wit' my boys." Yet, he hesitated.

Carl stood taller. "Go ahead … test me." He picked up the phone.

Devin stood with his hand on the doorknob for a full minute, until finally he threw his keys on the table and stomped back up to his room. The bedroom door slammed, and Carl relaxed. He had won. He had kept Devin from leaving the house.

He finished putting on Jasper's lead and scratched him behind the ears. "I should've forced him to move home years ago," he whispered. Then, he paused. It was much too quiet.

Hunched over his dresser, Devin was just about to sniff up a thick line of cocaine when his father threw open the bedroom door.

"Give it to me!" Carl's voice hit full volume.

"Fuck, Dad! Don't you knock?" Hands shaking, Devin brushed the coke back into the package.

"Give it to me," his father ordered again.

"No way!" Devin replied.

His dad grabbed at his wrist, but Devin twisted sideways. With both hands, he held the package tightly and lunged for the door, but his father leapt onto his back and wrestled him into a headlock. Prying at

Devin's fingers, he tore the bag apart and white powder scattered all over the floor.

Devin gasped. Mind raging and wild, he whipped around and slammed his fist into his old man's face. Then he sucked in his breath and froze.

His father barely flinched. Standing to his full height, he slapped Devin hard and grabbed him by the shoulders. "Look at you! What have you become?"

Devin winced. His dad's eye was already starting to swell. Horrified by what he had done, he tried to speak, but he couldn't find any words.

His father released him. "I'm done with this, Dev. I won't put up with it any longer. You need help, and obviously I can't give it to you. Paul will be here in the morning. I suggest you stay in your room tonight, get sober, and think about what you want to do. Get the help or you're gone. I've done everything I can for you. I did the best I could … for you and your brother … and I can't take this anymore. Get the fucking help!"

As the bedroom door slammed shut, Devin sank to the ground. Arms wrapped around his knees, he cried like a little boy.

~Wha's Da Haps~

It was late at night, and Kiio's Bar roared with voices and music. A warm breeze blew through the open patio doors, bringing with it the smell of salt water and kelp. People trudged in and out of the lounge—mainly lobster-red tourists seeking relief from the heat and humidity.

Travis slid some money across the bar and handed a beer to Brady. Along the back wall, a DJ spun some discs on a small turntable, and the rhythm surrounded them, pumping.

Brady shouted over the noise, "You try an' surf again, hah? Tha's where you went all week?"

Travis shrugged. It was a good guess, but he wasn't in the mood to talk about it.

Brady looked him up and down. "Kay-den. Wha's up with you and Mika?"

Travis took a long sip of beer and the alcohol helped

to loosen his tongue. "She was pissed I went away without telling her. Almost ripped me a new one when I called her today. I decided to break it off with her though. I'm gonna tell her tomorrow."

"For real?"

Travis shrugged again and nodded. "I can't fake it no more. It's gotta end. But I feel like an ass for ditching her … like Devin did to Lea."

Brady shook his head. "You can still be a dad to that kid."

"I know, but she wants someone there for her day and night. I can't give her that."

Brady ordered two shots of whiskey. He slid one over to Travis and slammed his down. Then he chugged the last of his beer and turned on his stool. "Shayla and Mika used to be tight, like sisters, yeah, 'til Shayla caught Mika with her guy. Walked in an' found 'em kissing. Knocked Mika out with one punch."

"Really?" Travis leaned forward on his stool.

"Heck yeah. An' I think she should' a done the same to Kane. Brah, that guy's a kook."

Travis put his drink down. "Kane?" He felt himself sober up a little.

Brady nodded. "Yeah, bro."

Just to be sure, Travis asked again, "*World Champion*, Kane Walker?"

"Yup."

His face screwed up in a scowl. Shayla couldn't have dated Kane. The news made his head hurt. He picked up his beer and swirled the remaining liquid around the bottom. The room spun, and he pushed the bottle away.

Brady gave him a curious look. "So, you and Mika, when did you guys hook up anyway?"

"At her party."

Brady's brow furrowed. "What party? The twins' birthday party?"

Travis tried to focus. Behind him people kept brushing up against his back, trying to get through the crowd. He pushed back.

Brady repeated the question. "Was that it? The birthday party? The night you met me there?"

"Apparently," Travis replied.

"*Apparently*?"

"Well, I don't remember anything. I was pretty loaded. I regretted it as soon as I woke up though."

Mouth open, Brady stepped off his stool. "Trav, you were smashed, bro. I helped you into bed that night. There ain't no way you could'a banged no one."

Try as he might, Travis couldn't remember. As usual, the only thing that came to mind was the morning after and his horrible hangover. "Well, do you think she could've … in my sleep?"

Brady burst out laughing, "No way, brah."

Travis squirmed on his chair. "I ... I blacked out. I just trusted what she said."

Brady shook his head and stopped chuckling. He glanced around the bar and spotted Ayumi and Mark. "Let's ask them. They were there."

Brady pushed through the crowd, and Travis followed, anxious to find out the truth.

"Ayumi. Mark." Brady demanded the couple's attention. "The night of your party ... how'd Travis and Mika end up in bed together?"

Ayumi seemed baffled by the unexpected question.

Mark piped up. "I carried her in there."

"That right? You put her in bed with Trav?" Brady placed his hands on the table.

Mark glanced at his girlfriend. "She passed out. Why? Wha's up?"

Travis swallowed hard. If Brady had put him to bed and Mark had carried Mika in later, there was little chance they had done anything.

Brady turned to him. "That kid's not yours."

"What kid?" Ayumi asked. "What's going on?"

"Mika told Travis the baby's his. Your sister's nothin' but a liar."

As the words reached Travis's ears, a tremor ran through his body. "I wanna see her. I gotta know for sure."

Ayumi asked again, "What baby?"

Mark stood up. "Yeah. Wha's da haps?"

Without giving them an answer, Travis and Brady headed for the door.

At two in the morning, Travis pounded on Mika's front door. He rang the doorbell again and again, and finally the lights came on. The door opened. Dressed in pajama pants and an old fleecy sweater, Mika stood in the entranceway, a surprised look on her face.

"We never did anything. That right? Why would you tell me the baby is mine?"

Her hand shot up to cover her mouth, and she started to sniffle. "I'm sorry, Travis."

"Why would you do this to me?"

She came outside and slumped down on the patio swing. The chair creaked as it swung on its chains.

Travis stopped it. "Tell me."

With panic in her eyes, she broke down sobbing. "I … I'm sorry. I just thought …well, the baby needed a father and … I thought maybe it would be a good thing if that could be you."

He stepped back. "How the hell would that be a good thing?" Barely breathing, he studied her face, searching for an answer. He found nothing.

Mika got up from the swing and moved away from him, down the steps. On the freshly mowed lawn, she started to pace. "You were all alone and staying around town... and with your accident and all...."

A dark shadow passed over him. The vein in his temple throbbed. "So you thought I was lonely? Is that it?"

Mika stopped pacing, and when she didn't answer, Travis snapped, "You almost screwed up my entire life with this."

"I wasn't trying to."

Needing something to alleviate his anger, he broke a branch off a eucalyptus tree and threw it into the bushes.

It didn't help.

"You did this for *me?* That's bullshit," he growled. "You did this for your own selfish reasons. I don't need anyone feeling bad for me."

She backed away from him.

"Who's the real father?" he asked. "Why didn't you go to him?"

Mika let out a wail and flopped down on the steps. "I can't tell him. It was wrong to get with him in the first place."

As she began to sob again, Travis's pulse slowed. For a moment, he almost felt sorry for the girl, but he made no comforting moves. He pitied Mika, and that took some of the edge off his anger, but as far as he was concerned his part in her life was over. Without another word, he turned and headed back to his truck. He slid into the driver's seat, looked at Brady, and shook his head. "I'm not the dad."

Mika watched Travis drive away in his truck, his tail-lights fading into the distance. He would no longer take care of her. She was alone.

She bit her trembling lip as the panic started to build and buried her face in her hands. Travis was right. She was selfish. She hadn't done any of this to help him. It was just an excuse to rationalize what she was doing. She shouldn't have lied. She should have handled her problems on her own.

Disgusted with herself, she wiped away her tears and hugged her arms to her chest. At least it was over and she wouldn't have to pretend anymore.

A cool breeze brushed past her, and she pulled her sweater tight. The only sound was the rustling of leaves and the *ko-kee* song of frogs in the trees behind her. The noise irritated her, so she headed back to the house and was just about to go inside when Ayumi and Mark pulled up to the curb.

Ayumi burst from the car. "Mika, what's going on? Why did Travis say you were having his baby?"

Shit. Mika hurried inside where she sprinted down the hall and made a quick dash for her room.

"Open up, Mika." Ayumi pounded on the door. The doorknob jiggled, but Mika had locked it.

"Are you pregnant?" her sister called out.

"Leave me alone. I don't wanna talk about it."

Ayumi pounded again. "Who's the father?"

Mika remained quiet. On the other side of the entrance, she could hear Ayumi sobbing. "How could you not tell me? I'm your sister."

Covering her ears, Mika crawled into bed. Her insides ached and her guts twisted. She clutched her feather pillow tightly. Lately she was doing all the wrong things, pissing friends off, and hurting the people she loved. What the hell was wrong with her? And how was she ever going to live this one down?

Ayumi knocked a few more times, but eventually she gave up. The house grew quiet, and Mika lay in bed crying, until finally, she fell into an uneasy sleep.

~Damned Devin~

While Devin talked with his lawyer in the living room, Carl took refuge in the kitchen. After their blow-out the night before, Devin had locked himself in his bedroom, and in the morning, when he'd come downstairs, he could barely make eye contact. "Maybe rehab will do me some good," he'd muttered. Then he had promised to straighten himself out.

Carl still couldn't believe he had heard the words.

Wondering how the meeting was going, he peeked into the next room, where Devin and Paul were sitting on the sofa, talking quietly. Devin nodded at something Paul said. The look on his face was pure determination. Carl was glad to see it.

He touched his eye. It was bruised, puffy, and tender, but he was no longer angry. Devin finally seemed willing to deal with his addiction, and if Carl had to sport a black eye for that to happen, he was more than happy to do so.

The familiar sound of a truck engine interrupted his thoughts, and he watched from the window as Travis pulled into the driveway. It was well past noon; the sun was high in the sky. *Another all-nighter.* Carl frowned. Yet maybe it was for the best. At least he hadn't been home to witness Devin at his worst.

Hoping his wounds would go unnoticed, Carl hid the left side of his face as Travis came inside. Unfortunately, Travis tried to cut through the living room, and Carl was forced to stop him. "Wait! Don't go in there," he hissed.

Travis stopped, and when he turned back, his eyes did a double-take. "What did he do?" he growled.

"*Shhh.*" Carl raised a finger to his mouth. "It's okay."

"No, it's not! Devin can't do something like this and get away with it."

Moving swiftly, Carl put his hand out and stopped his son from going past him. "Trav, please be quiet. I think your brother's finally getting help."

"But...what the hell."

"Never mind this." He touched his swollen eye. "It's fine. We got into a fight last night, but I told Paul it was someone else who hit me, so please keep it down."

Looking agitated, Travis pulled away and peeked into the living room. "Well, what's going on? What kind of 'help' do you mean?"

"He's agreed to rehab. They're talking about it now.

They're going to try to get the judge to go along."

Travis rolled his eyes. "I'll believe that when I see it."

With a sigh, Carl pushed his son gently back toward the door. "This could be a start at least. Now go find something to do for a while. We can talk more later."

Small waves lapped at Travis's feet as he hung them over the seawall at the edge of his father's property. Holding a bottle to his lips, he took a long stinging swallow, and then another, hoping to take the edge off.

Damned Devin! How could he stoop so low?

The day had started out great. Without Mika or a baby to worry about, Travis had thought things were making a turn for the better. Now that he was surfing again, he had hoped he'd be able to get his life back on track.

He rubbed his temples and flinched. Why couldn't he have just one day where nothing went wrong? He took another drink. Already, he could feel the effects of the booze.

The sound of footsteps broke his thoughts, and he looked up. It was Devin.

"Dad sent me to get you. He wants a family meeting."

Travis leapt to his feet and rushed forward. He rammed his shoulder into his brother's ribs and knocked him backward onto the rocks. "Asshole! You beat up Dad?"

Devin caught himself from falling and held his stomach, breathing hard. He straightened up. "Watch it, bro."

"For why? You gonna hit me too?"

"Travis, stop it already. I had enough fightin', brah."

Fist clenched, Travis took a step forward, but his brother shook his head and lunged at him first. As they wrestled each other across the rocks, Travis managed to get his arm free and punched his brother square in the jaw.

Devin stumbled backward. His foot missed the edge of the seawall and he fell into the water. Soaking wet, he stood up and touched his fingers to his mouth; blood oozed from his bottom lip. His expression twisted from shock into rage. Travis planted his feet, anticipating another strike.

A loud shout rang out. Their father raced toward them, screaming, "Break it up, both of you!"

Devin froze. He looked again at the blood on his fingers, shot Travis one last glare, and climbed back onto the seawall where his father examined his face.

"Go back to the house." Carl ordered. Then he turned to Travis. "You cool off. We'll talk about this later."

Travis shuffled back down to the water's edge. He

picked up the bottle of booze and chugged what was left. He stared down at the water. A bruise had already started to form on his knuckles. "*Fuck!*" He shook the hurt away and kicked some rocks into the sea.

Shayla saw the fight. She saw Carl run through the yard, and she saw Travis kick the rocks in frustration. She knew he'd be angry with her for watching, but she couldn't seem to look away. She stood frozen on the shore, waiting for him to notice her—and at the same time, scared that he might.

He looked shocked when he finally spotted her; humiliation covered his face. "What do you want?"

Shayla shrunk back. "I'm … sorry. I didn't mean to see anything. I was just going for a walk."

"And you ended up *here*?"

A whale breeched in the distance. It appeared a second time and disappeared. Shayla kept her eyes fixed on the spot. Truth was she had wanted to see him. She had wandered toward his house, hoping to run into him, but now she had no idea what to say.

With more intensity, Travis asked again, "What do you *want*?"

Her throat cramped. She ambled forward along the rocky beach and stopped, leaving a good three feet between them. "I just wanted to make sure things were okay with us. I know we haven't talked much since you told me about Mika."

Travis looked out at the water. She could see his jaw was clenched.

She picked up a seashell and brushed the sand off it with her finger. "Me and her ... we kind of have some bad history."

"Yeah. Brady told me about *Kane*."

Shayla cringed when she heard the name and hung her head. "He's an ass. I didn't even like him that much, but still, Mika was supposed to be my friend. She shouldn't have done what she did."

"Why are you telling me this?"

Shayla felt her cheeks flush. "I don't know."

With fire in his eyes, Travis wound up his arm and threw something into the water. It was an empty liquor bottle. Shayla watched it hit the ocean and looked Travis up and down. Was he drunk? She backed up further.

He shot her a fierce look. "It doesn't matter what you say. Go back to Chun's with your surfer-boy and leave me alone."

Shayla gaped at him. "What's that supposed to mean?" Chun's? *Surfer boy*? Then it hit her. *Kimo.* Travis thought she was interested in her cousin.

The thought almost made her laugh, but she stopped herself. Travis didn't know she and Kimo were related, but that didn't give him the right to treat her like crap. And besides, she fumed, who was he to talk when he was the one with the girlfriend?

Hands on her hips, she faced him. She wanted to scold him—to tell him exactly what she thought of him—but tears began to well up, and she didn't think she could shake them away. "Sober up, Travis!" She whipped around and left the way she had come. "And just so you know," she called out over her shoulder, "Kimo's my cousin."

~A Promise~

In the tool shed sat a rusty lawn mower and a quiver of old surfboards. No one went in there anymore, so it was the perfect hiding place. From a small crevice above the door, Devin pulled a small plastic bag—containing half the cocaine he had bought from Vince—and headed off to find a place where he could be alone.

His feet followed an old familiar route, and soon he stood on top of the cliff, looking out across the sea. An image of his mother flashed in his mind. Young and beautiful, she stood at the edge of the rocks. Strawberry blond hair billowed behind her as she tilted her head back to watch the clouds drift across the sky.

Devin wavered a bit and stepped backward. Never had he seen his mother so clearly in his mind. He opened his hand and stared down at the white powder. What the hell was he doing? Only half an hour earlier, he had told his lawyer he wanted to quit.

And he really did. For the first time since he had started the drugs, he understood the true extent of his problem. He was addicted to cocaine, and it was not only ruining his own life but destroying his family as well. If he didn't stop, the addiction was going to keep festering until he had nothing left.

Devin looked back at the house. How could he have punched his own father? And now he was fighting with his brother as well. Travis hated him. He had every reason to.

Devin wound up his arm and almost sent the drugs hurtling out over the cliff, but at the last second he caught himself. He needed some.

Leaning against a large rock, he scooped some of the powder onto his fingernail and was just about to inhale when he heard a noise behind him, footsteps scuffling up the path. He dumped the powder back into the bag and hid the package in his lap.

Travis stepped out from between the trees, stopping when he saw Devin. "Oh ... I thought I was the only one who came out here."

"Mom used to." Devin watched a lizard disappear under a tree fern. He clamped his mouth shut. He hadn't meant to be so open.

Travis looked Devin up and down. "What are you doing? What's in your hands?"

Cursing under his breath, Devin stuffed the bag of drugs into his pocket.

"I thought you were quitting," his brother accused.

"I am. It's jus' real hard, bro." Devin ran his fingers through his hair, stopping for a second to pull on it like a mad man. He could feel the drugs pressing against his leg, calling to him. He should've at least taken the hit before Travis found him.

Slowly, he rubbed his forehead, trying to think of something to say. Finally, he decided on the truth. "I can't take it anymore. There's jus' a lil' bit left."

Travis didn't know what to say. Glancing up at him with tired eyes, his brother seemed wrapped in misery. He felt his anger fade, and he sat down on the boulder. "I can get rid of it. Then you won't be able to...."

"No!" Devin slid his hand over his pocket. "I can't jus' quit cold turkey, bro."

"Yes, you can. You got to. I mean, look what happened. You lost everything, got busted ... *hit Dad*."

Devin said nothing. He put his head in his hands and looked even more miserable.

"You can do it," Travis continued. "You just have to *want* to."

Devin got up and started pacing. His face was flushed and he kept clenching and unclenching his fists. "I do want to," he groaned. "But bro, I got my hearing tomorrow, and this is the last of it, I promise. Don't tell Dad. I wanna stop, and I'll get the help. For real."

Travis relented. Cornering his brother wasn't going to work. In fact, Devin looked ready to leap off the edge of the cliff to protect the drugs in his hand.

Neither of them spoke for a while, and eventually, his brother returned to the rock. As they sat side by side, staring out at the ocean, Travis thought about the comment Devin had made about their mother. She used to come out to the cliff a lot. It was her favorite place to watch the sunset. That was the reason Travis came out here so often, but it surprised him that Devin had admitted as much.

He was about to mention the fact when Devin said, "You with that Mika chick, bro?"

"No." Travis felt a touch of annoyance, but he wasn't sure if it was hearing the girl's name or the sudden change of topic that bugged him.

"Well, what about th' other one, that hottie you work with?"

Travis shrugged. Girls were not a concern at the moment. Something much more important had been weighing on his mind, and he wanted to talk about that. Back when they were younger, before their mom died, his brother used to take him surfing almost every chance they got. They would get up before dawn, strap their boards to their bikes, and cruise along the North Shore on a mission to find the best, most deserted waves.

Travis remembered one day in particular when the surf at Rocky Point was cranking and they'd managed to be the first ones out. Feeling as if they were the only people in the world, he and his brother had paddled out and caught some perfect waves, side by side. It was one of his favorite memories.

"Remember when we used to get up early and go surf?"

Devin nodded.

"You taught me everything I know."

When Devin remained quiet, Travis frowned. "We used to rip," he said. "I miss that."

Fidgeting with a stick from the ground, Devin closed his eyes. Travis wondered what he was thinking.

His brother turned to him. "You started surfing again, huh? At Aunt Kendra's?"

Slowly, Travis nodded.

"You get up?"

He nodded again. It wasn't the direction he had wanted the conversation to go, but it was better than nothing.

"You scared?"

"Hell yeah." Out of habit, Travis massaged the stump of his arm, as an image of a sharp-toothed mouth, open wide and rushing at him, ran through his mind. A shiver traveled up his spine. "Hardest thing I ever did."

Devin gave no reply.

The two brothers sat perfectly still, each wrapped in individual thoughts. Travis's confession of terror hung on the air like a thick cloud. The warm tropical breeze seemed stale and the sound of the surf—usually so soothing—was almost deafening. Travis tossed a pebble over the edge of the cliff and watched it plunk into the water below, startling a pair of white terns that flew away crying.

Beside him, Devin took his hand from his pocket and extended it outward. "I'm scared too," he said. His hand shook as he offered Travis the package of cocaine. "Take it. But promise you'll gimme a 'lil before bed and in the morning … jus' to take the edge off so I can face the judge."

Travis held the drugs like they were fragile. Too shocked to reply, he looked at his brother and nodded.

Devin got up and shifted from foot to foot. There was a sad look in his eyes as he turned to leave. "I miss it too, little braddah."

Had he imagined his brother's words?

Pressing his fingers into soft, white powder, Travis glared at the substance that had robbed him of his older sibling. He could still see Devin shuffling through the backyard, shoulders slumped and head hanging. Handing over the drugs must have been difficult. Then again, this probably wasn't even the last of it.

Travis's fist tightened over the package. He wanted to

toss it over the cliff, but he tucked it into his pocket instead. He had made a promise, whether he liked the terms or not, and he never broke his promises.

As he lingered on the boulder, the trade winds blew steadily, cooling the air and mixing with the fragrance of mandevillas that grew in the gully. On the shore below, waves fought each other, trying to get over the jagged rocks. It wasn't a good place for surfing.

One day, when Travis was ten years old, Devin had gone surfing at Sunset with some friends, forbidding him to tag along. Seeking revenge, Travis had dragged his brother's favorite board down to that rocky beach and had put so many dings in it that Devin had stopped talking to him for a week.

"What a stupid fight," he whispered. Nothing like the ones they had now.

Flexing his fingers, he looked at the bruise that had darkened across his knuckles. He no longer felt buzzed from the booze. His anger had sobered him up.

Now he sat, contemplating his actions. He had wanted to get revenge on his brother for hitting their father, but punching Devin wasn't the answer. Fighting violence with violence. What had that solved? *Nothing.*

He hid his hand behind his back, cringing when he remembered what Shayla had seen. Her words finally reached him: *Kimo's my cousin.* His shoulder's drooped. "I'm an idiot."

~Back in Da Water~

Travis stood at the edge of the path leading down to Rocky Point. The view in front of him was gorgeous, a perfect day, sunny and warm, without a cloud in the sky. The surf rolled in on the small rocky beach, brilliant blue and clean with the late afternoon swell pushing in from the northwest creating some of the glassiest barrels he'd seen in a long time.

Rockies was a fun break that produced fast rights and hollow lefts, and because the waves were smaller than Pipe, they were less threatening. The smaller surf brought larger crowds, but the waves were easy to rip.

Travis watched Kimo charge down a smooth wall. The surfer hit the lip and pulled an extremely long floater. Seemingly weightless, he hovered along the peak of the wave for so long that the people on the beach started cheering well before he dropped back in. Travis smiled. He knew what it felt like to wow a crowd.

He spotted Shayla sitting on some lava rocks next to a local surf journalist who was snapping photos with a large-lensed camera. Moving down the stone steps and onto the sand, Travis snuck up beside her.

"Howzit?"

Shayla jumped. Her eyes grew wide when she saw him. She frowned and turned back to the waves.

Travis felt his cheeks flush. "I didn't know Kimo was your cousin," he confessed.

She brushed some sand off her leg. "Yeah, so?"

"So, I was wrong, and I want to show you something." He hurried back up the steps and grabbed the surfboard he had hidden behind some guava bushes. With it tucked under his arm, he raced past her.

"What are you doing?" she called out.

At the edge of the water he stopped, strapped his leash to his ankle, and pulled his paddling glove onto his hand with his teeth.

He turned toward her. "You know how I went away last week?"

"Yeah."

"You know what I did?"

She shook her head.

"I'll show you." He rushed into the water.

"Travis, don't!"

He heard her, but he didn't stop. Forcing himself

under and through each wave, he paddled out to the lineup, sat up, and pushed a strand of wet hair from his eyes. A nearby surfer stared at him, mouth open and gaping. Kimo looked over and nodded a greeting.

A hush fell over the group. Travis glanced around at the rest of the surfers. Most of them he knew—locals and old friends he'd grown up and surfed with all his life—yet nobody said a word.

A set formed, and everyone in the lineup sat motionless. Instead of bickering over right-of-way, they waited for Travis to make a move.

He swallowed hard, licking salt off his lips as he stared at the nose of his board with unseeing eyes. *Damn it.* Why had he chosen to do this today, in front of all these regulars?

The first wave went by, unridden, yet no one in the lineup complained. Travis's gloved hand shook so badly he didn't know if he'd have the strength to push himself up. Then he remembered. Pipeline was just up the coast. He was very close to where he'd been attacked by the shark. Muscles tensed, he gripped the edge of his board, as an overwhelming urge to flee flooded over him.

He forced himself to loosen his grip and shook the fear away. He couldn't wimp out now. Not with everyone watching.

Another wave approached. Again, everyone waited.

Travis got into position. He took a deep breath and charged.

All thoughts of killer fish left as he paddled like mad, letting the tremendous force of the water drive him forward. With his hand on the center of his board, he pushed up and planted both feet firmly into position. He dropped down the glassy surface and pulled into a small blue-green barrel. The sea whirled around him for a second and spat him back out. He tore from the pit, flew up the rushing water, spun his board in a 360, and landed the trick with ease.

The crowd cheered, and Travis did too. He was surfing. At Rockies. In front of everyone!

As he came in from the ocean, Shayla ran up to him, squealing. With a huge smile, she threw her arms around him. He dropped his board and spun her in a circle.

Her eyes shone bright and unbelieving as he put her back on the sand. "Unreal!" she cried. "You're surfing again!"

She beamed up at him, and he was swept away by her beauty. He loved the way she got so excited about things. It was contagious and drew him to her like the ocean on a blue-sky day.

"I'm stoked," she said. "I always knew you could do it."

He reached for her hand, and she took it, letting him

pull her to him. Then she frowned and pulled away.

His stomach lurched. "What's wrong?"

"You're still with Mika." She lowered her gaze. "I shouldn't have gone to your house today."

Travis shook his head. "It was a lie. She's not having my kid."

"What? *Really*?"

Travis grinned. With her mouth slightly parted like that, Shayla looked so shocked and cute that all he wanted to do was kiss her. But he held back. He needed to explain. Standing on the small rocky shoreline, he told her all about passing out at the twin's party, Mika's lie, and how he found out the truth.

"Wow." Shayla's eyes narrowed. "That's pretty low."

He nodded. "The girl's messed up, but I'm done with that now."

"So she's out of the picture then?"

He nodded again.

Shayla blushed and gave him a sly smile. "Do you …um… wanna go on a date some time?"

Travis laughed. He pulled her forward and pressed his lips to hers, enjoying the rush that traveled through him as she wrapped her arms around his neck and kissed him back. His heart swelled. She was his.

Kimo came out of the surf and joined them on the beach. He looked them up and down and ruffled

Shayla's hair. "Ho, cuz', not even! You goin' be his beach bum now?"

Shayla giggled. "I'll be sitting on the sand putting wax on his board."

Kimo chuckled and gave a loud hoot. "Yessah! Travis-man back in da water! I was scared you was neva' coming back."

Travis gave him a nonchalant shrug. "I just started again. It's not like I'm back."

Kimo slapped the front of his surfboard. "Nah, braddah, you no fool me. No real surfer would leave all dis." With a giant swoop of his arm, he gestured toward the ocean. In a serious tone, he leaned forward. "So, how is it? Scary or w'at?"

Travis's mouth tilted into a smile. "Heck yeah."

Holding onto Shayla's hand, Travis told the two of them all he had been through that week at his Aunt's. "At first, I panicked going back in the water. I needed to get over it, you know? Get rid of the sharks in my mind."

"I know, brah." Kimo nodded. "I used to be scared of big waves, especially at Pipe, but now I get em', piece of cake."

Hearing the name of his old favorite break, Travis glanced up the coast toward Keana Point. At that moment, Pipeline was certain to be pounding the shores.

In his mind he could see it—the gaping tubes exploding over a merciless lava-slab reef; the bone-crushing wipeouts; the surfers dodging death. The thought made him shudder. "Man, that place is cursed."

Kimo gave him a nudge. "Eh, brah, w'at you scared for? You use to do it before. W'at's da difference now?"

Tightlipped, Travis shrugged.

Kimo let the subject drop. With another grin, he smacked Travis on the shoulder. "Travis-man back in da water!" he hooted again.

Dark thoughts fading, Travis smiled back, and it was then he noticed the crowd. People had been listening to him talk story. They closed in on him, everyone speaking at once. They knew his name and his past accomplishments. They knew about the shark. Someone patted him on the back. Someone else took his picture. He grew dizzy as he looked around at the faces—some were familiar, some not. Where had they all come from? He backed away.

A man with a clipboard moved toward him, followed by another man with a video camera. Travis picked up his surfboard and turned to Shayla, "I gotta go. I'll call you tomorrow." He flew up the steps and onto the bike path beyond.

~Craving~

Outside, the sky was ablaze with red fire as the sun plunged toward the horizon. Devin stood at his bedroom window, tapping his fingers against the sill. Headlights shone in the distance. He pressed his face closer to the glass and cursed when he saw it was a car, not his brother's truck.

"Hurry up, Travis!" he hissed.

Why had he given away the last of his cocaine?

A sharp craving jerked him into motion, and he pulled apart his dresser drawers, checking all his old hiding places. *Nothing.*

He opened his bedroom door and peeked over the second floor railing. In the living room below, his dad sat wrapped in a blanket, watching TV. The coast was clear, so he crept stealthily into Travis's room and started rifling through his brother's things. He pulled open drawers and hunted through the closet, checking the pockets in every article of clothing.

What started as a careful search soon turned frantic. Reckless, with beads of sweat running down his forehead, Devin pulled open the top drawer of his brother's desk, spilling stuff onto the floor. He swore and slammed the drawer shut, and once again turned his attention to the closet. Travis's belongings lay in piles as Devin's craziness grew.

Carl charged into the room. "What are you doing?"

Devin jumped backward. He hadn't realized he was being so loud.

"You're looking for drugs, aren't you?"

When he didn't answer, his dad pointed to the door. "Out! You have no right to trash Travis's room, and he wouldn't ... or he *better* not ... have anything you could find in here anyway."

Devin didn't say a word. He knew enough not to repeat the same mistake he had made the last time. Veering around his father, he stormed back down the hall. As he entered his room, he kicked a towel on the floor, but it barely moved and he tripped on it instead. He picked it up and threw it against the window. Weak. Useless. *Pathetic!* That's was he was.

Panic hit. Would he feel this way in detox?

No, that would be worse.

Quickly, he pulled on a t-shirt. He could run. He could

hide at Jonny's. He didn't have to show up at the courthouse the next day. His friends would help him out.

Then he stopped—his hand an inch away from the doorknob—and swore. Making a fist, he wound up his arm, about to take his rage out on the wall, but then he stopped that too. His father would hear.

He slumped on the bed and put his head in his hands. He imagined himself sleeping in a cell every night with guys who were twice his size and harder than he. The thought made him shake. If he left now he'd get caught, and he'd end up in jail for sure.

Carl entered the room with a glass of water and a small blue tablet. "Take this. It's Diazepam, for anxiety. It'll help the withdrawals."

Devin tossed the pill down the back of his throat. He didn't touch the water. "Why d'you even care what I do? I only disappoint you anyway."

His father nodded. "You're right. I am disappointed. I hate the way your life's turned out. You never should've started hanging out with the *scum* you call friends. You shouldn't have disowned the mother of your child, and you shouldn't have started taking –and *selling*—drugs."

Devin's whole body shook as he looked out the window. They were horrible accusations—and true.

"You've made some bad choices," his father

continued. "But underneath it all, you're a good person. You just need a chance to recover, to get off the drugs that are holding you back."

Devin's eyes flicked to the man's face. Was it true or was his dad just saying that to keep him from running?

He looked out the window again. Where was Travis? If only he'd gotten home when he was supposed to, none of this would've happened.

His dad sat down on the bed beside him. "You turned your back on your family, Dev, and on yourself too. I want to know why."

The words made Devin's stomach twist. He tried to look away, but his dad gripped his shoulder, forcing eye contact. "Where did I go wrong?"

Devin chewed on the inside of his cheek.

"You're not going to tell me are you?"

Shaking his head, Devin pulled away. He hurried into the bathroom and locked the door behind him.

It took well over an hour to lose the persistent reporter. Dave Mutch, from the local news, had chased Travis all the way from the beach to the parking lot where he'd started asking a ton of questions—all of them personal.

After trying a few times to be polite, Travis had

jumped into his truck and threatened to run the guy over if he didn't leave him alone. Yet still Dave had pursued him all the way down the highway and along the coast until Travis made a few quick turns and lost him in a residential area. There he had sat until it was safe to venture out again, and when he finally got home, the sun was down and the stars were out.

He hurried into the house and locked the door behind him, scowling as he passed his dad in the living room.

"What's wrong?" Carl asked, deep lines furrowing his brow.

"Nothing." Travis rushed up the stairs. Then he rushed back down. "What happened to my room?"

His father planted his hands on his hips. "Seems your brother was looking for something."

"Well, there's nothing in there."

"There better not be. If you're on drugs too ..."

"I'm not." *Damn it, Devin!*

Travis stomped back up the steps.

"So, there's nothing in your room?"

"No!" he shouted. It wasn't a lie. The drugs weren't in his room—they were in his pocket—but he still had them, and he felt horrible for keeping the filthy secret.

Back in his room, he surveyed the damage and kicked a pile of clothing back into his closet. He didn't go to his brother right away. Instead, he straightened up his room and waited until he heard his father leave the house to take the dog for a walk. Then, he entered the bathroom that joined the two rooms and knocked on his brother's door.

Devin answered it immediately, looking pale and strained. "What took you so long? Where is it?"

"I got it. Stay over there."

While his brother sat on the edge of the bed, Travis took the powder from his pocket and poured some out on the dresser. A small amount.

"Yeah right, bro."

Travis didn't budge.

"Come on," Devin pleaded. "I need more than that. Shit. I never should'a given it to you."

"No. I shouldn't be giving it to *you*."

"Whatevahs." Devin moved over to the dresser and inhaled the little bit of coke.

Travis rolled his eyes and left.

Back in his own room, he walked to his window and opened it. Far out on the beach below, he watched his dad throw a stick into the ocean. Jasper swam to get it.

He turned away from the view. Lying down, he stared at the picture of his mother that he kept by the bed. Then he turned away from that too.

~Disappointment~

Carl hurled a stick into the ocean and watched it disappear into the waves. Barking joyfully, Jasper bounded into the rolling water, rescued the wooden toy, and dropped it back on the sand. The golden retriever shook the moisture from his coat, but Carl barely noticed the spray. He flung the stick again, this time with more vigor.

His gut tightened as he glanced back toward the house. It didn't make sense. Why would Devin go searching through his brother's things? Was Travis giving him drugs? Was he helping Devin get stoned?

Self doubt washed over him as he walked along the shoreline. Waves licked at his feet, and Jasper bounded in front of him, moonlight flickering off damp fur. A million stars covered the sky, and as Carl glanced up at them, he frowned. Could his wife see him? Had she been watching all this time?

Tears threatened to spill from his eyes. *Victoria.* He

could barely picture her face anymore. Nor could he recall what her voice sounded like. The memory of the woman he had once loved was fading. A moan tore from his lips. "I'm sorry," he mumbled into the night. "I don't want to forget you."

Regret hit him hard as he remembered the promise he'd made the last night they were together. Sitting next to the hospital bed, he had clutched his wife's frail fingers, trying not to notice how thin they had become. Looking deep into tired eyes, he had whispered softly, "Don't worry, I'll take care of them."

Taking her final breath, she had nodded. She had believed him. She had trusted his words. And he had failed her miserably. Devin had closed out on him a long time ago, and now, so had Travis.

Carl patted the key in his pocket just to be sure it was there. He had noticed the bottles missing from the liquor cabinet. He knew Travis was the culprit, but aside from locking the cupboard doors, he had said nothing.

"What am I supposed to do?" he spoke aloud. "Lecturing never helped with Devin. I don't want Travis running away too."

Pushing branches out of the way, he took a shortcut down an overgrown path. To his right, Jasper leapt through the underbrush, barely visible. The night had grown darker, with less than a quarter of a moon to light the way.

The house was quiet when Carl returned. Devin's trial was in the morning, and he knew he should go to bed, but he slumped down on the couch instead and reached for the remote. Flicking through channels, he searched for the late night news.

He bolted upright. Travis was on TV. Surfing!

Scarcely able to believe what he was seeing, Carl blinked his eyes and shook his head, yet there it was on screen—his one-armed son dropping down the face of a wave and pulling into a small barrel.

As he held his breath, Carl listened to the reporter confirm it was the first time anyone had seen the pro surfer enter the water since the shark attack the year before. As the news report ended, a heavy ache hit Carl's chest. "He didn't even tell me."

Quietly, he crept upstairs and paused in front of Travis's door. He raised his hand to knock, but then he changed his mind and headed back down to his own room instead. He crawled into bed and his lungs grew heavy, as if all the air had been sucked out of them. As usual, he ignored the sadness and switched off the lamp.

Travis's eyes were closed, but he wasn't sleeping. He heard his bedroom door open, the quiet shuffle of feet, the soft rustle of fabric. He opened his eyes and found his brother rummaging through the pockets of the shorts he'd been wearing earlier.

"What do you think you're doing?"

Startled, Devin dropped the clothing and shifted from foot to foot. "You gotta gimme some more, bro."

Travis rolled onto his side. "No way. We had a deal."

"Come on. I'm goin' nuts in there. I can't sleep. I can't even think right. Not when I know y'got it in here."

Travis pulled the cocaine out from under his pillow and stood up. "Fine," he said. "I can fix that problem." He rushed into the bathroom, lifted the toilet seat, and flushed the package down the drain. Devin ran in after him and leaned over the swirling water, watching his drugs disappear down the hole.

Hands shaking, he grabbed Travis and threw him up against the wall. "What the hell did you do that for?"

Travis shoved his brother back and he fell onto the side of the counter. Some bottles of cologne smashed to the floor, filling the air with a spicy fragrance. Devin came at him again, and this time he landed a few good punches before their father rushed into the room. "What the hell is going on here?"

The boys froze. The side of Travis's head ached where his brother's fist had landed, but he barely noticed. He had bigger things to worry about.

Carl stepped up to him. "You have it don't you?"

Travis shook his head. "I...don't..."

His father's eyes flashed with rage. "Give it to me!"

Travis stood taller. He tried to return a glare but the

look of disappointment in his old man's eyes was too much to take. Without bothering to defend himself, he slipped past his dad, and raced back into his room, slamming the door behind him.

Fuck Devin!

~Plea Deal~

Wearing a suit he had borrowed from his brother, Devin sat on a wooden pew in the courtroom, waiting for his attorney to cut him a deal. On the bench sat the judge. Devin couldn't help but stare at her thick black eyebrows. They seemed to grow more menacing by the second.

In the center of the room, his lawyer, Paul, was hunched over a table talking to the district attorney in a low voice. Every time the prosecutor shook his head a knot of anxiety formed in Devin's stomach. He leaned forward, trying to hear what they were saying.

A craving wrapped around him like a dark, vindictive shadow, and he dug his nails into the sides of his leg trying to force it away.

Clenching his teeth, he wiped a bead of perspiration from his forehead. Seconds passed. He glanced at the clock. The big hand had only moved an inch since the last time he'd looked, and that felt like ages ago.

At one point, drowsiness overtook him, and his head nodded to his chest. The bailiff snapped at him and he jerked upright. "Sorry," he mumbled. Heat rose to his cheeks. Hopefully that wouldn't cost him.

Sweat trickled down his back. He pulled his shirt away from his skin to let it breathe. What the hell was taking so long?

Shoulders tensed, he held his breath and fiddled with the sleeve of his jacket. It was baggy and didn't fit him properly. When had Travis grown so much bigger than him? He looked around at the faces in the room, but no one was paying attention. Not even his father, who sat at the back, face lined with fatigue.

At least the black eye had faded.

Devin was certain his nails had drawn blood through his pant legs by the time Paul came over to update him on the proceedings. "It's a good deal," his lawyer told him. "I think you should take it."

With a twitch of his head, Devin agreed. He just wanted it all to be over.

"Sign here." Paul slid some papers toward him and pointed to the dotted line.

Devin chose not to read it. His hands shook as he scribbled his name on the page.

A few minutes later, he was lead by the bailiff to a space before the bench. To the right of him stood Paul.

To his left, the DA. Devon's legs tingled from sitting so long, and he flinched when he put pressure on his foot.

The judge looked at no one in particular. "Plea?"

"Yes, your honor," the prosecutor responded.

She addressed Devin. "Has anything been promised to you for this plea?"

"No," he said, quietly and wondered if she'd heard him.

"Do you understand what you are agreeing to? Are you doing so of your own free will?"

He nodded, but then remembered his place. "Yes, Your Honor." He spoke more clearly.

The prosecutor stated a few more sentences full of legal jargon.

"No objection," his attorney barked.

What did that mean?

"Plea accepted." The judge shuffled some papers on the bench. Up close, her eyebrows were even hairier. "This state supports and accepts this plea deal and hereby sentences you to a two thousand dollar fine and two years probation, with conditions to abstain from nonprescription drugs and complete three months in a rehabilitation facility."

Devin swallowed the lump in his throat. Paul informed him he was free to go, with a stern warning to check himself into the rehab facility within three days as agreed upon.

Devin exhaled. He wasn't going to jail. A weight lifted from his shoulders and a smile crept to his lips, but his elation vanished when he turned to meet with his father and saw the look on the older man's face. Carl gave the judge a somber nod. He ushered Devin down the aisle and out the thick, heavy doors. Travis met them on the steps of the courthouse and followed behind with Paul.

When they reached the parking lot, Carl pulled a dufflebag from the back of his SUV. "I packed you some clothes," he said. "The judge gave you three days, but you're going to treatment now. I'd like to drive you, but I've got to get back to the office. Paul will take you. The clinic's in Honolulu. It's an excellent program with a great success rate. I'm trusting you won't run to your friends once you get there. If so, we'll have to send you out of state."

Devin glanced over at his attorney and nodded. He didn't want to go, but he wouldn't run. At least he didn't think so.

Clutching his luggage tightly, he looked for his brother, but Travis had already gotten into the truck. Devin trembled inside. Was he was ready for this?

Carl placed a hand on his shoulder. "Do you have everything you need?"

Devin shrugged and nodded at the same time.

"Well, if you forgot anything, I can bring it when I come see you next week."

"Thanks," Devin murmured. It surprised him that his father would even want to visit.

He glanced toward home and swallowed back another craving. If only he could get high one more time, just to stop the shaking.

"You'll be okay." His dad squeezed his shoulder.

The gesture filled Devin with remorse, and suddenly all he wanted to do was go back in time, to the old days when he and his father used to fish and camp and build wagon-carts with running motors. "Sorry 'bout your eye," he whispered.

"No worries." Carl nodded. "Make me proud, son. I know you can do this."

Devin slid tentatively into the front seat of his lawyer's car, and as they pulled away from the curb, he waved.

His father waved back. Travis didn't even look at him.

Tension hung in the air as Travis and his father drove through Wahiawa and up highway 99, past the Dole Plantation. In the passenger seat, Travis sat, staring out at the pineapple fields that stretched toward the mountains. The green rows of spiny leaves contrasted sharply with the deep red clay, and his mouth watered for a taste of the fruit, warm from sitting in the earth.

Mouth dry, he licked his lips. He almost asked for the bottle of water that was tucked in the cup-holder on the driver's side door, but he held his tongue and pushed the thirst from his mind. From the corner of his eye, he saw his father glance over at him. They hadn't spoken since the fight the night before, and Travis wasn't about to start now. He twisted his body and looked out the window.

Carl cleared his throat. "Devin will be okay. This is the right thing for him."

Travis rolled his eyes. He'd read the statistics. The failure rate for abstaining from cocaine was eighty percent for a first time patient, and Devin had been a junkie for way too long. He gritted his teeth. Rehab might help, but there was a larger chance it would do nothing. Devin would come out of therapy and go straight back to his old ways.

His dad turned on the radio, and for a while it helped to drown the silence. Then he switched it off. "Why didn't you tell me?"

"Tell you what?"

"About you ... surfing at Rocky Point yesterday?"

Travis sat up straight. "How'd you know?"

"I saw it on the news."

Great. He slumped back down. "It wasn't supposed to be on TV. It was Dave, that stupid anchorman."

His father frowned. "I've been trying to fend that guy off since your accident. He doesn't give up."

"I know. It took me over an hour to lose him yesterday."

But that was talking and Travis didn't want to talk. With a frown, he turned back to the window and refused to say anything further. His father didn't ask any more questions about surfing, but as soon as they pulled into the driveway, he reached out and put a hand on Travis's arm. "Before we go in, I want to talk about what happened last night."

"For why?" snapped Travis. "I ain't no druggie, Dad. Maybe if you'd asked why we were fighting in the first place, I could've told you I'd just flushed his drugs down the toilet."

Without waiting for a reply, Travis jumped out of the vehicle and headed straight for Shayla's house. It was the one place he knew he could find some peace.

~Scumbag~

Surfboard tucked under his arm, Travis led Shayla down an overgrown path and through the lush bamboo jungle. When they came out onto a secluded white sand beach, he propped his board up and smiled. "This is it. The first place I surfed."

Shayla looked around the lagoon. "It's gorgeous." She smiled back. "I didn't even know this was here, and I thought I'd been everywhere on the island."

Travis nodded. "It's one of my favorite spots."

A breeze spun around them, light and peaceful as they stood looking out at the water. With a giggle, Shayla tapped the nose of his board and pointed to the tiny waves. "Pretty gnarly surf," she teased. "Good thing you brought your best board."

"Well, I didn't really plan on surfing," he confessed. He drew her over to him and kissed her gently on the lips. She laughed, danced in a small circle around him, and tugged him into the sea.

The next few hours, they played in the surf and lounged on their boards. Travis talked about his brother's plea bargain, and once again, Shayla listened without judgment. Even better, when he pulled off his rash-guard and let her see his arm for the very first time, she didn't cringe.

Back on the beach, they threw down their towels and made themselves comfortable on the sand, soaking up the last of the afternoon heat as the sun plunged toward the water's edge. A beautiful orange and pink sky reflected onto the ocean, making for a picture-perfect sunset.

Lost in memory, Travis watched the descent. "When we were kids, my mom used to tell us if we listened hard enough we could hear the sun hissing as it hit the horizon. But really she just wanted to shut us up."

Shayla chuckled. "My dad used to do stuff like that too."

Travis rolled on his side and placed his head in his hand. It was the first time she'd ever mentioned her father. "Where is he?"

She frowned. "My parents split up a while ago."

"Oh, sorry."

"Don't be. We're better off without him. My mom wanted to move to the North Shore to get away, so we wouldn't run into him as much. It was a good move. She seems happy now with her new job."

"And you?"

Shayla didn't answer. Instead, she stared out at the sea.

Travis took the hint and remained quiet.

She pushed a lock of hair out of her eyes. "So, what about your brother? Are you happy he's in rehab?"

Travis shrugged. "I don't think it'll do him much good."

She wrapped her arms around him. "Maybe it will."

"Maybe." He shrugged. "But probably not."

In silence, they watched the sun dip lower, until it was almost out of sight. It didn't hiss.

Later that evening, Travis and Shayla sat under the thatched umbrellas at Kiio's Bar, eating supper and drinking pina coladas. Leaning back in his chair, Travis listened as a fat man in the corner of the patio played "Tiny Bubbles" on a ukulele.

He pushed away his empty plate and looked over at the huge Hawaiian buffet. He and Shayla had loaded up their dishes, sampling everything from *poi* to *lomi* salmon to chicken long rice—which wasn't rice at all, but long transparent noodles.

Shayla took one last mouthful of dessert and patted

her stomach. "I can't eat another bite." She gave him a lazy smile. Then her eyes grew wide, and she motioned toward the bar. Mika stood behind it filling drinks. "I didn't know she worked here."

"Me neither." Travis leaned forward. "Guess she got another job to save money for the baby."

Mika glanced over and saw them. She quickly looked away.

The musician switched to a steel guitar, and Travis ordered another round of drinks. The bar grew busier. The lights dimmed and people started to dance.

"Oh great," Shayla hissed. "Look who else is here."

Kane walked in. The pro surfer greeted a bunch of friends at the other end of the patio, and Travis couldn't help but scowl when he heard someone ask about the Bonzai Classic.

For the last week, he'd been trying to avoid any mention of the surfing competition. Unfortunately, it was all around him. Everywhere he went people were talking up their favorite surfers and betting on those they wanted to win. Both the trials and the first few rounds had already taken place, and if the waves held up, the finals would start the very next day.

Kane's voice traveled across the lanai, as loud and irritating as ever. From where he sat, Travis could feel the arrogance radiating from the surf champion. It hit him like a gnarly stench.

"Are you pau?" the server asked, collecting the empty plates.

"Yeah, we're all done." He handed her his credit card and stood up. "I'm gonna hit the bathroom," he said to Shayla. "Then we'll go."

As Travis walked away, Shayla hid behind a vase of purple orchids, hoping her ex-boyfriend wouldn't notice her. Luckily, Kane didn't even look her way. He was too busy waving at Mika. Standing behind the bar, Mika saw him, grimaced, and turned away. Shayla wondered what had happened between them.

Two months had passed since she had walked into Kane's apartment to find them wrapped in each other's arms, kissing on his living room sofa. Her boyfriend and her best friend.

At first, she had just stood there, too shocked to do anything else. Then, without thinking, she had flung herself over the coffee table, her fist making contact with Mika's face.

Stomach turning, Shayla forced her hands under the

table. No matter how betrayed she felt, she shouldn't have hit the girl. It wasn't right.

Feigning an interest in something sweet, she picked up the dessert menu and pretended to read until she felt someone beside her. Mika stood next to the table, wiping her hands on her apron. "So ... you and Trav, huh? That's cool."

Shayla didn't know what to say.

Mika sat down. "No really, it's cool." She brushed some crumbs off the table, her mouth turning into a frown. "I miss you, Shay, and I wanna talk. I'm sorry for what I did." Her voice wavered slightly as she spoke.

Shayla reached for her water glass and took a small sip. "Why did you do it?"

Mika blinked. "I had too much to drink, and Kane told me you guys broke up. Not that it matters. I shouldn't have touched him. You were my best friend. He's such a *scumbag*." She spit the word out venomously.

Shayla shook her head. "I don't care about Kane. I was talking about Travis. How could you tell him the baby was his?"

Mika gasped. "*Shhh!*" Cowering in her seat, she crossed her arms over her belly and shot a nervous glance in Kane's direction. "Please be quiet. I don't want anyone to know."

Shayla followed the glare and her heart skipped a beat. Could it be? Was *Kane* the father?

"Look," said Mika, in a hushed voice. "I just wanted to tell you I'm sorry. I didn't mean to hurt you … or Travis." With that, she jumped off her chair and faded back into the crowd.

Travis was just washing up when Kane walked into the men's room. With a nasty smirk, he looked Travis up and down and headed over to the urinal.

Travis's blood began to boil. Standing a shade taller, he turned off the faucet and wiped his hand on his shorts. He wasn't a coward, and he needed Kane to know that. He stayed where he was, watching the back of the guy's head in the mirror. Thick gelled hair poked out of the top of a red bandana. Was he trying to look like a gangster? Travis rolled his eyes.

Kane sauntered up to the sink next to him and ran his hands under the water. "Wazzup, Kelly-man?"

Travis leaned against the counter. Hatred flowed through his veins and prickled his skin as he thought about all the times Kane had thrown him a snide remark or goaded him on before a contest. He gripped the edge of the sink, wishing he could think of something clever to say. He knew he was the better surfer. In a little over a year, he had moved up the ranks to compete for the number one spot—something that had taken Kane ten years to do.

But that meant nothing now.

Kane pressed the button on the hand-dryer and held his hands underneath. As if to show Travis he still had two, he made a huge show out of rubbing them together to dry. When the machine shut off, he turned to leave. "I see you tomorrow at Pipe. Oh wait … you ain't coming."

Kane snickered as he headed out the door, and Travis had to stop himself from slamming his fist into the wall. It took all of his control not to run after the kook. Everything about Kane sucked—his arrogant stance, his smug grin, the way he flashed his money around.

Travis's heart knocked rapidly in his chest as he stared at his reflection in the mirror. All he could see was his stump, his shirt pinned up on one side. Like that even hid anything. His eyes darkened. Why had this happened to him? It wasn't fair. All Kane cared about was what he could get for free or how many times he could get his picture in one of the surf magazines. If anyone, it should have been Kane who was missing an arm.

Mind filled with malicious thoughts, Travis stormed back to the table where he signed the credit card receipt and motioned for Shayla to get up. "Let's go," he grumbled. "Your ex-boyfriend's a dick."

~Pure Agony~

As he paced back and forth in Shayla's backyard, Travis said every foul thing he could think to say about Kane. "I can't believe you went out with that guy."

"Me neither." Shayla shook her head and sat down on one of the patio chairs.

"Why did you date him anyway?"

"I don't know." She shrugged. "We dated for a year, but I barely knew him. He was always on tour, and when he was home, he'd throw on the charm. I didn't know he was such a jerk. He's good at pretending he's something he's not."

Travis thought about his ex-girlfriend and stopped pacing. "Yeah, I guess I know what that's like. I dated Hayley for six months with no idea who she really was."

Shayla gave him a questioning glance.

"She only dated the pros," he explained, "and only if they were winning. Acted like an angel, but what a joke.

Kicked me to the curb right after the accident. Didn't even visit me once in the hospital."

Shayla shook her head. "That's awful." She paused. "I would've come to see you, every day."

Travis smiled. Breathing easier, he pulled Shayla to her feet and held her close. Yellow and silver lights reflected off the house and shimmered across the water in her small swimming pool.

"You want to go swimming?" she asked.

"I don't have anything to wear."

"That's okay." She gave him a devilish grin.

Travis's eyes widened, and he glanced toward the house. "What if your mom comes home?"

Shayla chuckled. "That's not what I meant, you perv." She gave him a shove, and he toppled backward into the pool. He came up sputtering and laughing, clothes clinging to his body. He wound up his arm to send a splash her way, but she jumped in with him, fully clothed as well. He pulled her over to him and wiped a wet strand of hair off her cheek. "We're supposed to wait half an hour before swimming, you know."

"That's okay. We don't have to swim."

This time, the look she gave him was pure agony. Stifling a moan, Travis backed her up against the side of the pool and kissed her fiercely. She returned the fervor, running her fingers through his hair and pressing closer to him.

A light came on in the kitchen. With a sharp gasp, Shayla pulled away and glanced toward the house.

She giggled. "Mom's home. I should go inside before we … you know."

Travis relented. "Okay." But he paused before releasing her and gave her one last kiss.

Shayla climbed the ladder, clothing sticking to her body as she got out of the pool. She wrung out her shirt and the water splashed at her feet. "Thank you for today. I had a lot of fun."

Still standing chest-deep in the pool, Travis laughed. "You're just going to leave me like this?"

She stared at him for a second and then chuckled. "Yeah."

As his girlfriend headed inside the house, Travis smiled and slumped against the side of the pool. The door opened again. Still laughing, Shayla threw him a towel, and by the time he reached out and caught it, she was gone.

On the dance floor, Kane pressed his hips against a pretty brunette, grinding to the music. Every now and then, he glanced over at Mika. She rolled her eyes and continued pouring drinks. Was he trying to make her jealous?

"Why should I care who he dances with?" she mumbled.

Through the thick haze of smoke, a strobe light flickered and people packed into the club. The air grew hot and stuffy, and as she tended the bar, a wave of nausea hit her. Whoever had named it morning sickness was out of their minds. Lately she felt sick all the time.

She popped the top off a bottle of beer and handed it to a redhead wearing way too much makeup. The girl handed her some money and told her to keep the change. Mika stuffed the bills into her apron. At least her new job was bringing in tips. She was going to need all the money she could get.

With one hand on her stomach, she stroked the soon to be growing bump through her clothing. Finally she'd made up her mind. No more games, no deception. Father or no father, she would raise the baby herself.

Frowning, she glanced over at Kane and the other partygoers. It wasn't fair. Here she was, alone and pregnant, working late into the night, inhaling tons of second hand smoke. Why had this happened to her? It wasn't like she slept around. Normally she waited a long time before having sex with someone.

Except for that one night.

That one night, he had made her feel special. She had thought he really liked her. She'd felt so happy in his arms...

"Stop thinking about him," she hissed under her breath.

Mika handed a customer a Mai Tai and placed some more money into her pocket. She turned back to the bar and Kane stood in front of her. Groupies surrounded him, vying for his attention, as he slapped some money down and ordered a round of drinks.

Mika fixed the beverages and handed them out. When she finally gave Kane his, he leaned across the bar. "Eh sista', we go party afta' work, yeah?"

"No way."

He gave her a winning smile. "I no see why not."

"I'm not going anywhere with you. Do you really think I'd make *that* mistake again?"

As she turned away, a tall Korean guy came up to the counter. He was handsome, with a chiseled chin and broad shoulders. Mika made a big deal out of smiling at him, tossing her hair and giggling, and only after stuffing a ten-dollar tip into her pouch did she turn her attention back to Kane. He mouthed something vicious and walked away.

Mika shot a spiteful look at the back of his head. She turned back to her work, and for the rest of the night, she took no notice of him—especially when he left the bar with the girl he was dancing with earlier.

~Detox~

A *shadowy figure swam underneath him, large and dark.*
Devin grabbed his surfboard and pulled his feet up as he
peered into the aquamarine depths. Another beast swam past,
and another. Sharks. At least five. Maybe more.

He lifted his head and saw his brother, sitting out in the
lineup, oblivious to the giant fish that were heading in his
direction.

Devin reacted. "Travis!" he shouted. "No!" He paddled
frantically toward his brother, the words echoing in the air as
the ocean swelled. A wave peaked in front of him, blocking his
path. It picked him up and tossed him under the rolling
current. He fought the wave, kicking and spinning, and came
up sputtering. He heard a scream and caught a glimpse of
terror in his brother's eyes. A shark clamped onto the lower
half of his body and dragged him under the water. Blood
bubbled up to the surface. "No!" Devin hollered again, and
one of the sharks turned toward him....

Temples pounding, Devin shot up in bed. He could barely remember what the nightmare was about, but in his mind's eye, he could see his brother laying in the hospital bed, covered in bandages and hooked to an IV. He pulled his knees to his chest, hugging them tightly. "I couldn't save him." His body shook violently and he gagged on a sob, almost choking as he pushed his covers away.

It took him a while to figure out where he was, but as he looked around the darkened room, the events of the day came back to him—the trial, the judge's sentence, the trip to the rehab center.

As soon as the intake director had signed him into the clinic, she had introduced him to the resident aides and checked through his bags to make sure he didn't have anything that could hurt anyone. She had confiscated his mouthwash and hand sanitizer—even though he'd promised not to drink them—and she'd administered a urine test to screen him for drugs.

He'd met his therapist next, a heavyset man with dark-rimmed glasses. "Welcome," the man said. "I'm Dr. Harold." He motioned for Devin to sit down and handed him an orientation package.

He told Devin the rules—no intoxicating substances allowed on the premises, no use of electronic devices for two full weeks, no glamorizing drugs with other patients—and waited for him to fill out some mood evaluation forms. They'd discussed his treatment plan and the expectations of the clinic. "This isn't a one-size-fits-all program. We work with you to create a plan that's successful. We want to get an idea of what has contributed to your substance abuse so we can set goals, identify triggers, and help you develop coping skills that will help you when your time here is over."

Devin had barely listened. He'd sat on his hands to stop the shaking and watched a fly that was trapped between the screen and the window pane.

The best part of the day came when the therapist finished the assessment and gave Devin medication to help with the anxiety and withdrawals. Devin popped the pills gratefully—not caring to ask what they were—and was finally shown to his room, where he'd crawled into bed and blacked out.

Meds must'a been strong, he thought now. The clock on the nightstand read four a.m.

Devin flipped on the lamp and shrank away from the light. On the wall hung an abstract painting in various shades of blue and purple. The shapes swirled on the canvas—an intoxicating illusion—and suddenly he felt as if the walls were closing in on him.

He hurried over to the window and opened it as far as it would go. A breeze floated into the room, caressing him with thoughts of escape. He absentmindedly patted his pockets, feeling for his cell phone, but it wasn't there. They had taken it, cutting him off from the world.

A surge of raw need hit him, sickly sweet and spiteful. The sensation threatened to choke off his breath. If only he could drive to Vince's house. A few hits of coke could end his misery. Or his life. What did it matter? He'd already destroyed anything worth living for.

The lump in his throat grew so big he couldn't swallow it, and soon he was gasping for air. Never had he felt so trampled on, so defeated. Depression, anxiety, chills, exhaustion, night terrors—the doctor had said they were all symptoms of withdrawal.

If only he weren't trapped in this place.

The noise of the overhead fan was way too loud. Irritated, he gritted his teeth and pressed a button by the side of his bed. Seconds later, a nurse appeared. "Are you okay? What can I do for you?"

The concerned look on her face made Devin sick. So kind and sympathetic. It made his stomach turn. At that moment, he would have sold his soul for just one line of blow, a tiny morsel of relief.

"Are you having cravings?" she asked. Everyone was always asking about his cravings.

"Christ," he snapped. "Can you jus' gimme some more meds?"

He took a breath and held it, but she didn't comment on his outburst. With a quick nod, she left the room and returned with a tiny cardboard container. A blue pill sat inside, the same kind he'd been given earlier. She handed him a cup of water, and he quickly swigged the tablet down.

"I'll be here if you need me." She turned out the light, and closed the door.

Back in bed, Devin waited for the pill to kick in. He squeezed his eyes shut, trying to control the turmoil that was swimming inside him. The edge of his fingernail was sharp and he ran it over his forearm, pressing until it drew blood. The pain gave him something else to focus on, but soon his sheets and arms were stained with red and he knew he was going to have to explain himself in the morning.

He pulled his blankets to his chin, clenching his fists around the fabric, and then he felt it. A foggy stupor washed through his brain and a murky wave covered him slowly until his eyes grew heavy. Relief filled him as he sank into the mattress, letting the darkness swallow him up.

~Bonzai Classic~

Travis sat on the hot sand watching the Bonzai Classic Surf Competition. Flawless waves—some twenty feet on the face—blasted onto Pipeline's legendary reef. Despite the perfect conditions, Travis couldn't keep the scowl off his face. Those were waves he should've been riding.

His jaw clenched as he tightened his grip on his bottle of soda. The rum he'd mixed into it buzzed in his veins, making his head swim.

In front of his eyes, the most experienced surfers tussled for the hollowest waves. They took off on vertical drops, emerged from life-threatening barrels, and pulled off crowd-pleasing maneuvers. Surfboards smashed into pieces as contenders pushed deeper and deeper for the highest-scoring tubes.

There were some great heats, yet Travis sulked through all of them. Sitting next to Shayla, he secretly downed hard liquor just to get through the day. Why had he agreed to come? He hated sitting on the sidelines while his biggest rival dominated the competition.

And Kane didn't even have to try. The only surfer who'd had any chance of beating him was eliminated early, and the rest were so far behind on points there was no way they could catch up to him in the ratings. Kane took his time, shredding the waves and showing off his fancy tricks, until the foghorn blew, and he came in from the water, triumphant for another year.

Everyone cheered, celebrating his victory. Travis stood up, fuming. Kane had won the title fair and square, but why couldn't somebody—*anybody*—else have won? It was ridiculous to pout, and Travis knew it, but he just didn't want Kane to win. Not for the fourth year in a row. Not when things could have been different.

As he stood on the beach, the heat combined with the alcohol made his head spin. The awards ceremony began, and Shayla put her hand on his arm. "I wanna go see Kimo. Wait for me, okay?"

Travis nodded. "Sure."

As she ran to the podium, he chugged the rest of his drink. He noticed a few people staring at him, so he moved into the shadows of an ironwood tree. From there, he watched the photographers snapping pictures of the pros. Cameramen and journalists surrounded the stage, all of them jostling for the surf champ's attention.

Kane stood on top holding his trophy in the air.

Jerk-wad.

Dave slid up beside him.

Travis glowered at the reporter. "Shouldn't you be over there talking to Kane?"

The anchorman fiddled with some papers. "I'm sorry I chased you down the other day," he said, "but I've been trying to get a story about you since your accident."

Travis barked. "Yeah, and you got one."

"Please?" Dave begged. "Just a few questions?"

"Brah, I said *no*. What do I have to do to get rid of you?"

Travis clenched his fist and the reporter backed away, but as he did so, he held out a business card. "Okay, but take this, and if you change your mind, call me."

To shut the man up, Travis stuck the card in his pocket. Then he went to look for Shayla.

Shayla crossed the sand with her cousin, gushing over him as they walked. During the contest, Kimo had surfed better than ever. Unlike Kane, he had concentrated most of his efforts on surfing Backdoor Pipe. Charging right instead of left, he had caught one amazing wave after another.

One ride in particular was incredible. After surviving a near vertical takeoff, Kimo had disappeared deep into a massive barrel. Just when the wave seemed to swallow him up, a blast of whitewater spit him back out again. It was the only perfect score all day.

"I can't believe you made that drop," Shayla babbled as she clung to his arm. "Fourth place! I'm stoked for you, cuz!"

The crowd was huge. Beachgoers cheered as pros posed for pictures and fans hurried over to offer their congratulations. In the yards of the sponsor houses, the surfers partied, cracking open bottles of champagne and making toasts. The commotion went on for quite a while, but eventually the excitement died down and the majority of people started making their way back to their vehicles.

As she followed Kimo up the beach, Shayla spotted Travis standing on the hilltop. Shadows covered his face as he waved her over. She could tell from his stance he wasn't happy. The sun blinded her as she turned toward him and she accidentally bumped into someone. She realized who it was and jumped backward.

Kane gave her the once over. "Howzit, Shay?"

She rolled her eyes and tried to step aside. He grabbed her arm and held her there. "Guess you still mad at me, hah?"

She pulled away. "Um ... you slept with my best friend. Or did you forget that already?"

He waved away an insistent fan. "I neva'. I told you dat."

"Whatever."

She crossed her arms and was about to congratulate him on being a *'father'*, when Travis pushed his way between them. "I don't think she wants to talk to you, man."

Kane returned his glare. "Dis not your problem, brah."

"Don't call me that ... and I think it is."

Kane turned to Shayla. "So, w'at? You wen hook up with dis punk now?"

Travis stepped closer.

"Trav, don't...." Shayla pleaded.

"For why?" He turned to her. "You actually want to talk to this kook?"

Kane stepped closer. "Who you calling one kook? Dat ain't funny. You see me laughing?"

"Stop it," Shayla said. "I don't want you guys fighting." She placed her hand on Travis's arm and smelled the alcohol on his breath. This was not good. Not good at all.

The pressure of Shayla's hand caused Travis to back down a little. Inhaling deeply, he looked into her eyes and his anger softened. Adrenaline rushed through his body still, but there was no way he could pound Kane now. Not in front of her. He threw his rival a nasty look and took Shayla's hand. "Let's go," he said and starting walking.

"W'at punk? Goin' already?" Following too closely, Kane gave him a shove. "You wish you can kick my ass, you one-armed freak. Brah, I take you out with one little pinky."

Travis whirled around. "What'd you call me?" With a sudden lunge, he slammed his fist into Kane's face.

Kane stumbled to the ground, and Travis leapt on top of him, smashing his face into the sand. Coughing from the dirt in his lungs, Kane managed to flip over, but Travis held him down with his knees. "Who's the freak now!" he shouted. He raised his arm to strike again, but two security guards pulled him away.

He bucked and kicked, straining against them. "Calm down," one of them said.

Beaten, with blood dripping from his nose, Kane stumbled to his feet. He tried to charge Travis, but security got to him too and held him fast.

Cursing loudly, Kane thrashed against the men, calling Travis back on. But Travis barely heard him. He was much too focused on his surroundings. He saw the reporters, and he saw the cameras. People everywhere were staring.

"Let me go," he ordered, pushing away from his captors. He struggled free and sped down the beach, sprinting past Off the Wall and all the way to the lava rocks at Rockpiles. Away from the crowds, he stopped behind a lifeguard tower and took his anger out on a tree.

He slowly turned around. "You didn't have to follow me."

Shayla stepped onto the grass beside him. "I know."

He wiped the blood from his knuckles onto his shorts. It was the second time Shayla had witnessed his temper—first with his brother, and now Kane. What was wrong with him? He had never been an aggressive person. Before his accident, he had always avoided brawls. He had even held his temper with Kane. Most of the time.

He stared down at his pinned-up sleeve. More than ever before, he hated his stump. He couldn't escape it. He could wrap it up and keep it hidden, but it was always there—or not there—to remind him he could never have his old life back.

A cloud of fury darkened inside him. With a loud grunt, he kicked at a dried palm branch lying on the ground. A giant wave crashed onto the rocks at the edge of the water; he could feel the impact through the soles of his feet, a thunderous boom.

"Travis..."

Shayla reached for him, but he pulled away and took off running. Flying over the scorching sand, he rushed back through the crowd and up the small hill, where he finally stopped in the shade of a kamani tree. Light-headed, he placed his hand on his chest. His head spun and his body tingled. He thought he might throw up.

A few moments later, the sensation passed. He still felt chilled, but his breathing and pulse returned to normal. It was the second time he'd had the feeling. *Must be the alcohol*, he thought.

He kicked a rock out of his shoes and continued walking. He didn't know where he was going, but it didn't matter. Putting one foot in front of the other, he ignored his surroundings and didn't look up until someone touched his shoulder. It was Kimo.

"Howz'it braddah? I heard you and Kane went scrap."

"He deserved it," Travis said, and kept going.

Kimo agreed and followed him. "He's a scrub, brah. You okay o' w'at? I know you no need my help, but I get your back if anything happen."

"Nah, I'm all right." Finally, he stopped and gave his friend an exhausted but grateful nod. "Thanks, though." He drew a deep breath in.

Kimo looked him up and down. "It's too packed over hea'. We goin' to Hale'iwa. You like come? I get one stick you can use."

Travis almost turned the offer down. Then he reconsidered. Suddenly the only thing he wanted to do was surf. "Okay," he said. "Let's go."

~Drunk~

Travis spent the rest of the afternoon with Kimo, surfing at Hale'iwa. The waves formed perfect walls for the surfers to carve, and together they ripped them up.

Kimo tucked into a small barrel, and Travis launched into an aerial. With little effort, he landed the trick and cut back through the water to slap hands with his pal. Both smiling, they headed back out for more.

On the next wave, Travis turned to hit the lip, lost his balance, and tumbled underneath the water. His knee smashed into a rock, and his rash guard protected him from a scrape across his shoulder. He came up sputtering, but he was fine. Blood trickled from his leg as he left the ocean. He shook it off and grinned.

What an awesome session.

As he stopped to wait for Kimo, who was still out in the surf, a girl in a tiny pink bikini ran up to him. She threw her arms around him. "Oh. My. God! I knew it was you out there!"

Travis backed away, and when he realized who it was, he had to force himself to keep calm.

His ex-girlfriend, Hayley, looked up at him through lowered lashes. "I'm sorry, Trav. I shouldn't have dumped you. It was a big mistake."

He snorted and shook his head. "Is that supposed to make me feel better? We both know why you were dating me, Hayley."

"But ... I don't want those things anymore." She put her hand on his arm. "I miss you, Trav, and it's so cool that you're surfing again. I saw you on the news and..."

Ah, so that was it. "Piss off, Hayley. I got someone way better than you."

Without a second thought, Travis turned and walked away. Suddenly all he wanted was to go and find Shayla. Why had he left her on the beach in the first place? He had been angry with Kane, not her.

Kimo caught up to him and motioned toward Hayley. She was standing where Travis had left her, arms crossed. "Who dat?" he asked.

Travis shook his head. "Just a dumb pro-ho."

Kimo chuckled and they headed over to the showers to rinse their boards. Travis stuck his head under the tap and shook the water from his hair. "You think Shayla will be at the awards party tonight?"

"For sure, brah," Kimo nodded.

"Kay den. I'm going with you."

The trade winds had shifted, closing out the surf at Pipe, but there were still a few surfers at Off the Wall. Shayla sat by herself on the sand, watching them, waves tickling her toes as they rolled up the shore.

For the last hour she'd been trying to make sense of everything that had happened with Travis. Why had he left her?

She thought about Kane—his arrogant smile, the grating sound of his voice as he taunted Travis on the beach.

"What a kook," she muttered, shaking her head.

She still couldn't believe he had called Travis a freak. The pain that had flashed in her boyfriend's eyes, the blood on his hands after he'd punched that tree—it was awful. He'd had every right to be mad at Kane. But why had he run away? Why did he seem so angry with her?

Then it hit her. The alcohol on his breath.

He was drunk.

Groaning inwardly, she hugged her knees to her chest. She hadn't seen Travis drinking during the contest. He must have been hiding it from her. That was even worse.

Feeling as if she'd been tossed by an angry wave, she walked back to her car and drove home, wanting nothing more than to sleep for the rest of the day. But when she pulled into her driveway, a truck blocked her path. She recognized it and her stomach lurched. What was *he* doing there?

On the front lawn, her mother and father stood, talking—or yelling by the sound of it. Her mother's high pitched voice traveled in through the open window. Her face was red, her lips puckered.

Shayla leapt from the car and ran to her mother's side. She turned to her dad. "You're not supposed to be here. There's a restraining order!"

"I know. I just wanted to see you."

He moved forward and Shayla wrapped her arm around her mother's waist. Nothing bad would happen this time. "Don't come any closer."

Her father stopped, shoulders sagging, and it was then Shayla noticed how tired he looked, so thin and pale. His skin had a strange yellowish tinge, and there were dark bags under his eyes. He looked worse than the last time she'd seen him.

"Okay, I'll go," he said. "But take this. I missed your birthday."

After handing her a wrapped parcel, he turned around and headed back to his vehicle. Shayla followed her mother into the house and dropped the package onto the table with a thud. "Does he think he can buy me off or something?"

Her mom sat down. "He's your dad. He misses you."

Shayla looked up. "You're not taking him back, are you?"

"God, no! I just feel sad for him, that's all. He's not a bad man. He just got himself messed up on booze."

The lines around her mom's mouth drooped, her green eyes squeezing shut as she rubbed the back of her neck. She looked exhausted.

Shayla stared at the wood grain on the table, tracing the patterns with her finger. She couldn't help but think of the days before her father lost his job as an engineer, before he started hitting the bottle. He used to be such a good dad, attending all her dance recitals and taking her to art museums. Why did that have to change? And why couldn't things ever be easy … or normal even?

She thought about Travis's behavior on the beach and her lip quivered. She accidentally bit down on it, tasted blood, and wrinkled her nose in disgust.

After a while, the gift aroused her curiosity, so she slid it toward her. It was hard and heavy, about the width of a boogie board. She broke the tape with her fingernail and tore the wrapping aside. It was an oil painting set, with very expensive brushes. The best kind.

Her mother got up and patted her on the arm. "At least you can use that to finish your projects."

Shayla took the set up to her room and slid it under the bed with the painting she'd made of Travis. She leaned against her desk and took a deep breath. Maybe it was a good thing her father had shown up. To remind her of what she *didn't* want in her life.

Grief hit and all she wanted was to crawl under her covers, but she forced herself into the shower instead. Kimo was expecting her to show up at the awards ceremony. It was a big day for him. She couldn't miss it. As she shampooed her hair, she threw on a bogus smile. She would go to the party, have a good time, and worry about everything else later.

By the time they arrived at Waimea Falls Park, the Bonzai Classic after party was in full swing, and Travis was drunk. It had taken all the liquor in Kimo's cupboards to give him the nerve to show up. He looked around the pavilion. Tables were decorated with linens and fresh flowers. Live music bellowed from the stage. People were dancing, eating from the large buffet, toasting the pros, and having a great time.

A small group surrounded Kimo. With huge smiles, they patted him on the back, congratulating him once again on his fourth place standing. They crowded Travis as well, clasping his hand and asking how he was doing. An old surfing buddy approached and tried to strike up a conversation. Other people stared, but Travis turned away from it all. His mind was set on one thing—finding Shayla—and the booze in his system made it easy to ignore everything else.

Finally, he spotted her talking to a couple of friends. She backed up when she saw him, eyes flashing with obvious irritation. "What do you want?"

"Kimo said you'd be here."

She pulled him away from the others. "You're drunk."

"Nah, I'm all right." He tried his best not to slur any words. "I came to apologize. I know you're pissed 'cause I was fighting with Kane."

Shayla shook her head. "I'm not angry about that."

"Then what...."

There was a sudden uproar as Kane arrived. A loud cheer rang out, and the hair on the back of Travis's neck stood up. He clenched his jaw as the reigning surfer walked by.

Nose swollen, Kane spat at him as he passed. "You goin' get it."

Travis tried to stand taller, but as his rival disappeared into the crowd everything started to spin. He stumbled backward, and Shayla caught him by the arm. "Look at you." She helped him stand. "You can barely walk. What's going on, Trav? You were drunk at the beach today too."

He reached for her. "Don't be mad."

She pulled away. "Travis, please … just go home. I don't want to deal with this."

His heart tore inside. He didn't understand. One minute she seemed totally into him and the next she closed out like the surf. To no longer have her in his life was something he couldn't even imagine, so he said the only thing he knew for sure. "I love you."

Silence followed. Shayla shook her head. "Tell me that when you're not drunk." She went back to her friends.

Travis slumped against an empty table and swallowed hard, fighting the alcohol that threatened to spew from his stomach.

Some girl put her hand on his shoulder. "Dude, you okay?"

"Leave me alone," he replied. He pushed himself to his feet, bolted outside, and threw up behind some red ginger plants.

~Feeling Bad~

Just before noon the back door opened and Travis hobbled into the house. Expecting an argument, Carl stood up and faced him. Then he took a step back. The stench from his son's body was appalling. Travis reeked of vomit and booze. His face was pale and hidden beneath dark sunglasses.

"Where were you all night?" Carl asked. He had to refrain from covering his nose.

Travis veered around him. "I stayed at Kimo's." From the fridge, he pulled a jug of water, poured himself a glass, and took a sip. He seemed to have trouble swallowing it.

Carl frowned and placed his hands on his hips. "What's this about some fight you got in?"

Travis pulled the cup away from his lips. "Where'd you hear that?"

"Dave Mutch. He called last night and told me all about it."

"Shit."

Shaking his head, Carl huffed. "How am I supposed to keep fending that guy off when you can't even keep yourself out of trouble? Drinking in public? Assault? You know you can be charged for stuff like that?"

Travis rolled his eyes. "Fights happen out at Pipe all the time. No one presses charges."

"You shouldn't be fighting."

"For why? Because I'm a cripple?" He slammed his glass down on the counter and water splashed onto the floor.

Carl took a step back. "That's not what I meant."

"Well, that's what Kane called me, right before I pounded him."

The pain in his son's eyes was devastating. Carl's voice grew soft. "He said that?"

"Actually *freak* was the word he used."

Silently, Carl cursed Kane out. "Yeah, I would've done the same thing," he admitted. "But still, you shouldn't be fighting. Be careful, okay? I don't need you ending up in the slammer."

Travis pulled away from him; his face turned from green to red. "Christ's sake, Dad! When are you going to get it through your head? I'm not Devin!" He spun around and headed back toward the door.

"Damn it!" Carl shouted. "Where are you going now?"

"Into town," Travis barked back.

As the door banged shut on its hinges, Carl swore as loud as he could. He was sick of being shut out and tired of hearing doors slamming. He threw his mug into the sink and the handle broke off.

The phone rang and he picked it up. It was that damned reporter again. "No. Travis isn't here," he hollered into the receiver, "and if you call again, I'm charging you with harassment!"

Travis pulled up to a tall town-house in Waikiki. As he turned off his ignition, a six-year-old girl came running down the steps. "Uncle Travis!" Allisa hurried over to the side of his truck, golden pigtails bouncing.

He opened the door and crouched down so she could give him a hug. The last time he had seen his niece was in the hospital, but he was so groggy from the pain medication he could barely stay awake. Now, as he felt her arms around his neck, some of the day's anger slipped away.

Allisa looked at his pinned up sleeve and touched it gently, feeling through to his stump. "Does that hurt?"

Travis smiled. "Not that much anymore."

A grin lit up her face and she gave him another hug. Her hair smelled like icing and cinnamon. Knowing he reeked of booze, Travis shrank away from her. His niece didn't seem to notice.

Lea rushed out of the house next. "Trav! It's so good to see you!" Her smile was as big as her daughter's. "Come in."

After setting a cup of coffee in front of him, Lea busied herself in the kitchen, where she was cooking up a batch of *malasadas.* The aroma of sweet pastry filled the air, and as she stood at the stove frying the pieces of dough, Allisa sat at the table with Travis, chattering. The rambunctious little girl had just started the first grade and had a bunch of stories to tell. Only after a lengthy show of school projects and report cards did she finally settle down in the living room with a puzzle, giving Lea and him a chance to talk.

"You don't look so good," Lea said, as Travis stirred some cream into his cup.

"I'm hungover," he confessed.

"I think there's more to it than that."

She waited and Travis frowned. "The Bonzai Classic

was yesterday. It's been exactly one year."

Lea nodded and brushed some sugar off her shorts. She set down a plate of goodies and joined Travis at the table. "Wanna tell me about it?"

"Not much to tell." He picked up a piece of pastry. The cinnamon sugar melted in his mouth, but not even the delicious dessert could take his mind off his woes. "Did you hear about Devin?"

Lea nodded. "Your dad called and told me everything. I think rehab is the best thing that could've come out of this. It'll be good for him."

"Not as good as it would've been six years ago."

Lea shook her head. "You got to stop feeling bad for your brother's actions."

With a tired sigh, Travis nodded. "I know, but every time I come here … I just don't understand it. Look what he's missing out on." He gestured toward his niece. Puzzle forgotten, Allisa had lined up her dolls on the couch and was singing pop songs to them. "She's grown up so much," he said. "But still such a cutie."

Lea glanced at her daughter and chuckled. "Yeah, sometimes." She sipped her drink. "There's no point in wishing for things to be different. You've been there for me, and so has your Dad, and now I have Duke. There's plenty of good that's come out of this."

Travis admired her optimism. He picked up a stuffed toy and played with its bow absentmindedly. "Wish I could think like that."

Lea shrugged. "Give it time."

~Nutz, Brah~

It was late afternoon by the time Travis left town. Allisa didn't want him to go, and it had taken a solid promise of taking her to the beach the next week to get her to stop hanging off his legs. Travis smiled as he thought about it. His niece was adorable.

Soon the drive was behind him and the North Shore was back in sight. As he sped up the highway and back into Hale'iwa, he could see whitecaps in the distance. He tried not to look at them.

The first place he stopped was the Surf Shop, where he found Brady sitting behind the counter, fiddling with his computer. "Hey, man." Brady looked agitated. "I been callin' you all day. Where you been?"

Travis leaned against the counter and patted his pocket. "I forgot my cell. I went to see Lea." He looked around. "Is Shayla in yet?"

"Nah, took the day off. Said she ain't feeling well."

The tone in Brady's voice told Travis all he needed to know. Shayla wasn't sick. She just didn't want to see him.

Brady flipped the laptop around. "Dude, you got bigger problems. Did'cha catch the news this morning?"

When Travis shook his head, Brady clicked the mouse and a video popped up. "You ain't gonna like this." It began to play.

First, there was a small clip of Travis wrestling Kane on the sand. Then, the dark-skinned surfer appeared on the screen, nose still bleeding a little. "Travis wen false crack me," Kane said to a news reporter. "Guess he cannot hand'o losing."

Giving the camera a compassionate look—that came across sickeningly genuine—Kane spouted out sympathy, saying he was sorry about the shark attack and that his *'braddah'* could no longer compete.

"Sorry, my ass!" Travis exclaimed. "And he ain't my brother!"

Brady shook his head. "Nutz, brah. He made you look brutal, but I didn't believe it. Not for a second."

Furious, Travis gripped the edge of the counter. He told Brady the real story. "It's bad enough he called me a freak, but now he's mocking me on the news too? Sayin' I'm jealous? What a douche! I wish I could tell 'em what really happened."

"So, why don't you?"

For a moment, Travis considered it. Then he let out a sigh. It was bad enough people stared at him every time he left the house. Why should he let them to do so from the comfort of their own homes?

He glared at the paused news video, wondering how many people had seen it. "I gotta go," he muttered.

When Shayla's mom opened the front door, Travis cleared his throat and ran a hand through his unwashed hair. Knowing he must reek of booze, he stepped back and nodded a greeting. "Howz'it? Is Shayla home?"

"She is, but she's not taking any visitors."

He let out a sigh. "Can you tell her to call me when she gets up?"

Standing with one hand on the doorknob, the woman gave him a sympathetic smile. Tiny wrinkles crinkled around large green eyes. *Shayla's eyes.* "I'll tell her," she said, "but between you and me, my daughter can be pretty stubborn."

Travis nodded. "Thanks."

Feet shuffling, he walked back to his truck and sat for a moment, letting the air-conditioning cool his forehead. Never had he felt so alone and humiliated. Bitter rage swelled inside him, and as he pictured Kane's busted up nose, a single thought ran through his mind.

Pipeline.

Teeth clenched, he pulled away from the curb and drove straight to Ehukai Beach Park. He ignored the stares of several people as he got out of his vehicle and kicked his door shut.

On top of the small hill overlooking the impressive waves, he leaned against an ironwood tree and stood, glaring out at the surfers. There it was. His old life, right in front of him, taunting him. The waves seemed to jeer, as if they knew what he had lost and were laughing because he didn't have the guts to enter the water.

Well, fuck that.

Travis rushed back to his truck, grabbed his surfboard, and stormed down to the water's edge. Shadows, sharks, the cursed ocean—none of it mattered. He wanted to surf Pipe again. Like he used to.

Disregarding everything around him, he waded into the water and jumped on top of his board, but as soon as he got out into the waves he realized he was in trouble. He had entered the ocean in the wrong spot. He hadn't stopped to time the sets and he wasn't anywhere near the channel.

A wave rolled in and knocked him backward. He came up sputtering and got slammed by another.

Moving faster than usual, the lateral current pushed him sideways over the sandbar, away from Pipeline and toward Rocky Point. Paddling harder, he tried to fight it but he couldn't seem to make any headway. Further and further away he drifted until the surfers looked nothing more than specks.

Travis knew had only two choices. Head back to shore, take the walk of shame, and start all over again, or move out to sea, behind the breakers, and paddle all the way back to Pipe.

There was no swallowing his pride. He chose the latter.

It was a long and arduous path back, and every moment of it made him angrier. Finally he made it into the lineup, out of breath and irritated.

A local veteran was the first to notice him. With a concerned look, he paddled over. "Eh, Kelly, should you be out here? Waves are pretty heavy."

Some of the others nodded in agreement.

Travis responded with silence. This was the crew he'd grown up with, guys he'd surfed with all his life. Quite often they took it upon themselves to keep the ocean safe, kicking inexperienced people out of the water and maintaining order within the group. Travis respected that, but Pipe was his home break, and he was not an amateur. He didn't budge.

"He ain't no barney," a former surf pal piped up. "Let 'im try."

Travis gave the guy a quick nod of thanks.

He took his place in the line-up, more determined than ever. No chickening out and no backing down. He would do this, heavy waves or not.

When the time came, he charged.

"Not this one!" someone hollered.

"Too big!" called somebody else.

Ignoring the warnings, Travis stroked as hard as he could. The wave peaked. He pushed up and tumbled over the falls, barely managing to take a breath before the lip beat down on him.

Swirling under the strong current, he struggled for control, but couldn't find any. He fought the surf, trying to locate the surface, but he didn't know which way was up, and the water was vicious. As the wave blasted him onto the reef, his face scraped the coral, and then his ribs. Rough edges tore through his rash guard. He tried not to panic; he tried to relax. The water tossed him again, forcing him to hold his breath even longer.

Finally he broke through and took a huge gulp of air. It cut into his lungs sharper than the reef. He heard a sharp call, and someone grabbed his shirt. Someone else pulled him onto a board. Weak and battered, he could barely hold on as a lifeguard and two old surfing buddies fought the ocean and hauled him back to the beach.

Once on shore, they dragged him onto the sand, and as he lay there gasping and sputtering, water rushed from his nose. Only after coughing up another mouthful was he able to gather a little strength. "I'm fine", he muttered, pushing his rescuers away. By then, a crowd had formed.

"You gotta get that stitched up." The lifeguard motioned to his forehead. "What were you thinkin' going out there?"

Travis put his hand up and it came away red. "Whatever," he said. "I'm all right."

Stumbling to his feet, he pushed his way through the people. Snapped by the surf, his leash dangled from his leg, so he reached down and tossed it away. He didn't even look for his board.

As he neared his truck, he heard someone call out, "Brah, I don't think you should drive." He didn't listen. He peeled out of the lot and tore down the highway.

He had failed. He could no longer surf Pipe.

Trembling, he started to hyperventilate, and suddenly, he felt as if he was going to be sick. He pulled his truck to the side of the road and tossed his guts onto the pavement. Then he sat, holding a dirty paper-towel to his wound, debating what to do next.

~Binge~

On the television, a spear-fisherman held up a giant yellowfin tuna. Carl rubbed his eyes and switched channels searching for something that could hold his interest. He looked up when he heard the front door open. Travis came inside, face caked in blood, with a six-pack of beer tucked under his stump and a large bottle of rye in his hand. He passed through the room and headed up the stairs.

"What happened?" Carl rushed after him. The bedroom door shut in his face. "Did something happen with Kane?"

Full of anxiety, he paced the hallway. He had seen the morning news and heard what Kane had said. Had Travis gotten into another fight?

Nah. He shook his head. It looked like the reef had delivered those blows.

Several times that evening, Carl pounded on Travis's

door, but there was never any answer. He knew his son was drinking, and one time, he thought he heard Kane's interview playing inside the room. His head throbbed with the start of a terrible headache.

After knocking one last time, he squeezed the pain from his eyes and went to his own room. Perhaps Travis would talk in the morning.

Morning came and went. In the afternoon, Travis stumbled from his room, smelling like stale whiskey. He snatched his keys from the kitchen counter and staggered toward the door.

Carl stepped in front of him. "Where do you think you're going?"

"To the store."

"Not like that, you're not. You can't keep driving around when you're drunk, Trav. You're going to get someone killed!"

Travis threw his keys down and swerved around him. "Fine, I'll walk."

Forty minutes later he returned with more alcohol.

"Travis, you've got to stop this," Carl barked.

But once again, his son pushed past him, rushed up the stairs, and locked the bedroom door. Carl sat at the kitchen table and put his head in his hands. He had never seen Travis act like this. Upstairs, a lamp crashed onto the floor, and Kane's interview started again.

For two days, Travis sat in his room, drinking and wallowing in misery. Over and over again, he watched Kane's interview. He turned his phone off. He didn't go to work. It was best just to stay home. That way nothing else could go wrong.

On the third day, he woke with a massive headache. Flinching from the pain, he pulled the last of his six-pack from under the bed and took a swig of beer. The foamy liquid was warm and made his temples pound even harder. He yearned for something stronger.

At the foot of the bed, Jasper raised his head and whimpered. Travis stroked the dog's thick fur and winced from the effort. Even the smallest amount of movement hurt; his body still ached from his wipeout. His skin was battered and bruised, and every time he moved, the gash above his eye reopened.

Let it bleed, he thought. What did it matter? He had messed things up with Shayla, his attempt at surfing Pipe had ended in disaster, and Kane had ruined his reputation. His old life was over, and it seemed as if his new life kept getting worse.

As he slid onto his stomach, Travis glared at the computer. He had pressed pause the night before, and Kane's face was frozen on the screen, blood caked around his nose. Travis smirked.

He heard footsteps on the stairs.

"Trav, you awake? It's time to stop this."

When the doorknob jiggled, Travis rolled over and stared at the ceiling, waiting for his old man to give up. There was a loud shattering noise, and then another, as his father threw his body up against the door and busted it open. Jasper sat up and barked.

Carl planted his hands on his hips and gave Travis a disapproving look.

Refusing to acknowledge the fact that his door now hung on one hinge, Travis took a long swig of his drink and pointed at the image of Kane on his laptop. "You see this crap?"

"I sure did." Carl picked up the remaining beer.

"What the hell are you doing?" Travis snapped.

"I'm saving you."

"I'm fine."

"Yeah? You don't look fine to me. You think locking yourself in your room watching this video over and over again is fine? Drinking yourself into a stupor? This isn't you, Trav. I've noticed the bottles missing from the cabinet. I'm not blind, you know."

Travis reached out his hand. "I don't want beef. Just give them back."

His father didn't budge. Eyes still flashing with anger, he lightened his tone. "I don't know what happened the other day, but I'm pretty sure getting plastered isn't the answer. Look at yourself. It's not even noon and you're at it already. Using alcohol to cover the pain. You're acting just like your brother."

Travis stood up. "I'm not Devin!" he shouted. But suddenly he wasn't so sure. Here he was, ready to fight his old man over a six-pack. He unclenched his fist. "I'm not like him," he murmured.

"Then find a new way to cope."

As his father stormed out of the room, Travis hung his head. His dad was right. He was using alcohol for comfort, and it wasn't even working. A half empty beer sat next to his bed. He kicked it over and foam poured onto the floor. "I may as well be a deadbeat drug addict."

He sat on the edge of his bed and stared at Kane's arrogant face. The surfer's deep brown eyes seemed to mock him. *Well, screw him!* Travis picked up his cell phone and dialed a number. Adrenaline raced through him as he waited for an answer on the other end.

Four days had passed and Shayla still hadn't heard from Travis. "This sucks," she whined to her mother as she picked at her breakfast. "He didn't come into work yesterday, and he won't return any of my calls." She stirred her omelet with her fork. "It must've been hard for him to sit through that contest, and even harder to see Kane win. Then I totally shut him out. He said he loved me and I sent him away."

Her mom gave her a sad smile. "He'll come around. Why don't you go talk to him?"

Shayla pushed her uneaten food away. "I think I will."

Before she could rethink the decision, she left the house and hurried through the gully between the two homes. Gathering her courage, she knocked gently on the back door of Travis's house. Carl answered, looking a bit too pale with dark bags under his eyes.

"Hi," she said warily. "Is Travis home?"

"Yeah, but I don't know if he'll come downstairs."

Fear leapt into her throat. "Why? What happened?"

Carl shrugged. "No idea. He won't talk. He came in the house the other day, torn up and bleeding, but he won't tell me why. I think it has something to do with Kane, but I'm not sure."

Shayla had seen the news and heard the nasty things Kane said. Holding her breath, she listened while Carl told her about Travis's multi-day binge. "I had to bust down his door to take away the booze, and now I'm not sure if I should go back upstairs."

"He's *still* drinking?" A crushing ache formed in her chest. Shifting from foot to foot, she glanced up the stairs. She knew she should go to him, but at the same time, how could she accept that kind of behavior? "What should I do?"

"I don't know." Carl shrugged. "But I have to leave soon to go visit Devin. Today's the first day he's allowed visitors. Maybe Travis will talk to you. Will you try?"

Shayla nodded and headed upstairs. A few seconds later, she rushed back down. "Travis is gone."

~A Clear Mind~

Outside the rehab center, rows of anthurium and ginger flowers framed the beginning of red shale pathways that wound through acres of tropical jungle. A rainbow glittered in the mist above the koi pond, and sunlight filtered through the open patio doors. Most of the residents lounged on lawn chairs enjoying the breeze and talking amongst each other. But not Devin. He stayed inside, choosing to sit by himself in a large overstuffed chair in the main common area.

Head down, he traced the pattern on the seat cushion with his finger. Sick of therapy sessions and tired of being around so many people, he wished he could crawl into a hole and disappear for the next three months.

Being sober was a totally new trip for him. With a clear mind, he had started to comprehend all the terrible things he had done. Anger, guilt, and regret hovered around him constantly. If he could just get his hands on some coke, he knew he could forget the awful feelings, but despite his cravings, he knew that drugs were no longer the answer.

There were no answers.

He looked at his reflection in the window. A monster stared back at him—a monster of lies, deceit and broken promises. A low-life junkie who had gotten baked out of his mind every day for nine years just so he wouldn't have to cope with his own issues.

Someone entered the room. Devin glanced into the eyes of his father. Surprised, he tried to smile, but all that came out was a grimace.

His dad sat down on the chair beside him. "How you holding up?"

"Could be better." Devin exhaled.

A week had passed since he'd started treatment, but already it felt like a year. Every day was the same: getting up early, going to lectures, talking to counselors and attending drug education classes. All meals were strictly scheduled and beds had to be made in the morning. Everyone had chores assigned to them and punctuality was mandatory.

Life sucked.

His hands shook as nausea rose in his throat. He rubbed his eyes and straightened out in his chair.

"Are they treating you well?" his father asked.

"Yeah."

"You look a little better. You've been eating?"

Devin nodded. "At first it was tough, but now I'm hungry all the time."

"Well that's good. How are the cravings?"

"I dunno. I just wanna go home."

Carl's chest grew heavy. He couldn't stand to see Devin so wrapped in anguish. Especially when he felt partially to blame. If only he'd done more as a father, perhaps his son's life would have turned out differently.

He thought about Devin at five years old, scared to go to bed at night until his father chased away the monsters in the closet. Back then, Carl was a source of security, a hero, a dad. It had been a long time since his son had looked to him for help.

Swallowing his guilt, he tried an encouraging smile. "Your doctor said it's normal to feel overwhelmed. You've got to come to terms with things. Early recovery is bumpy, but it'll get better. This is the best place for you right now."

"I know," Devin mumbled.

Carl patted him on the back. "Just because it's hard

doesn't mean you can't do it. Stay strong. Deep down your heart is in it—even if your head sometimes isn't."

Devin nodded, but he didn't look convinced.

Moving into the center of the gardens, they met up with Dr. Harold for a family therapy session. "Welcome," the doctor said, shaking Carl's hand. "Courtyard and paths are open to visitors, so I thought it'd be nice to have our chat outside today." He pushed his glasses higher onto his nose and led the way down a winding red shale path. He encouraged Carl and Devin to talk freely while he listened without judgment.

Carl didn't quite know where to start, so he told Devin all about Kane's interview and Travis's drinking. "I'm sorry he couldn't come today. He was gone when I left. Breaking down the door seemed like my only option, but maybe I shouldn't have done it. I don't want to end up pushing him away, like I did with you."

Devin stared at the ground. He didn't comment on Carl's confession, but he kicked a rock on the path and his face screwed into a scowl. "Wish I could'a been there when Kane called him out. I would'a liked to see Trav pound that guy."

Carl paused. It was nice to see Devin so concerned about his brother—or anyone other than himself for a change. Standing in the shade of a large tree fern, he waited, hoping Devin would say more.

Devin opened his mouth for a second and shut it again.

Dr. Harold gestured toward Carl. "Tell your dad what you're thinking. It's important to be honest, to get things off your chest."

Devin heaved a sigh. "It's Trav. All this time, I should'a been there for him. I should'a helped him through stuff." His face looked pale as he shook his head. "I'm an asshole brother… and an asshole son."

Carl stepped back. This was a side of Devin he hadn't glimpsed in ten years. He put his hand on Devin's shoulder. "You had your horrible moments, but we knew it wasn't you."

"No." Devin shook his head. "I got myself into this mess. I'm the one who couldn't handle shit, who wanted to party all the time. After Trav's accident, I couldn't face him, and now he hates me." He looked over at the doctor, his eyes turning dark. "I'm done with this," he said, and hurried away.

Carl turned to the doctor. "Can I go speak with him alone?"

Dr Harold nodded, and Carl headed down the path Devin had taken. He found his son sitting on a bench by a koi pond, trailing a stick in the water.

Carl sat down beside him. "I want to apologize," he said. "I was an asshole too. I never should've kicked you out of the house when you were younger. I didn't know how to help, but as your father, I should've done more."

Devin turned to him. "Nah, man, I wanted you t' kick me out."

"Why?"

It took a moment, but then Devin spoke quietly, "When Mom died I stopped caring about shit, an' I didn't want you to care either."

"Why?"

Devin looked at the ground. "'Cause then it wouldn't matter what happened to me."

There was a long pause, as a lump formed in Carl's throat. The substance-induced mask was off. Finally, he could see his son. He reached out his arms. "I'm always going to care."

Devin clung to him. "I screwed up."

"It's okay." He held his son tight. "I'm just glad you're back."

Devin walked his father to the lobby and gave him a hug goodbye. He no longer looked into the eyes of the enemy. Now he saw a friend. He stood taller, feeling stronger and more assured. "When you find Travis, tell him to come see me, yeah?"

Carl nodded. "Sure, but I don't know if he'll listen."

As his dad headed back to the parking lot, Devin sat once again by the window in the common room. He watched his father drive away. If only Travis was with him too, he thought, as he stared down at the road. But there was no chance of mending that relationship. There had been too many times when his brother had needed him, and he had been too stoned and stupid to realize it.

A craving hit, but Devin pushed it out of his mind. He breathed deeply, forcing himself to actually feel what he was feeling. "It should'a been me," he whispered, the words cutting into his soul. "I should'a lost my arm to that shark."

He leaned against the window sill and laid his head across his arms. Exhausted, he stayed that way, half sleeping, until he felt a tap on his shoulder.

Blinking, he bolted upright. Lea stood in front of him.

He felt his cheeks flush; he knew he looked like crap.

"You look awful," she confirmed.

"Thanks." He gave her a weak smile.

"You okay?"

"Sure" he replied. "Why you here?"

Lea backed away a little. "I knew you could have visitors today. Maybe I should go."

He stood up. "No, stay. I was jus' askin'."

She paused and shifted from foot to foot. "I wasn't sure I should come, but ever since I saw your brother, I've been thinking about you ... or wondering about you, I mean."

She seemed nervous and frightened. Devin could barely stand it. Here was a woman who had loved him more than anything, and vice versa. She was the love of his life, yet he had treated her like crap.

Without warning came a memory of their one year anniversary. Lea had just found out she was pregnant, Devin was no longer working, and they'd just been evicted from their one bedroom apartment in downtown Honolulu. He remembered the tears in her eyes as she begged him to stop taking drugs.

"How are we going to raise a child when you're high all the time and spending all our money on blow?"

She had sobbed and pleaded, but Devin's only concern was how he was going to keep getting high if he had to spend all his money on some kid? He had walked out on her then. With an unclear mind, the decision was easy.

He stared down at the carpet and felt the full agony of it. How could he have been so stupid?

As if sensing his distress, Lea knelt beside him. She pulled him close, and he buried his face in her hair. "I'm sorry, Lea." It felt strange to be in her arms again—and stranger still to hear himself apologizing—yet relief surged through him as he said the words.

Slowly, he pulled away. A tear slid down her face, and he could see the love she still felt for him. Gently, he touched her cheek. She inhaled slightly and shivered.

Then, she pulled away and showed him the diamond on her finger. "I'm with Duke now."

With all the willpower he possessed, Devin pulled away and nodded. "I really am sorry," he whispered.

"Me too," she replied. She got up to leave, but before she could, Devin gathered his nerve and asked the one question he had never cared enough to ask, until now. "When I get outta this place, could I come an' see Allisa?"

Lea's face lit up and her eyes glistened with a fresh batch of tears. She threw herself back into his arms. "As soon as you're better," she answered.

Devin held her tightly, knowing it was the last time he ever would.

~Sentiment~

As he sat on the front porch swing, Carl puffed a cigar, the strong-smelling smoke wafting around him as the rings that he blew faded into the darkness. A pair of headlights shone in the distance, and he stood up. The vehicle passed, and he sat back down.

His mind twisted with a mix of emotions. He couldn't remember a time when there was such a large gap in his relationship with Travis, yet his bond with Devin was stronger than ever. In the span of only a few hours, he had reunited with one son and driven the other away.

Closing his eyes, he took another drag, drawing the smoke into his mouth and holding it there for a moment, savoring the flavor before pushing it back out with his tongue.

Finally the familiar sound of a muffler filled the air, and Carl breathed a bit easier as his son's truck pulled into the driveway. He readied himself for another fight, but Travis smiled as he walked up to the house. And he looked sober.

Carl held out his hand, offering Travis his cigar as he came up the steps. Travis took a drag, coughed out a large puff of smoke, and handed it back. "*Bleck.*" He made a face and waved the cloud away.

Carl laughed. "You're not supposed to inhale."

Travis sat on a chair opposite him. "I think that's the first time you've ever offered me some of your cigar."

Carl smiled. "Well, I guess I'm celebrating a little. I had a good visit with your brother today."

Finally able to loosen up and unwind, Carl told his youngest son all about the conversation he'd had with Devin. "I think there may be some hope for him yet."

"Unreal," Travis replied; yet he looked skeptical.

"You should come to the next family session," Carl said. "He asked for you."

Travis shrugged and the quiet of the evening surrounded them. Carl blew another ring of smoke and watched it slowly dissipate. He frowned. "I'm sorry for what happened earlier, taking your beer and all, but I hope you know I was only trying to help."

"I know Dad, and you were right. What I was doing was wrong."

Carl stopped rocking. For once, he done the right thing? Giving Jasper a pat on the head, he smiled.

Travis smiled back. "You know that douche-bag anchorman? I finally gave him that interview."

Travis couldn't help but laugh at the astonished look on his father's face. After all, it was pretty amazing. He had spent the entire day shooting an extensive interview for the local news. Dave Mutch had wanted live and still shots of everything from the exact spot where he'd been attacked, to the strap that he'd rigged on his board for duck diving. He'd wanted footage of Travis surfing before and after his attack, along with pictures of his arm during and after recovery.

Travis's blood curdled while the photographer took pictures of his unwrapped arm, but once the whole thing was over, he was glad he'd gone through with it. He was ready to be seen and ready to be heard. He had sulked in the shadows for too long.

After hearing the story, his father got up and stood beside him. "That's great, son. I can't wait to see it."

Pride shone in the older man's eyes. Travis glowed. With no hesitation, he embraced his father.

"Wow," Carl smiled, "Hugs from both of my kids in one day."

Travis chuckled. "Should I get you a t-shirt that says *World's Greatest Dad*?" His cheeks grew warm; he wasn't used to showing so much sentiment.

Laughing, his father slapped him on the back. Then he

turned serious. "That shark attack scared the shit out of me, Trav. I lost my wife and my oldest son. I couldn't stand the thought of losing you too."

Surprised by the confession, Travis swallowed hard. He hadn't thought about what the incident had done to his family and friends. He'd only ever thought about himself. Drowning in his own misfortune, he'd been blind to the hands stretched out to him. Hell, even the damned reporter had only wanted to help.

As he squared his shoulders, determination buzzed through his veins. It wasn't too late to change. He could overcome his weaknesses and turn his life around. Shayla was right. He could still be great.

Again, Carl held out his cigar, and this time, when Travis took it, he didn't find it quite so disgusting.

~Stupid Bet~

Hands on her hips, Mika stood in front of the opened refrigerator. "Where'd all my coconut pie go? It was in here last night!"

Eyes flicking with irritation, Ayumi charged into the kitchen. "Mark and I ate it. So what?"

Mika winced. *Oops.* It was the first she had spoken to her twin in over a week. Clamping her mouth shut, she turned around and headed back to her room, but her sister followed. "You're gonna have to tell me sooner or later, you know."

Stopping beside her bed, Mika pushed her hair back from her face and let out a sigh. She was sick of giving everyone the silent treatment for her own stupid mistake. "It was some random guy at a party, a one-night stand I never should have had." She bit her lip. At least the last part was true.

Arms wrapped around her knees, she held her breath and hoped her sister would believe her. But Ayumi had one more question. "What party was that?"

As soon as the words came out, Mika knew she'd messed up. There was no way she could answer that. Apart from their birthday bash, there was only one other party she and her sister had gone to in the last few months and none she had attended by herself.

She stood up and grabbed a towel from her door. "I have to take a shower."

Before Ayumi could respond, she ducked down the hall and into the bathroom, and as she locked the door behind her, a fresh batch of tears fell down her cheeks. She turned the water on, but instead of getting into the tub, she slumped against the wall, waiting for the inevitable.

Not two seconds passed before her sister pounded on the door. "Kane's party? Open the door, Mika!"

Mika took a breath and tried to control her shaking as she let her twin into the room.

"This is because of that stupid bet, isn't it?" Ayumi demanded.

Mika could feel the shame creeping onto her face.

"Oh, Mika. You didn't. Not with *him*!"

"I'm sorry."

"You told me you guys didn't do anything."

"I lied." Mika hung her head. "I'm sorry. I didn't want anyone to know. Not even you."

Her sister's eyes grew wet with tears. "You could've told me, Mikki."

Mika's lip quivered. "I don't know what I'm gonna do. I've made so many mistakes. Everyone's pissed at me."

Ayumi held out her arms. "It'll be okay. We'll figure things out. We always do."

~Lessons~

The newscast had already started.

Travis stood on the beach at Pipeline, talking about the shark attack. He described what had happened to him and his recovery afterwards. Then, after a short segment on his life previous to the accident, along with his pro tour ratings, they re-ran the clip of him surfing with one arm at Rocky Point and talked about how he had started again.

Dave held a microphone. "Do you find surfing more difficult now?"

"Paddling is pretty hard, and I get drilled when I wipe out, but other than that it's about the same." Travis touched the gash above his eye.

The reporter eyed him curiously.

"A year ago you came in second place in the world tour ratings, and you could have won first. Do you think you will ever compete again?"

"Nah. I just surf because I love it."

"And what about Kane Walker?"

"What about him? He and I both know who would've won the title if I hadn't lost my arm." Travis held up his stump for the world to see.

"Was that what you were fighting about the other day?"

"Nah," Travis replied. "Kane likes to run his mouth. Called me a one-armed freak, yeah, and I didn't like it much."

Taken aback, the reporter nodded.

The scene switched, and Travis sat on a plush blue chair in a small studio. No longer shirtless, he seemed much more relaxed.

"So, what are your plans now?" Dave asked him.

"Don't know. I got a few things to sort out. Not sure what I'm gonna do. Take one day at a time I guess."

"How do you feel about people wanting to hear your story?"

Travis shrugged. "It's a bit strange. It's nice they care and all … but I don't want a lot of attention, ya know?"

"Well you might get some now." The anchorman laughed and leaned forward. "What about your family and friends? Who has been your main support through all this?"

Eyes glued to the television, Shayla sat in bed watching Travis's interview. With nervous fingers, she fiddled with the bow on her pajama pants. "That's where he went yesterday," she whispered.

Her mother sat on the edge of the bed. "See, I told you not to jump to conclusions."

When the segment ended, the anchorman stood up and wished Travis the best of luck. As they shook hands, Shayla tried not to focus on how wonderful Travis looked or the way his mouth tilted to the side when he talked. His last statement rang in her ears. *She means a lot to me.*

Her mom gave her an encouraging smile. "Sounds like he still cares about you."

Shayla shook her head. It didn't matter. She had already made up her mind. "I can't see him anymore." She frowned.

"Because of your father?"

Shayla nodded. "I promised myself I'd never end up with someone like that. Someone who drinks.'"

"Oh, Shay." Her mom wrapped an arm around her shoulders. "Your dad was an alcoholic for years. I should have left him sooner, before it got as bad as it did. But you don't know Travis has a drinking problem. Maybe he's just going through a hard time."

Shayla didn't say anything. Instead, she stared out the window toward the rocky cliff. A year had passed since the night her father had come home, trashed from a party, screaming about nonsense. Shayla had run into the kitchen just in time to see him strike her mother across the face. Eyes raging and reeking of booze, he pushed her mom up against the stove and would have done more, but he stumbled over a floor mat and landed flat on his face.

Grabbing hands, Shayla and her mom fled the house together, and afterwards they took out a restraining order. They hadn't seen him since.

Clutching her blanket to her chin, Shayla tried to force the memories away, but they lingered and filled her with doubt.

The doorbell rang. It was Travis.

Taking a deep breath, she answered the door.

He looked sad as he stepped over the threshold. "Shay, I know you're mad about what happened at the Bonzai Classic, but please listen. Last year at Pipe, I was winning that competition. It was unreal. When I was little, I never would've thought I'd be one of the pros shredding the waves and winning. I almost made it to the top. I'll never have that back, and it sucked to watch Kane take it. I was stressed, and I had way too much to drink. I didn't mean to take it out on you."

"You never mean to," she whispered.

He inhaled sharply and ran his hand through his hair. Obviously at a loss for words, he cleared his throat and looked away.

She had to tell him. "My dad was a drunk."

In a small voice, Shayla told Travis all about her father's lies, the cheating, and the abuse. "I want to be there for you, Trav, but I just don't think I can be with someone who drinks, someone who gets angry."

Travis took her hand. "I didn't know about your dad," he said. "But I'm not like that, and I would *never* hit a woman. I don't need to drink. For real. I don't want it anymore. I love you, Shay, and this time, I'm not drunk when I say it."

Shayla's heart unleashed and she melted into his arms. "I love you too."

It was a day for apologies. An hour after he and Shayla made up, Travis sat in the office at Brady's Surf Shop.

Once again, remorse filled him. "Sorry I left you hanging, bro. If you want I can stay on for a bit, but I've been thinking, and working here just isn't my thing."

"You sure?" Brady asked with a frown. "You sold mo' boards this month than anyone I ever hired."

Travis shook his head. "I'm sure."

Brady gave a disappointed shrug. "No worries, bro. I get it. You gotta find your own way."

With an appreciative nod, Travis left the office and joined Shayla at the cash register.

"What'd Brady say?" she asked. "Is he mad?"

"He understood." Travis smiled. He was glad he had come. Already a huge weight had lifted from his shoulders.

He gave Shayla a kiss. "Want me to pick you up after work?"

"Of course." She nodded.

Someone tapped him on the back, and a young voice stated, "I saw you on da news. You owe me some lessons, brah."

Lessons? Travis turned. It was the same young grom that had accosted him the day Kimo returned—the local boy whose cousin was also a one-armed surfer. Travis remembered telling him if he ever got back in the water he'd give him some pointers. Speechless, and slightly amused, he shook his head. The kid had some nerve.

He looked at Shayla.

She spread her hands and smiled. "A promise is a promise."

He looked the grom up and down. "Kay den. I got nothing to do. My board's in my truck. You got one too?"

The kid pointed to a small surfboard leaning up against the front wall, and Travis felt a hint of excitement. "What's your name anyway?" he asked, as they walked out of the shop.

"Makani," the boy returned.

"Let's go see what you got."

~Haole~

Standing waist deep in the ocean, Travis shouted with pride as Makani tore up the wave and smacked the lip. For the last three hours, they had practiced everything from cutbacks to airs. On clean, shoulder-high sets, the boy showed great promise. He caught plenty of good waves and learned a bunch of new tricks.

"Guess I can't call you grom no more," Travis said as they rode the foam in. "You were killin' it out there."

A huge grin lit up Makani's face. As they rinsed their boards under the showers, he rattled on about how stoked he was to be catching waves with his favorite surfer. "*Mahalo*," he kept saying over and over again.

Travis laughed. It was nice to have someone look up to him. In fact, aside from his ethnicity, Makani kind of looked like him. He had the same shaggy, blond hair and similar red shorts. Travis would have bet money the kid was trying to copy him. But he didn't mind. It reminded him of the way he used to idolize his brother.

Weaving through the parking lot, they made their way back to Travis's truck. The sharp sound of squealing tires split the air. A red sports car flew toward them. Travis tossed his surfboard and yanked Makani aside just in time. The car stopped inches from his body, dust flying in all directions.

Travis made sure Makani was okay. Then he turned to the driver, trying to see who it was through the tinted windows. "Watch where you're going, kook!" He stormed around the side of the car.

The door opened and Kane got out.

"Oh, big surprise," Travis snapped.

Kane's fists folded as he stepped forward. "I heard you was talking shit about me on da news. You think das funny?"

"Hey, man, it's a two-way street. At least what I said was the truth."

As they stared each other down, a bunch of locals stopped to watch. Travis saw them and backed away. Kane was trying to get him to throw the first punch—to make him look like the bad guy again—but he wouldn't do it. Not in front of witnesses, and not in front of Makani.

Kane's passenger door opened, and a red-haired girl got out of the car. It was Hayley, and as she stepped up to Kane's side, Travis snickered. "Snagged another pro surfer, hah?"

She touched Kane's arm. "This ain't worth it."

Kane shrugged her off, but it was obvious he recognized defeat. "Nuff already. We go."

Travis retrieved his board from the ground and chuckled again. "Yeah, get lost. Wouldn't want to ruin your rep by beating up a cripple ... or gettin' beat by one."

Kane looked ready to explode. "I no care what you say. You neva' can surf as good as me."

Travis scoffed. "Oh, yeah? You'd be scared shitless if I entered the next contest."

A smidgen of fear crossed Kane's face, but it faded quickly. He placed an arm around Hayley's shoulders and laughed. "Yeah, brah? I heard w'at happened to you at Pipe da other day. Das how come your face bust' up. You might be surfing Rockies, haole, bu' no can handle Pipe."

Kane and Hayley got back into the car. The engine roared and the tires spun a massive show of smoke as they burned out of the parking lot. Overly aware of the blood thumping through his veins, Travis glared after them. The small crowd broke up, and he and Makani continued to his truck. Now the mood was somber.

Makani slid into the passenger seat and glanced over

at him. "You way mo' bettah than Kane."

Travis started the vehicle, and as he pulled away, he tried to push the whole thing from his mind. Unfortunately, Kane's words had burned into his brain. Nothing could erase them.

Following the boy's directions, he rounded the turns and cruised over the small bridge passing Waimea Bay. He pulled up to a small house, surrounded by a forest of palm trees, and waited while Makani pulled his surfboard from the back of the truck. After promising they'd go surfing again soon, he sped away.

An hour later, he pulled into the parking lot of the drug rehab center in Honolulu, but he didn't go in. Instead, he sat there, staring at the door. His stomach turned. Why had he driven there to begin with?

Letting out a frustrated breath, he spun his truck around, and by the time he got back to Brady's Surf Shop, Shayla was off work and sitting out front waiting for him. "You took forever," she said as she got into the truck. "I was almost ready to go home."

"Sorry," Travis mumbled. Then he turned to her. "You wanna go away for the weekend? I can ask my dad if we can borrow the boat."

"Sure," she answered. "That sounds awesome."

~Refreshed~

Carl stood on the back deck, sipping tea and staring at the horizon. Except for the occasional car and the odd chatter of geckos and frogs, the evening was extraordinarily quiet. The sun had started to plunge toward the sea; the sky showed the orange hues of its descent.

He took a deep breath, inhaling the aroma of his warm drink. Things were looking up. He'd had a positive therapy session with Devin over the phone, and Travis had taken Shayla away on the boat for the weekend.

Stretching his arms above his head, he smiled. He still couldn't believe the changes he had witnessed in his boys.

"Hello?" someone called out from the front door.

Carl hadn't even heard a knock.

"Yeah?" He hurried through the house. "Sorry, I was out back."

A Polynesian woman about Carl's age stood at the

front entrance. Long black hair framed charcoal eyes as she peered around the door. She hesitated. "I looking for Travis Kelly. I Makani's mother, Iva." She extended her arm. "Travis took my son for surf lesson today, and Makani won't stop talking my ear off ever since. I jus' want meet him."

Surprised, Carl stepped forward and shook her hand. "Really? He didn't tell me about that."

Captured by the gentle expression in the woman's dark brown eyes, he held her gaze for a moment, as well as her slender fingers.

Her face flushed as she removed her hand from his. "I'm sorry fo' bother you," she said. "I jus' protective of my son. If he goin' surf wit Travis, I jus' want meet him."

Amused by her repetition, Carl smiled. "Then I'll make sure you do," he replied. "Travis is away for a few days, but would you like to come in? There's tea brewing, and I could tell you all about him."

Iva hesitated. Then, she nodded. "Yes. I like that."

The small yacht cruised through open water, bumping gently along with the darkened waves. Stars covered the sky, peeking though a blanket of black, and behind them, Shayla could just make out the shoreline growing smaller as they moved further out to sea. She stood beside Travis as he steered the boat. She slipped her arms around his waist and ran her fingers lightly over his chest. "Are you gonna tell me why we're running away?"

He gave her a half-hearted smile. "It was either this or get drunk again, and I wasn't about to do that."

She frowned. "No jokes. Something happened didn't it?"

Pulling away from her, he released the anchor and ensured it was set. Then he stood at the side railing, staring out at the ocean. In the distance, the lights of another boat crossed the horizon. Shayla waited, watching it with him, until the lights faded and he started talking.

Voice tensed, he told her about his day in the surf with Makani, his confrontation with Kane, and his trip to the rehab center.

"Why didn't you go in?" she asked. Then she paused. Devin was a touchy subject.

"It wasn't visiting hours." His voice was barely audible.

Shayla hugged Travis tightly and laid her head against his back. She stayed that way until she felt him relax. Eventually, his breathing slowed, and he loosened up again. She closed her eyes. His skin was soft and warm, and it made her happy that he was comfortable enough around her to go without a shirt.

With a loving caress, she traced the design of the tattoo inked across his shoulder blades. A strand of hair clung to his cheek, shining golden in the moonlight. And his lips ... she couldn't stop looking at them.

Rising on her tiptoes, she kissed the nape of his neck and whispered something that made him tremble. Without a word, he whirled around and pulled her to him, kissing her passionately as she pressed her body to his. He smiled—the cute half-tilted smile she loved so much—and pulled her down the stairs to the cabin below deck. She climbed onto the bed, and he slipped in beside her.

Travis awoke the next morning feeling alive and refreshed. A ray of sunshine shone through the porthole casting warmth onto his pillow. The boat rocked gently and Shayla snuggled close to him. With dreamy eyes, she gave a content little sigh and ran her fingers across his shoulder and down his arm. He froze when she touched his stump, and he shivered, but he didn't stop her. She loved him, and he trusted her.

"I have something for you," she said, sitting up quickly. She hurried to her suitcase, pulled out a framed picture, and brought it back to him. It was a painting of the cliff outside his house. And there he stood on top of it, holding his bright blue surfboard.

He took it and held it carefully. "This is from that day on the cliff. You said you were painting me."

Shayla got back into bed and nodded. "Sometimes you're sad when you go up there, so I hope it doesn't bring any bad feelings."

Travis shook his head. "Nah. It's beautiful. I love it."

He gave her a kiss and she snuggled up next to him again. Eyes closed, he savored the feeling of her body next to his. Wrapped in her arms, he felt stronger somehow. All his worries faded away, and in that moment, he was happy.

~A Clean Life~

Makani held his trophy high in the air, and Travis cheered loudly. For the last three months he had been coaching the boy, training him for this very day. Winning the Menehune surf competition was a huge accomplishment. It was his first real victory.

As the boy jumped off the podium and into his mother's arms, Travis smiled proudly.

Makani rushed over to him and leapt into the air. "Yessah! We did it!"

Travis ruffled the kid's hair. "Nah, little man. You did this one all on your own. You practiced hard. Five days a week. You deserve this win."

Makani beamed.

Iva stepped forward and handed Travis a check. "You do more than you think."

He looked down at the amount of money and gasped. He shook his head and thrust it back. "I can't take this."

"Yes ... you take." Iva pushed his hand away; her tone was serious. "I no see my son so happy since his papa die. The hours you spend teaching, I should give you more than that."

At the mention of the boy's father, Travis grew quiet. One evening, while surfing, Makani had told him about the man. Like Travis's mother, Makani's father had died of cancer a few years earlier. It was just another thing they had in common.

"I did it because I wanted to," he said.

"I know you do. Now you take."

"Please, Trav," Makani insisted. "Was my idea too."

Travis didn't want to accept such a gift, but he knew Iva wasn't about to take no for an answer. Reluctantly, he took the check and put it in his pocket.

Satisfied, Iva smiled. "We have barbeque later, to celebrate. You like come?"

"Yeah, yeah, *please*?" Makani begged.

"Of course," Travis replied. "I wouldn't miss it."

"Bring Shayla too, and your Dad," Iva added.

The side of Travis's mouth turned into a grin. The relationship Iva had struck up with his father was starting to get serious. Or at least he hoped so. Iva was an awesome match for his dad, and it would be nice to have a family again.

Iva gave him a tender look. "Devin get out of rehab tomorrow?"

Travis nodded. "Yeah."

"You excited to see him?"

He shrugged.

She smiled encouragingly. "Maybe you go surfing, huh?"

The idea took him aback. He opened his mouth, but he didn't know what to say.

Iva patted him on the shoulder, called out to Makani, and started up the beach with their things.

"You come?" Makani asked.

"In a bit," Travis replied. "I'm gonna catch some waves."

Out in the ocean, clean lines were coming in with some juice still left in the sets. Travis strapped his leash onto his leg and headed out into the surf. As he paddled, he noticed two teenage boys sharing a wave and laughing, and for the first time in months, he allowed himself to think about his brother. His father had told him about Devin's progress, but so far he'd refused to believe it.

He couldn't help but wonder. Was it real?

Travis caught the next wave and rode it straight to shore. Curious to find out the truth, he rushed across the sand and headed for his truck. He needed to see it for himself. Had his brother really changed?

After his final group therapy class, Devin wandered down the hall. Today was his last day at the clinic, and it was strange, but he was actually going to miss the place. Over the last three months, it had become a haven for him. Was he ready to leave?

He felt better, that much he knew, but sometimes he wondered if he could have gotten clean without rehab. *Probably not*, he decided. Here, he'd had to deal with his emotions without drugs. He'd had help. Tomorrow he was going home.

"It'll be hard," Dr. Harold had told him. "You need to start new, not have anything to do with your old life."

But how easy would that be? Once he got out, would he be able to start all over? What if Vince called, or Jonny? Would he be strong enough to ignore his old friends?

As Devin dragged his feet down the corridor, he heard someone call his name. Recognizing the voice, he spun around and stopped. Travis stood in the lobby.

Devin froze. Elation, curiosity, nervousness, shame—all of it hit him as he watched his brother walk toward him. Why had Travis come to see him now, after all this time?

He didn't know what to say, so he reached out and

gave Travis an awkward hug. They released each other, and he cleared his throat. "You smell like the ocean."

Travis nodded. "I just got outta surf."

Devin's face lit up as a wave of pride washed over him. He knew his brother was surfing again, but hearing the words spoken aloud made his heart swell.

His smile faded. "Kane still giving you trouble?"

Travis shrugged. "Sometimes."

"Wish I could'a been there when he called you out."

"Yeah," Travis mumbled. There was bitterness in his tone.

Devin let out a breath. He didn't deserve this visit. A rush of guilt hit him as they started down the hall, and he swallowed it back. "There's a rec room. Wanna go shoot some pool?"

"Okay." Travis nodded.

Side by side, they walked to the recreation area where senior clients were allowed some leisure time, playing pool or various board games. A few of the residents sat around a big screen TV watching movies. Others worked out, lifting weights on the exercise equipment.

Devin moved over to the pool table and racked the balls. It took Travis a while to figure out how to shoot with one arm, but by the third game he seemed to get the hang of it. Just as he would have when they were younger, Devin taunted his brother every time he missed a shot. He wouldn't let Travis use the rake or give him any sort of advantage because of his disability.

Finally, during the fifth game, Travis made a few good shots and took the lead. He called the corner pocket and hammered the eight ball into the hole. "Take that," he gloated, sending Devin a smug look.

Impressed—and a tad surprised—Devin slapped his younger sibling on the back. "Unreal, brah." He smiled as he put down his cue. "You gettin' good at doin' stuff with one arm. I could never do that."

Travis shrugged. "It's getting easier."

As they walked back down to the front lobby, Devin listened while his brother told him all about Makani. "He looks up to me," Travis said. "Kind of reminds me of the old days, when you and I used to surf."

Devin grinned. "Yeah, you always were a lil' tagalong."

Feigning offence, Travis punched him in the arm.

"Ow!" Devin rubbed the spot. "Dude, you got way too frickin' strong."

They both laughed, and the air in the room felt lighter.

"Want me to pick you up tomorrow?" Travis asked. "I could bring some boards."

Devin nodded cheerfully "Fo' shua, brah."

Travis looked surprised. "For real?"

The stunned expression on his face made Devin laugh.

If anything could help mend his relationship with his brother, it was surfing.

They continued through the front lobby in silence and at the front entrance, Travis paused. He gave Devin a tentative frown. "Sorry I didn't come sooner ... to the family sessions and stuff."

"It's all right," Devin shrugged. "I wouldn't have come see me neither."

This time when they hugged it wasn't so awkward, and as he watched his brother walk away, Devin smiled. Tomorrow he would start his new life—a clean life with his dad, his daughter, his brother, and the surf. *Strange*, he mused, but he wanted it more than anything.

Full of energy and joyful spirit, Travis bustled around the kitchen packing food for the BBQ and babbling about the surf competition. Shayla sat motionless on a bar stool watching him and listening while he described almost every wave Makani had caught that day.

"I still can't believe it!" he blabbered. "First place in his very first contest! He was rippin' all day. You should've seen him."

His excitement was contagious; and she couldn't help but smile. It was the happiest she'd ever seen him.

He plucked some grapes from a bowl on the counter

and popped them into his mouth. "Guess what else I did," he said as he chewed. "I went and saw Dev."

Shayla gasped. "Really?"

"Yup." He popped another grape into his mouth.

"And how'd it go?"

"Good."

It wasn't much of an answer, but before she had a chance to ask more, Travis picked her up and carried her over to the living room sofa. With a huge grin, he threw her down, and kissed her breathless. Letting out a giggle, she rolled him over, and straddled his lap as she pulled an envelope from her pocket. "I got some news myself," she said, waving the paper in front of him. "I got into art school. I got the letter this morning."

Travis took the packet and read it. "That's sick!" he exclaimed. "I'm stoked for you!"

Shayla smiled. "They especially liked that picture I painted. The one of you on the cliff."

Travis squeezed her tightly and kissed her again. "I guess there's a lot to celebrate tonight."

Shayla nodded. "Is your dad coming to the BBQ?"

Travis shrugged. "I don't know. I can't get a hold of him. He's acting so weird lately. He's never around."

She smiled again. "Well I'm sure he'll make it."

Her cell phone rang, and her father's name popped up on the screen. She groaned and climbed off Travis's lap.

"Doesn't he understand what a restraining order means? This is the fourth time he's called me this week."

Travis's brow furrowed. "Want me to answer? I can tell him where to go."

Shayla shook her head. "No, it's okay." Her thumb went up to reject the call, but she paused. What if it was important? What if something awful had happened?

"Hello," she answered, and instantly regretted it.

"Yur my daughter an' I wanna see ya." His words were slurred. She had to strain to understand them.

For several minutes she tried to explain why they weren't allowed any contact, but her father was so drunk none of it made any sense. He just kept apologizing and repeating things over and over.

"I'm yur dad," he griped again.

"I know," she replied. "And I miss the old you, before you started drinking. Why won't you get help? If you went to rehab and stopped…"

"I ain' doin' that." His voice sounded frustrated.

Shayla sighed. "Then, I'm sorry, Dad. I can't see you."

Clicking the phone shut, she slumped against Travis's chest; she could feel his heart pounding.

"It was the right thing to do," he said.

Swallowing the sad lump in her throat, she nodded and nuzzled into him. He was right. If she'd learned anything in the past few months, it was that people didn't get help until they truly wanted to. She couldn't let her dad's decisions affect her life. No matter how much she loved him.

"Maybe someday he'll change his mind," she said. "But art school is starting up soon, and I got surfing, and dancing, and you." She smiled up at him. "Forget about it, okay? No gloominess. Today is Makani's day, and we should be out celebrating."

~Epic Session~

The smell of barbecued ribs and roasted corn on the cob lingered in the air and mixed with the sweet fragrance of plumeria trees that grew in Makani's backyard. Stuffed from the feast, Carl patted his stomach and handed his plate to Iva. As he watched the beautiful woman take her collection into the kitchen, he smiled. It had been a long time since he'd felt this attracted to anyone. Since his wife, he hadn't dated at all, but the more he got to know Iva, the more he felt the spark.

Inhaling deeply, he forced himself out of his chair. He was so full he could barely move, but he could hardly sit back and let Iva clean up by herself. He gathered some of the leftover food and joined her in the kitchen.

"Thank you for supper," he said, as he wrapped up one of the containers and put it in the fridge. He moved over and gave her a kiss.

She smiled bashfully and glanced outside where Travis was still eating. "You tell him yet?"

Carl shook his head. "No. Tomorrow, I think."

Shayla came into the kitchen. "Do you guys need any help?" She took up a position at the sink and starting scrubbing the dishes.

As Carl went back outside, Makani ran past him with Jasper in tow. Barking, the golden retriever hopped on his back and wrestled him to the ground with sloppy kisses. Makani covered his head and let out a fit of giggles. Carl smiled and joined Travis on the lawn. "You sure made a difference in that little boy's life."

Travis shrugged. "Nah, Mak had the talent to begin with."

"Come on. You've got to take some of the credit."

Again, Travis shrugged, but there was a glimmer of satisfaction in his eyes, and for reasons of his own, Carl was glad to see it.

"I've got some stuff to do tomorrow. You said you were picking Devin up from rehab, right?"

"Yeah." Travis eyed him curiously. "What stuff?"

Carl ignored the question. "You boys going surfing?"

Travis beamed up at him. "I hope so."

"Okay, then let's say we meet at home afterwards. Around six o'clock?"

"Sure," Travis replied.

Carl smiled, and as he took a quick glance at his son, he was certain he had made the right decision. He would tell Travis about it tomorrow, and if all went well, he would include his other son as well.

After Travis picked up Devin the next morning, they drove down the highway searching for some late season waves. They pulled up to Sunset Beach and got out of the vehicle, smiling.

Boards tucked under their arms, they stood on the warm sand, staring out at the ocean. It was the middle of March. Soon the North Shore would be flat and would stay that way for most of the summer, but on this day, the swell beckoned. Clean conditions with a light offshore breeze. The waves were cranking four to six feet on the back—twice that on the face. Some were almost double overhead and bigger than anything Travis had surfed since his return, but it didn't matter. The surf couldn't have been any more perfect.

"Been a long time," Devin stated. "Hope I still got it."

As they headed into the water, Travis felt the excitement hit him. He was at Sunset! Surfing with his brother!

As they paddled into the lineup, the other surfers stopped to stare. An older veteran's mouth dropped open, and Travis heard someone say his name, but most of the other surfers ignored him. They were too busy gawking at his brother.

Either Devin didn't notice or he didn't care. He took his place in the lineup and when a nice set approached, he smiled. "Let's see what you can do, lil' braddah."

With his gloved hand, Travis took long, deep strokes and dropped into a sweet wave. When he got to the bottom, he looked over and saw his brother riding with him. They turned up the face, carving the liquid together.

The next wave was even better. The wall jacked up and Travis sped through it. He pumped up the face, did a big snap, and threw out some spray. Water splashed over his head. Behind him, Devin pulled an aerial. Not a huge one, but enough to catch a bit of air, land on the face and keep going. Travis hooted; pride filled him. His brother was a little rusty, but he still had talent.

All smiles, Devin paddled over to him and held up his hand for a high five. "That was sick, brah!" Straddling his stick, he looked out at the ocean and sighed. "You dunno how good that felt."

Travis thought about the first wave he had caught

after his accident. "Trust me, I know."

Stoked for more, they paddled out again and shared the waves together, surfing frontside and backside. Cranking out some nice turns, they ripped up the inside bowl sections and caught some amazing barrels. They rode for hours until the surf closed out, destroying their fun. Devin managed to catch one last incredible wave that seemed to peel on and on, giving him a long and exhilarating ride.

Travis caught that one too.

Back on the beach, they carried their boards up the sand. Dripping from head to toe, Travis smiled. "Epic session, bro. I'm wiped."

"Me too," his brother replied. "My body feels like mush."

Devin stretched his arms above his head, and Travis noticed he was heavier than he used to be. "You've been working out, haven't you?"

Devin chuckled. "Yeah, and it's a good thing. I gotta get back in shape if I'm gonna stomp you in the water."

Travis kicked some sand at him. "You wish."

With a crooked smile, Devin lunged, knocking Travis sideways. The two boys wrestled on the ground, laughing until they were winded.

Back on their feet, they wiped themselves free of dirt. Travis grinned, and the day was perfect.

"Hui!" The call was sharp and shrill. "Ho, Dev!"

Travis turned toward the sound and his good feelings faded. Devin's best friend, Jonny, walked toward them, with some of his hooligan friends.

Gripping his surfboard with white-knuckled fingers, Devin froze. A grin plastered Jonny's face as he approached, but Devin could barely force a smile. He glanced down the beach and considered running. Could he do this? It just wasn't fair.

When Jonny reached them, he clasped Devin's wrist with one hand and thumped him on the back with the other. "Eh brah, why you neva' call me and tell me you was back?"

"Sorry J-man, I just got out today." Devin glanced at Travis and saw him scowl. He straightened his shoulders and took a deep breath.

"That's solid, brah." Jonny tapped Devin's surfboard and looked him up and down, but he didn't mention anything about surfing. "Eh, we get one party tonight. I pick you up if you like."

Devin shook his head. "Sorry, bro, I can't."

"For why? Your dad not goin' let you?"

"Nah, that's not it." Leaving his board in the sand, Devin led Jonny away from the others. "It's jus' ...now that I'm outta rehab, I gotta stay clean, Jon."

"It's all good, bu. Jus' cruise with us an'...."

He stepped away and locked eyes with his pal. "No, you don't get it. I need to stay away from drugs, Jonny, an' anyone who does 'em."

The smile left Jonny's lips and his eyes narrowed. "So, w'at'? Das it den? I thought we wuz boys?"

The words ripped Devin's soul. "We are," he replied.

For a moment, Jonny just stared at him. Then he whirled around. "Whatevas', brah."

Devin watched him go. His hands shook; his palms grew sweaty. Why had he done that? How could he tell his best friend to go away? Sure Jonny was addicted to cocaine, but he was a good guy, and he'd always been there whenever Devin needed him.

A craving swelled and hit him hard. He almost ran after his friend, but when his brother stepped up beside him, the clouds cleared a little.

"You tell him you couldn't hang out anymore?" Travis sounded suspicious.

Devin nodded.

"It had to be done, man."

"I know."

"I'm glad you did."

Devin saw the pride in his brother's eyes and suddenly nothing else mattered. Despite the fact that he had just lost his best friend, he had gained another — and blood ran thicker than water.

He smiled. "Let's go home."

~Commitment~

Sparks from the bonfire in Carl's backyard crackled and melted into the star laden sky. Dancing in the dark, the orange flames burned bright, illuminating the faces of Travis, Devin, and Shayla as they roasted hot dogs and popped blackened marshmallows into their mouths.

Carl picked up his guitar and sang as he strummed, choosing a humorous song he knew the boys would remember from their youth. When Devin grabbed a harmonica and tried to join in, Travis and Shayla laughed until tears came to their eyes.

At the end of the song, Carl chuckled too. He leaned the instrument against his chair. On the other side of the fire, Travis nuzzled his face in Shayla's neck and whispered something that made the girl giggle. Carl smiled when he saw it.

He stood up and demanded everyone's attention. There was a lump in his throat as he looked at his sons.

"It's not easy to make such drastic changes, but you did it, and I'm proud of you both. It's so good to have you home again."

He turned to Shayla next. "You've done wonders for my boy. He's finally smiling."

Beaming up at him, Shayla blushed.

A tear formed in Carl's eye and he quickly wiped it away. He laughed at himself. "There's a reason I started all that. I have something to show you. Come with me."

Everyone piled into Carl's SUV. Devin jumped up front, and Travis and Shayla slid into the back. Travis shrugged when Shayla nudged him. He had no idea what his father was up to.

"Where are we going?" he asked, but Carl said nothing. His eyes glinted mischievously as he drove along the highway.

A short while later they pulled up to a large building in Hale'iwa. Moonlight glinted off the freshly painted exterior. It was obvious the place had just been renovated—evidence of construction littered the ground, and the landscaping had yet to be completed.

A mural of an enormous wave was painted on the side, and when Travis looked at Shayla, she smiled knowingly. "That's the project I've been working on."

He realized his mouth was hanging open. He closed it. Shayla was in on this too?

Through the front window he could make out a lobby and a large quiver of boards. His interest peaked. He'd driven down this road plenty of times, yet he'd never noticed the place. What was it?

Above the main doors, a large portion of the building was covered in a huge orange tarp. Carl wasted no time in tearing it down. "Hope you like it," he yelled, from the top of the ladder. It swung free. The sign above the door read: *Kelly Bros' Surf School.*

It took Travis a moment. A grin spread over his face as he glanced at his brother.

Devin's mouth hung open. "This is for us?"

Carl nodded. "If you want it."

As Travis looked up at the tall building, a tingling sensation ran through his entire body. Was this for real? Had his father set them up an entire business? Their very own surf school?

Carl climbed down the ladder. "I figured my sons needed a fresh chance at life."

Feeling a little unsteady, Travis put his hand on Shayla's shoulder. He thought about Makani and how much he loved coaching the boy. All those nights he had lain awake wondering where his life was headed—he should have thought of something like this.

He stared at his father. Then he gave him a hug. "I don't know how to thank you for this."

Carl smiled and patted his shoulder.

Devin bounced from foot to foot. "Guess you and me are gonna be partners, lil' bro."

Travis grabbed his brother around the neck. "This is unreal!" he shouted, as Devin picked him up off the ground and whirled him sideways.

He looked up at the sign again.

Kelly Bros' Surf School.

Awesome.

The two boys moved about, peeking in windows and admiring the mural, and when they finally settled down, their father turned to them. "In order for this to work, I want a commitment from both of you. That means working normal hours. No partying."

They both nodded.

"Devin, you have to give this your all…."

"I will, Dad, no worries."

Travis beamed.

"And I can't afford to just pay for it all. Both of you are going to have to contribute some of your inheritance money until the business picks up. Rent isn't cheap."

"Fine wit' me," Devin said.

"Me too," Travis agreed.

With a satisfied nod, Carl wrapped an arm around them both. Two sets of keys dangled from his fingers. "All right then. It's all yours," he said.

Travis took his keys and held them like a fragile seashell. Then he and his brother ran to the doors, laughing and wrestling, as they each tried to be the first to unlock them.

~No support~

You'll be fine," Ayumi insisted, as they pulled up to a large brown house. "Just go in and ask for him. I'll be right here."

Mika hesitated. Slowly, she opened the passenger door. "Are you sure I have to do this? He's not going to like it."

Ayumi shook her head. "He's the father, Mikki. Like it or not, he should know."

Mika squared her shoulders and took a deep breath. Then she stepped outside the vehicle. Quickly, before she could change her mind again, she walked up to the house and knocked on the big wooden door.

She knew what would happen. He would deny it. He would turn her away and leave her to raise the child alone, with no support. Her baby would never know the joy of spending time with its own father.

She swallowed the lump in her throat and wondered as she always did. Why'd she have sex with such an asshole to begin with?

But she knew why. That one night, he wasn't an asshole at all. He was kind, funny, and charming. She could still remember the way he'd looked at her as he'd stroked her face and told her she was special. It was all lies, of course, and all because of a stupid wager.

Mika wrung her hands furiously, and as she stood there, waiting for the door to open, she remembered the night of Kane's birthday party. He had bet one of his friends he could sleep with her, and now, because of that, she was five months pregnant.

Hearing footsteps, she almost turned and ran, but it was too late. Her whole body trembled.

The night of Kane's party, she hadn't slept with him. He had lost the bet. But because she was hurt and feeling so lonely, she had slept with someone else. Someone worse.

The door opened and Devin stood in the entrance. His eyes narrowed when he saw her. "What are you doing here?"

Mika looked down at the bulge in her stomach and said, "I have something to tell you."

Pregnant? With *his* baby?

Gaping at the girl, Devin shook his head and crossed his arms. "It ain't mine," he stated.

Or was it? He had slept with the girl at a party a few months ago, and her stomach was about the right size. But wouldn't she have said something sooner? Besides, he'd seen her out with other guys since—including his very own brother.

His head whirled. *Travis.* What would he think of this? And his dad. What if he found out?

Finding it difficult to breathe, Devin leaned against the doorframe. A huge weight pressed in on him, choking him, and he pulled at his shirt collar.

"What's going on?" Travis stepped up behind him. He looked Mika up and down. "What do you want?"

"I came to talk to Devin," she murmured.

Devin shook his head. "Go home, Mika." He shut the door in her face, rushed through the house, and flew out the back door. Breathing heavily, he jumped in his car and sped out the driveway, barely missing Travis's truck as he squeezed between it and the fence.

Travis opened the door again and watched his brother's car peal away.

"What's going on?" he demanded.

Still standing there, Mika started to cry. "Devin's the father." The words burst from her lips.

Travis's mouth dropped. "Huh?'

Eyes filled with shame, Mika nodded. "It's true," she muttered. "The baby is Devin's. I knew he wouldn't want it, and so I told you it was yours, because then it would be closer to its real daddy. It would still be in the family."

As she sobbed even harder, Travis stood speechless. In a strange way, her explanation made sense, yet it all seemed surreal.

"Please don't hate me," Mika begged him. "I was out of my mind. I wasn't thinking properly."

Travis didn't know what to say.

Ayumi got out of the car and headed toward them, but Travis didn't stick around to hear what she had to say. He leapt down the steps, leaving the twins on the porch, and jumped into his truck.

"Get in," he shouted to Shayla.

In complete silence, they drove up the highway and down every side street. They checked all of Devin's usual hangouts—the gas station, the basketball courts—but it was early in the morning and those places were empty. They found nothing. Devin was gone.

Travis pulled over to the side of the road and sat. A thin salty film covered his windshield, and he wiped it with his hand creating an even bigger smudge. He turned to Shayla. "There's one place we haven't looked."

~Selfish~

Standing on the front steps of a redwood bungalow in Wai'anae, Devin pounded the railing with his fist. He barely felt the pain in his knuckles as they smashed against the tattered wood. A large sliver jabbed under his skin and a thin path of blood trickled out from the wound.

"How the hell did I let this happen?" he yelled.

Vince grabbed his hand before he could slam it into the banister again. "Whoa, brah. Nuff already. Try dis." He pressed an eight ball of coke into Devin's fingers and patted him twice on the shoulder.

Devin's whole arm shook when he realized what he held, and as he looked down at the white powder, his breathing came in shallow rasps. Why had he come here? An intense craving grew as he clenched the cocaine. He closed his eyes and breathed deeper.

"I dunno, brah," he said. He squeezed the package

again and was just about to hand the drugs back when the sound of tires squealed around the corner. A black truck came to a stop just inches from Vince's sedan. Travis burst from the driver's side door.

Devin froze. A thick haze of dust hovered in the air as his brother stormed over the grass and up the front steps toward him. Eyes flashing, Travis snatched the drugs from his hand. "Damn it, Devin! I knew you couldn't stay off the stuff. You're not even going to try!"

Vince took a step between them, but Devin held him back. "Travis... I wasn't gonna..." he stammered.

His brother shook his head. "No. Don't bother. You've been out of rehab for two days, and you're back here already. You're the most selfish person I've ever known, Dev, and if you go back to this shit, I'll never talk to you again. It's your choice!" Travis threw the cocaine back at him and whirled around.

"Trav!" Devin rushed after him. "Wait."

But Travis had already jumped into his truck. Devin ran to his car and leapt inside, but by the time he turned the ignition, his brother was gone.

Careening around turns, Travis tore down the highway. "Slow down!" Shayla cried, gripping the dash as they fishtailed around a bend.

Hearing the panic in her voice, he braked hard and swerved to the side of the road. "Stay here," he ordered and opened the door.

As his feet hit the pavement, his cell phone rang. Devin's name lit up the display. He threw the device as far as he could. It hit the cement and broke into pieces. He stood, glaring at the ground. How could Devin do this to him, *again*?

He felt Shayla step beside him. His breathing was ragged and uneven as his anger turned into heartache. She reached for him and he grasped her tightly. Holding back a sob, he buried his face in her hair and cursed his brother. "Why can't he see what he's doing?"

He released his grip and turned away so she wouldn't see his tears. "I'm sorry," he mumbled.

She shook her head. "You don't have to be."

In silence, they drove back home. When they pulled into the driveway, Travis waited for Shayla to get out of the truck. Then he tossed her his house keys and locked the doors. "I'll be back in a bit," he called and took off, tires spinning.

Devin sat on the beach at Makaha, sulking. One by one, he tossed every stone he could find into the ocean. Locals and tourists came and went; he barely saw them. The afternoon passed in a moment as he wallowed in the mess he had made. Why had he called Vince? Why had he gone to his house?

He pulled the package of cocaine from his pocket and pressed his fingers into the thin plastic, pushing the powder around. He had kept it. Was he trying to fail? If he screwed up now, no one would ever trust him again.

Swallowing hard, he trembled. The lump in his throat ached for relief, but he held back, and as he sat there, he remembered the people he had met at rehab. Some were so sick with addiction they reeked of death, and he could still hear the moans coming from detox. How horrible those first few weeks had been. He couldn't go through that again. He wouldn't. And besides, even if he wanted to, he couldn't snort the stuff now. He'd fail his next drug test and go to jail for sure.

Devin ran a hand through his hair. Then, he shook his head. It wasn't just detox or jail that scared him. It was lack of control. The white dust had stolen his family and his life. It had held him captive for far too long.

He thought about Travis and the surf school and his

dad. The last few days had been great. Did he really want to give all that up?

Eyes closed, he listened to the surf and felt himself back on the waves at Sunset with his brother, water splashing over his head as he sliced through that perfect barrel. The feeling of his feet on a board was ten times the exhilaration of any high he'd found snorting coke. That was the rush he needed.

Sitting straighter, Devin clenched his fingers around the small bag of coke and wound up his arm, about to throw the drugs into the water. Then he stopped, thought for a moment, and tucked them back into his pocket.

~Terrible Father~

Devin cruised down the freeway and into town. The thick Honolulu traffic, combined with his broken air conditioning, made for a slow, stuffy drive. He wiped the sweat from his brow and stuck his arm out the window trying to create more air flow. "Come on," he grumbled to a car in front of him. "Move it already."

Finally he found the exit he needed and turned up a slow curving ramp. He reached his destination, climbed the steps of the town-house, and rang the doorbell.

Lea answered the door. "Devin." She looked surprised to see him. "Howzit? You want to come in?"

He shook his head. He didn't want to talk. "Can I take Allisa to the beach? I'm good, I promise. Done rehab, no drugs. I'll be careful with her and have her home for dinner."

Allisa squealed when she saw him and peeked out from behind her mother. "Please, Momma? Can I go?"

Lea studied him for a moment. "You're all clean? You'll take care of her?"

"For real," he replied. "I swear. It's all good."

Lea nodded and packed some towels and sunscreen. "Just down the street, okay? One hour, that's it." She handed him the bag, but hesitated before letting go. "I'm trusting you, Devin. I don't wanna regret this."

Hand in hand, Devin and Allisa walked through Waikiki, weaving around surfboards, beach boys and outrigger canoes. Pale tourists hung leis of orchids on the Duke Kahanamoku Statue, and tanned girls in bikinis lay on grass mats catching the last few rays before sunset.

Allisa chattered up a storm, and Devin couldn't help but think she was adorable. Kneeling on the sand, he helped her build a castle, and as he did, he thought about Mika. Was he really having another child?

The tower collapsed, and Devin's world crashed along with it. Could he do this? What if he couldn't stay clean? What if he made a terrible father?

As he filled another bucket with sand, he glanced at his little girl. She took his hand, dragged him up to his feet, and pointed to a seashell that had just washed up on shore. Shrieking, she jumped up and down and rushed into the water to grab it, only to get tossed by a rolling wave. She laughed as he helped her up. Then she gave him a hug and handed him the shell.

"Here, Daddy. This is for you."

Devin looked down at the precious gift and smiled.

"It's to make you feel better. 'Cause you were sick for a long time. Mommy told me. But you're not sick anymore right?"

He shook his head.

"I like the beach," she said. "Can we do this next time too? Are you gonna come back?"

Her fearful expression tore his heart.

Kneeling down, he nodded. "I'll come," he replied, "and maybe you can have a sleep-over with me and Grandpa and Uncle Travis soon."

Allisa's face lit up and she fell into his arms. "I love you, Daddy."

The words struck him, and as he held her, he realized something. She was part of him. She was his family too. All of her life, he'd abandoned her, treated her like a piece of dirt, yet she still loved him. She still wanted him by her side. He didn't deserve it. But he wanted to. And if she was open to loving him and giving him another chance, then maybe the others would too.

Shayla sat on her bed, rocking back and forth, arms wrapped around her knees. Darkness had settled over the island. Stars littered the sky. Hours had passed since Travis had taken off in his truck and she had walked home, determined to let him handle his problems on his own. But as the evening wore on, her anxiety grew. Goosebumps prickled her flesh. Where had he gone? Was he okay?

She picked up her phone, but she had already called everyone. Carl hadn't seen him, neither had Brady, and nobody could get a hold of Devin.

No longer willing to just sit there and wait, she grabbed her keys from her pocket, hurried to her car, and drove down the coast, slowing to a crawl as she passed Travis's favorite surf spots.

After checking the parking lot at Pipeline, she pulled onto a side road near Rocky Point. Frustrated, she sat behind the wheel and stared at the familiar landmark across the street—a large totem pole with a rock on its head. Vacant eyes stared into her soul as if they could see all her fears, and suddenly she knew where to look. Fingers locked on the steering wheel, she drove straight to the nearest bar. Sure enough, Travis's truck was parked alongside.

As she went in, it took a moment for her eyes to adjust to the darkened interior, but when they cleared, she found Travis sitting in a booth at the far back corner. He had his back to the door. A tall drink sat in front of him.

A lump formed in Shayla's throat as she stepped up to the table. His head hung low as he circled his straw around the glass. She watched him for a moment and cleared her throat. He looked up with a tired expression.

She slid into the seat across from him. "Why'd you come here?"

He said nothing.

"I thought you gave up drinking."

Travis pushed his glass away. "I did."

It was full.

Shayla studied him. He looked sober.

"It's never going to work." He let out a grunt.

"What's not?"

"The surf school." He groaned again. "Devin's gonna wreck everything, and even if he doesn't do drugs now, how long until he does? A month? A week?"

Shayla put her hand on his. "You'll make it work, with or without your brother, but you got to give him a chance."

"I did, and look what happened." He pulled his hand away.

Shayla sat for a while in silence. She ran her finger

along the rim of his cup. "You didn't drink any."

Travis shrugged. "I promised I wouldn't."

The server came over. "Can I get you anything else?"

He handed her back the drink with some extra cash. "Nah, I'm done here."

~Fear and Longing~

As a light, hypnotic rain hit the living room window, droplets of water streaked down the dark glass, reminding Mika of all the tears she had shed since leaving Devin's house earlier. Now it was well past midnight, and she sat sipping tea with her sister on the sofa. Her head hurt and her nose was raw.

Inside her belly, the baby kicked. It was a weird sensation, but one she had grown to like, and as her stomach fluttered, she rubbed the growing bump. Only a few more months and her child would join the world.

Without a father.

A weary sound escaped her lips and she turned to her twin. "Why do I even care? I knew this would happen. Devin already has one child he doesn't take care of, so why should this be any different?"

Ayumi's eyes narrowed. "He's a kook, Mikki. I don't know why you fell for his crap to begin with."

"He was different the night we were together. He was sweet."

"He sent you home in a cab."

"That was the next morning!"

Clearly frustrated, Ayumi got up and moved into the kitchen to clean up the dishes. "He's a jerk."

Mika looked away. "I know."

Flicking through the channels on the television, she tried to find a program that could distract her from her misery. Regret whirled through her mind. If only the father were someone else. Even Kane would have been a better choice.

Exhausted, she placed the remote on her lap, closed her aching eyes, and started to doze off. The doorbell rang. Her sister answered it and came back. "It's him."

Devin stood on Mika's front steps. "Is it really mine?" He gripped the doorknob with clammy fingers.

Mika nodded. Her eyes were puffy and her cheeks were flushed; it was obvious she had been crying.

"Can I come in?" He stepped over the threshold.

In the living room, he glanced around, and his eyes traveled to the picture window at the front of the room. Vaguely, he remembered putting someone through it. He winced. Then he thought about their last party, when the twins had thrown him out for snorting coke, and he grimaced.

Mika cleared her throat. "Have a seat."

Devin sat on the sofa and tapped his foot, fidgeting with the edge of the cushion. Silently, he watched the girl as she went into the kitchen to pour him a cup of tea. Nodding his appreciation, he accepted the drink and took a sip. She sat beside him, but said nothing.

Eyes flicking around the room, he licked his lips and picked at a hangnail on his finger. He remembered the night of Kane's party. Mika was upset over something Kane had done, so Devin had offered to take her home.

Try as he might to forget, he could still feel her soft skin, her hair falling across his chest, and he could still see the way she'd smiled up at him while he lightly stroked her face. That night was great, he thought, but he cringed as he recalled his actions the next morning. After injecting some cocaine, he had smoked a big joint, and by the time Mika woke up, he was angry. He had yelled at her and sent her home in a cab.

His mouth grew dry, and he took another sip of tea. He looked at her—really looked. Elbows propped on her knees, she held her drink with dainty fingers. Her deep brown eyes were bloodshot from crying, and her forehead was creased. He almost reached out for her, but he stilled his hand and stared into his cup.

"I'm sorry I was such a dick to you," he mumbled. "I shouldn't have sent you home like that. I was stoned and girls were..." He shifted in his seat. "I dunno. It's been a while since I dated anyone."

She put her hand on her stomach. "I'm sorry too." Her voice was clipped and bitter.

"Guess we should'a been more careful."

"Or not done it at all!"

Five minutes passed and neither one of them spoke. Once in a while they glanced over at each other, and Devin wondered what Mika was thinking.

"Why didn't you tell me sooner?" he asked.

"'Cause I knew you wouldn't want it." Her voice wavered, and Devin felt like a moron. She'd expected him to flake.

With a frown, he reached out and brushed away a piece of hair that clung to her cheek. She jumped at his touch and froze, but she didn't pull away. Her sobbing ceased, and he cleared his throat.

"I have another daughter," he confessed.

"I know."

Of course she did. Everyone knew that.

He hung his head. "Allisa's six. I hardly ever saw her, but she always knew who I was ... even when she hadn't seen me for a year."

When Mika didn't respond, he kept going. "You know I got outta rehab yesterday?"

She nodded.

"I've been clean for three months." He paused and shook his head. "Treated my family like shit."

Why was he telling her all this? Blood rushed to his cheeks and his ears grew warm. He felt like running, and was just about to get up to leave, when Mika turned toward him. With a tender expression, she gently touched his arm. Flustered, Devin stayed put.

Mika's mind whirled with hope, sympathy, fear, and longing. So many times, she had thought about Devin—their night together and how wonderful she had felt in his arms. She had seen this side of him once—the nice side—but what if he changed again? What if he went back to his old ways?

There was an awkward silence, as she worked up the courage to ask, "So, what now?"

Devin shrugged. "We have a kid, I guess." He smiled weakly. "I know I've been an ass, and I don't have the greatest track record, but if you want I'll stick around."

Mika let out the breath she was holding. She took his

hand and laid it on her stomach. "We'd like that."

As their unborn child kicked at his fingers, a sense of wonder crossed Devin's face. His eyes met hers, and as the motion settled down, he cleared his throat and removed his hand. "It's getting late. You should sleep."

Frowning, Mika nodded. "Where you gonna go?"

Devin shrugged. "I dunno, but I ain't goin' home. I can't face 'em yet."

"You can't just sleep in your car."

"I can stay at the hostel."

With a shake of her head, Mika got up, headed down the hallway, and came back with a blanket and a pillow. "You can crash here," she insisted. The bedding was hot from the dryer, and she held it for a second, drawing in some warmth, before placing it on his lap.

"Thanks." He paused, and then he said quietly, "I was pissed at myself, you know? That's why I sent you home that mornin'."

Mika's heart lurched. "Why were you pissed?"

"'Cause I liked you so much."

The words sounded sincere, and Mika was drawn into his somber, grey-green eyes. She hesitated, but only for a second. "That couch is kinda lumpy. There's room in my bed if you want."

Carl stood in front of the big picture window, staring outside at the road. "Devin's been missing all night," he told Iva on his cell phone. "He's probably out getting high. Shayla's here with Travis. She told me everything. If it weren't for her, I'd still be in the dark."

"I hope he come back soon." Her voice was always so soothing.

Outside a rooster crowed, and the first rays of sunlight spread across the yard as a swirling pink sunrise faded into blue. There were very few cars on the road.

"Sorry for calling so early. I didn't get a wink of sleep last night."

"I just glad Travis safe. You want me to come there? I look for Devin with you?"

"Nah, there's no point." Carl sighed. "I'll call you as soon as I hear anything." He clicked his phone shut and moved into the kitchen, where he poured some hot water into a cup and waited for his tea to steep.

Breathing in the sweet jasmine scent, he rubbed the kink out of the back of his neck and took a long sip, hoping the drink would soothe his nerves and give him some strength. Just as the warm liquid slid down his throat, the back door opened, and Devin walked in. Carl put his cup down and gave a sigh of relief.

Devin froze. Then he rushed forward. "Where's Travis? I gotta talk to him." He hurried into the living room and started up the stairs.

Carl chased after him. "He's not up there. Where were you all night? Shayla told me about Mika. You got another girl pregnant? And calling your dealer! What the hell is going on, Devin?"

With his hand on the top of the stair railing, Devin stopped. "Sorry, Dad. I should' a come home."

"You're damned right you *should'a.*"

Shoulders sagging, Devin came down the steps and stopped in front of him. "I didn't know about Mika 'til last night, but I'm gonna do things right. I'm gonna take care of her and the baby."

Carl shook his head. "And what about your other daughter? Are you going to take care of her too?"

Devin nodded. "Yeah. I saw Allisa yesterday."

Carl took a step back and studied his son. Looking him straight in the eyes, he leaned forward. "Did you do any drugs?"

Devin matched his stare with sober integrity. "No."

Relief vanquished the last of his anger, as Carl sat down on the living room sofa. "Good. Then we can work through the rest." He motioned toward the other chair. "Tell me everything."

Devin glanced at the door. "I will, but can it wait? I really gotta find Trav."

Carl nodded. "He's at the beach with Shayla. Chun's, I think."

~Like Beef~

The surf at Chun's Reef sucked. The waves were inconsistent and kept closing out. "Why'd we even come here?" Travis barked. "It's impossible to surf in this mush." He smacked the top of the water and grumbled, "Let's go in."

Shayla nodded. Then she frowned and pointed.

Kane Walker paddled over and sat up on his board. He shot Travis a hateful grin and snickered.

"You still with dis punk?" he asked Shayla.

Travis rolled his eyes. "We're not goin' do this today."

A half decent wave approached, so he turned to catch it to shore. Kane gave a loud hoot and dropped into it as well. Turning sharply, he cut Travis off, knocking him off his board and over the falls. Travis tumbled under the curling water and came up coughing and spitting.

He paddled after his assailant, and when they reached

the beach, he threw his board on the sand and faced the guy. "You're the big shot surfer! You got the title! So what the hell is your problem?"

"Yeah, *loser!*" Shayla said, coming out of the surf as well. "You're just mad because Travis would've beat you last year. You're only the champion 'cause Trav lost his arm."

From the neck up, Kane turned a deep shade of red. The vein on his forehead bulged. Eyes narrowed dangerously, he stepped up to Travis. "Like beef?"

Travis felt his whole body twitch, but before he had a chance to react, someone hollered, and the noise turned their heads.

Devin ran toward them, shouting, "You goin' scrap with my bro, you get through me first!"

Speechless, Travis stood there, while his brother advanced on Kane. The two young men made a small circle in the sand. Kane threw Devin vicious stink-eye. Then he snarled at Travis, looked at them both, and backed away in defeat. Hissing some curse words, he grabbed his surfboard and took off down the beach. At a safe distance, he called out over his shoulder, "Eh, Trav, if you like see who's the bettah surfah, I be at Pipe tomorrow mornin'."

Devin flipped up his middle finger. "He'll be there, kook."

A smug grin crossed Kane's lips, and he stuck out his thumb and pinky finger, throwing them a sarcastic *shaka* as he fled.

Travis turned to his brother. "What the hell did you say that for? I can't surf Pipe! And what are you doing here anyway?"

Devin shrugged. "I came to find you."

"No one asked you to."

Shifting from foot to foot, Devin frowned. "Trav, come off it, okay? I dunno why I called Vince. I snapped, tha's all, and I thought about takin' a hit, but I didn't. I swear."

"I'm supposed to believe that?"

"For serious, brah. I'm done wit' that stuff."

Travis shook his head. "Whatever. You don't care about getting clean. You just don't want to go to jail, and rehab was your ticket out."

"Screw that!" Devin raised his voice. "You think I liked being in there, bro? It was hell. And not jus' detox. I had to give up everything, change my whole life. You don't know the shit I went through."

Travis swallowed hard. His whole body shook. "Giving up things? Changing your whole life? Sure, Dev. I don't know how that feels at all. Try living without an arm for a day and then tell me that."

With Shayla in tow, Travis stomped through the sand. As far as he was concerned, the discussion was over. He was done listening to his brother.

Shayla sat on the edge of Travis's bed staring at the back of his head. He had his face buried in the pillow, and when she touched his back, he flinched.

"Is there anything I can do?" she asked.

He shrugged away from her. "Nah, I just wanna sleep."

She stood up. "I'll go then."

With a shake of his head, he rolled over. A crease ran across his forehead. "Please don't. Just wake me in half an hour, okay?"

Taking her cell phone with her, Shayla left the room and sat down on the couch in the family room. She browsed through her contacts, dialed Brady's number, and frowned when he didn't answer. She saw Mika's number and paused. If there was ever a time she needed to talk to the girl, it was now. But should she?

Without willing it, her thumb hit the send button, and the phone rang on the other end of the line.

"Shay?" Mika answered. Her voice was quiet.

Shayla cleared her throat. "Yeah, it's me."

For a moment there was stark silence. Then they both started speaking at once:

"I don't know what to do about Travis."

"Devin's here, and he's pretty upset."

"What happened?"

"What did he say?"

For a good hour, she and Mika chatted about everything the guys were going through. It was strange, Shayla thought, but they seemed to have more in common now than ever before.

"I wish there was some way to help them," she said.

"Me too," Mika replied. "Let me know if anything changes, okay? And I'm sorry, Shay. For everything. What I did to you. And Travis. I don't know what I was thinking. I was lonely, I guess, but that's no excuse. I talked to my parents yesterday. They're gonna put me through nursing school after the baby comes. I'm gonna go to counseling and get my life straightened out. I just wanted you to know."

"Thanks, Mikki. That's good to hear. We'll talk again soon, okay?"

Shayla clicked her phone shut and headed back upstairs. Travis was still lying face down in bed, but she could tell from his breathing that he wasn't sleeping. Sitting beside him, she reached over and gently massaged his neck and shoulders. "Are you thinking about your brother?"

With a small grunt, he rolled over. Moonlight shone through the open window, illuminating his troubled expression. "Nah. I'm not going to bother with him anymore."

Running her fingers across his temples, Shayla continued her massage and waited.

"There's a storm in the North Pacific." His voice cracked a bit as he spoke. "Surf's supposed to be huge tomorrow."

She gave him a curious look. "So?"

"So...Devin told Kane I'm gonna show up at Pipe. But I can't do it. Not again."

"*Again*?" She glanced at the scar above his eye.

His cheeks flushed, and he turned over to face the wall.

"That's how you hurt yourself, isn't it? You tried to surf Pipe."

Silence rang out. His breathing was shallow.

"Trav, please tell me."

Gradually, he turned back. "I just wanted to prove it to him—*to everyone*—that I could still do it." In a voice filled with frustration, he griped, "Devin should've kept his big mouth shut. I'm gonna look like a wuss."

"Well, you're not a wuss," Shayla insisted.

After a moment of silence, she rummaged through her overnight bag and pulled out something she knew he'd recognize. Travis took the object from her and turned it over in his hand. "My trophy ... I threw this away. Where'd you get it?"

She didn't answer. Instead, she pointed to the award. "You won that at the Bonzai Classic. It's proof you've mastered Pipe. So why do you need to do it again? Does Kane's opinion really mean that much to you?"

Travis dropped his gaze and stared at his blanket. Nostrils flaring, he ran his thumb across his bottom lip and remained quiet.

"Does this have to do with your brother?"

His head snapped up. "No." He threw the trophy under his bed. "I just want my old life back. That's all."

Slumping back down, he turned over and pulled his blanket across his shoulders. Shayla wanted to say more, but she held back. She crawled in beside him and wrapped her arm around him. Eventually, his breathing slowed. He twitched a few times and fell asleep.

"Promise you won't surf Pipe," she whispered.

He didn't respond.

~Surf Kook~

The ocean was flat black and the sand was sharp under his feet—sharp enough to draw blood. Travis's surfboard floated nearby, but when he waded into the water, it moved away. No matter how many times he tried to reach it, it always remained a few feet ahead.

Breathless, he stopped, his eyes fixed on the board. The fiberglass surface started to bubble, and soon the whole ocean was in turmoil—boiling and gurgling.

A group of surfers surrounded him, chanting, "Surf, kook. Surf, kook."

On shore, his parents stood, watching. His mother cast her eyes to the ground, while his father shook his head in disgust.

A tremble ran through Travis's body, mixed with a sweltering rage. Pushing harder, he reached again for his board, but the water swept him off his feet and he landed on his back on the speckled earth.

The sky swirled red and orange overhead, and Devin leaned over him, laughing. Blood gushed from his right arm...

On the verge of screaming, Travis opened his eyes. He clamped his hand over his mouth and glanced around the room. The sun has risen, and he could hear the surf coming in through his open window. Beside him, Shayla slept soundly. Shifting positions, she pulled the blankets up to her chin, but she didn't wake.

He willed his body to stop shaking. He could feel it building, a panic attack. He hadn't had one in awhile—not since he'd started surfing again—but he recognized the symptoms: the rapid heartbeat, the nauseating dizziness, the tingling in his body, the tightening in his throat. He had read about it all on the internet.

"Control yourself," he mumbled, as he crawled out from under the covers. He dressed quickly and slipped out of the room.

A few minutes later, he stood on top of the cliff, holding his blue pipeboard. His grip on the fiberglass intensified as he stared out at the waves, and as the North Shore pounded the shores, his dream flashed before his eyes. *Surf, kook. Surf, kook.* He could still hear the obnoxious chanting.

His heart started to race again, the anxiety returning, and in less than a minute his mind was made up. Taking his surfboard with him, he sprinted past the house and jumped into his truck.

Still dressed in pajamas, Shayla burst through the

front door and ran toward him, flinching when her bare feet hit the sharp, rocky lane.

"Where are you going?" she shouted.

"I'm sorry," he mouthed through the window, as his foot pressed down on the gas pedal.

Surfers hovered on the horizon as spectators spread across the sand. From the top of the hill, Travis stood, watching it all. Pipeline was going off. It was firing double overhead, solid eight to ten feet, Hawaiian scale, with water glistening so clean he could see right through the waves.

Right away, his eyes found Kane. The reigning champion dropped down a twenty-foot face, caught a wicked barrel and leapt off the shoulder. Travis felt his determination rise. Crossing the beach, he headed for the water's edge and inhaled deeply as the spray of the sea splattered his skin, giving him goose bumps. A shiver ran though him. What if his board was really cursed?

He shook his head. That was stupid.

Strapping his leash to his ankle, he stood up, and once again, he watched. Though he knew Pipe better than most, he felt as if it were his first time out. He needed a plan. He needed to know exactly what he would do when he got out there.

Studying the sets, he memorized the patterns, the consistency, the molds. Some waves were bigger than others. Some steeper and faster. The second wave looked best, he decided. That was the one he wanted.

Stomach churning, he readied himself, his fingers tightening on fiberglass as he thought about the last time he'd tried to surf Pipe. He could still feel the fury of the ocean as it sucked him over the falls, swallowed him into the depths, and spewed him back onto the jagged reef.

Running his fingers over the scar on his forehead, he shook the thought from his mind. "It's not the same," he said. "Last time I was hungover. I wasn't focused."

He headed out.

"Wait!"

With one foot in the water, Travis turned.

Shayla ran toward him. "Trav, please don't." Her eyes flashed with fear and anger. Further up the beach, his father appeared. Devin followed behind.

"What'd you do? Tell everyone?" He shook his head.

"You don't have to do this," she pleaded.

His family drew closer.

Travis nodded. "Yeah, I do." He pushed some hair off her cheek and gave her a kiss. "It'll be okay," he said, and took off.

Paddling with all his might, he made it through the first bit of whitewater and glanced over his shoulder expecting to see his brother chasing him. But Devin remained on shore. He hadn't brought a surfboard.

Slowing down, Travis conserved his energy. The current of the channel worked with him, and he made it out to the lineup fairly easily, where he found Kane harassing a sun-freckled surfer.

"These all your waves or somethin'?" Travis sat up on his board.

Kane turned, and his mouth dropped open. The surfer he'd been taunting dropped into a sweet wave, but Kane didn't notice. He was too busy staring at Travis. "I thought you was goin' chicken out."

"You seem to think a lot of things. Like I care what you think, for one."

A local surfer paddled over. "You sure you wanna be out here, Kelly? I heard you ate it bad the last time."

Travis glared at him. "I'm gonna surf."

The guy threw his hands up. "Kay-den. It's your funeral."

~Heavy Juice~

Squinting into the distance, Shayla tried to spot Travis in the lineup. A tear slid down her cheek as she pictured his face covered in blood, his head cracked open on the reef.

Carl wrapped an arm around her shoulder. "Thanks for letting us know," he said.

She nodded but said nothing.

Next to them, Devin held a pair of binoculars to his eyes. "Damn it! Why didn't I bring my board?"

Shayla gave him a dirty look. "This is all your fault, you know."

With bated breath, they watched Travis choose a wave, and for a moment, it looked as if he might make it. Then he fell. His surfboard flew over the falls, and so did his body.

Shayla cried out. She knew she couldn't reach him, but she rushed into the water anyway. The current forced her to the side and she stumbled. Carl caught her in his arms and brought her back.

Steadying herself, she grabbed the binoculars from Devin's hand and peered through them. Something broke the surface. It was Travis. She pointed as another wave crashed down on him.

"No," she sobbed, as he disappeared again.

"Over there!" Carl exclaimed.

Travis's bright blue surfboard floated in the white water. Travis popped up beside it. *Thank God*, Shayla thought, as he reached for his stick. But he didn't come back to the shore. He turned around and paddled back out again.

"You're right." Devin stepped up beside her. "He's out there 'cause of me."

A surfer walked by, and Devin snatched the board from his hands. "I gotta borrow this," he said, and took off into the water.

Travis mustered his strength and headed back toward the breakers, struggling as he tried to duck-dive. One of the oncoming waves slammed him, setting him back a few feet, but he forced himself to keep going. His chest burned after taking such a massive pounding, and there was going to be some nasty reef rash on his leg. But he was alive, and he had almost gotten up.

The conditions of the last wave had been absolutely perfect. With the help of his paddling glove, he'd been able to slice through the water with enough momentum. The wave had lifted him; he had started to soar. If only he hadn't hesitated, he would have made it for sure.

Rejoining the lineup, he took his place next to the freckle-faced surfer Kane was harassing earlier. The guy stared at him, an awed look in his eyes. "You're a bit psycho, mate," he stated. He had an Australian accent.

Kane paddled over. "Brah, fo' real. You bettah stop it. You made your point already."

Travis scoffed at him. "Scared I'll catch the next one and show you up?"

"Whatevas'." Kane turned away.

The Aussie surfer rolled his eyes. "That bloke's really up himself."

Travis laughed and decided he liked the guy.

Still a bit winded from his wipeout, he relaxed on his board, letting the waves roll by. The whole time, Kane sat beside him, goading him on with nasty looks and snide remarks. Nothing he said mattered anymore, and finally, Travis turned to him and chuckled. "You gonna surf or just be a little bitch all day?"

"I waitin' for you, punk. You start 'em."

A dark depression formed on the horizon. The wave looked ideal, and Travis was in just the right spot. He threw out stink-eye, daring the others to try to stop him. This one was his. This time, he was going to make it.

He charged. He felt the wave lift his board. His feet hit the deck, and for a moment he was flying. Until the lip snatched him up and slammed him toward the ocean floor. Salt water burned up his nose and down his throat as he flailed and kicked, fighting the madness. His head broke the surface, and he managed to gulp a single breath of air before another giant sent him twirling all over again.

As his back scraped the reef, a piece of his rash guard caught on the coral and held him there. Twisting and thrashing against the rapids, Travis clawed at the fabric, and finally it ripped apart, freeing him.

The current whipped him around again.

As he twirled beneath the heavy juice, Travis started to panic. He didn't know how much longer he could hold his breath. There was a freezing pain in his temples, and a pounding in his ears. The tremendous pressure made him feel as though his limbs were made of mush. There was nothing left to do but pray—and try not to inhale the water rushing up his nose.

Dizziness overwhelmed him, and his body went limp. *There's no use*, he thought, as he let the ocean take him.

A hand grasped his arm, and he came up, choking. The air stung his lungs, piercing like needles. "I got you," someone said, as another wave crashed over them.

~The Real Problem~

Fighting the vicious waters, Devin hoisted his brother onto the surfboard he had borrowed. It tipped to one side, and Travis started to slide. "Hold on!" Devin pulled him back on. Travis's eyes rolled back into his head and he made a weird gurgling sound. Devin cried out, terrorized by fear. He had to make it back to shore. He had to save his brother.

He heard someone shouting, and two lifeguards arrived. They transferred Travis onto a rescue board and rode the whitewater in with him.

Devin followed, sputtering hysterically, "Is he gonna die? He's blue. I tried to get him."

As they reached the beach, Shayla and Carl came running up with more help. Another lifeguard joined in and helped the others carry Travis away from the lapping waves. They laid him on the ground and hovered over him. A large crowd pressed in on every side. Devin pushed through the people, trying to see. The rescuers blocked his view. He couldn't tell what they were doing, but he caught a glimpse of a resuscitation mask.

Devin froze, unable to move. This was it. Travis was going to die, and once again, he couldn't do anything to stop it.

Travis shuddered and gagged, spitting up a mouthful of sea and foamy white bile. With unclear eyes, he looked around. He took another breath and started coughing again, his lungs wheezing with every breath.

"Easy now." The lifeguard helped him sit up. "You swallowed a bunch of seawater, but you weren't out for long. Just relax and take it slow."

Travis's head spun and he blinked a few times, trying to stop it. Blood dripped into his eye, and he wiped it away. The cut on his forehead must have reopened.

"I'm sorry, Trav! I should'a got here sooner. I could'a stopped all this."

It took him a moment to realize who was talking. Devin knelt beside him, holding onto his arm. His dad was there, and Shayla too, her shoulders heaving with sobs. Travis shrank away from them all. He noticed all the people standing around, but they blended into one. He heard someone ordering the crowd to clear out and one of the lifeguards asked him his name. "Do you know where you are?" he questioned.

"Pipe," Travis mumbled.

The man tried to fix an oxygen mask over his mouth, but he pushed the contraption away. "I'm fine," he insisted. "I don't need any more help."

Travis sat up straighter and started coughing again.

"I think you should see a doctor," his father said.

"No," Travis barked. "I'll be fine. Please, everyone just go away." He shook his head, trying hard to clear his mind. "Where's my board?" The words came out slurred. "I gotta go back out."

"I'm sorry." The lifeguard shook his head. "We can't let you do that."

The fuzziness in Travis's mind rolled into turmoil. "I'm one of the top surfers in the world," he growled. "You can't stop me."

"We know who you are," the man stated. "But you're not in the right state. If you go back out there now, you'll be a hazard to yourself and the other surfers."

"Travis, listen to him," his father commanded.

"No. I have to do this!"

Travis stumbled forward onto the sand, and his vertigo returned full force. He wiped some bile off his cheek and got to his feet; stars blurred his vision.

Devin stepped in his way. "Are you tryin' to get yourself killed? You're not goin' surfing, bro. I ain't gonna let you!"

Travis stopped staggering, and with a half-crazed grunt, he smashed his fist into Devin's face. With a startled cry, Devin dropped to the ground, but he was quick to jump back up again. He stretched his arms out to the sides and stepped forward. "Hit me again!" he shouted. "Come on! You think you're goin' back out there? So, you make that wave. Then what? You need a bigger one and bigger? You gonna tackle Waimea next?"

Travis backed up.

His brother kept on him. "What you trying to prove? You here to show up Kane? I doubt it. You're not here for him. You're here 'cause of me. So hit me again, if it'll make you feel better!"

The world spun, and Travis fell to the side. He dropped to his knees and put his hand to his head. His fingers came away red. His stomach heaved, and he spewed another gut full of seawater onto the sand.

Devin quit yelling and knelt beside him—as did Shayla and his father. But Travis barely noticed them. Everything around him twisted in and out of focus. His chest burned from the salt in his lungs.

When his mind finally stopped spiraling, he looked up

and saw that his board had washed up on shore, broken in two pieces. Then he noticed Kane and several other surfers watching from one of the sponsor houses. Darkness and fatigue flooded up from within. "Get me outta here," he said. "I wanna go."

His father and Shayla helped him up and he leaned on them for support as they headed toward the parking lot. He refused to ride with his brother, so they took him to Shayla's car and settled him into the passenger seat. His dad grabbed a towel from the back and wiped the blood from his face. "Trav, why'd you go and do this? You don't need to prove yourself to anyone."

Travis pushed the towel away. "Yeah, right. You're the one who wanted me to compete in the first place. After Devin quit, you pushed and pushed. You wanted me to win that title."

Carl stepped back, the lines on his forehead growing deeper. "That was because you had talent. I didn't care if you won. I only pushed you to do it because I was trying to be a good father. I wanted you to do what you loved."

He wrapped the towel around Travis' elbow. It was covered in blood and sand from scraping across the reef.

He continued. "You didn't choose what happened to you, Trav. It's not your fault. It's no one's fault. And surfing Pipe isn't going to fix anything. I know it's hard, but it's how you handle these things that make you who you are. You need to figure out what you're angry about."

As his father spoke, Travis took a deep breath. His

pulse thumped so hard he could feel it in his temples. He slumped forward in the seat. His dad was right. His inner torment had nothing to do with riding waves, beating Kane, or mastering Pipe. Going out in heavy surf wasn't going to solve anything, because it wasn't the real problem. Neither was losing his arm.

The problem was Devin. It always had been.

Swaying slightly, he got out of the vehicle. He steadied himself and faced his brother. "You think I'm mad because you called Vince, but it's so much more than that. Ever since you left home, I've been trying to fill your shoes. Why do you think I joined the world tour? To make everyone else proud. To make up for *your* mistakes. I wanted to be great ... like you should've been!"

Devin heard the words, but even more so, he felt them. The accusations stabbed straight at his soul, as did the disappointment in his brother's eyes. It was all true. He should have been a better brother, a better person, but he had failed, and nothing he said could change that.

Yet he had to try.

From his pocket, he brought out the package of cocaine Vince had given him and thrust it into his brother's hand. "Here. I don't want this and I didn't take any. I kept it for you. So you'd believe me."

Travis held up the package with obvious doubt. "How do I even know this is the same stuff?"

Devin met his stare. "Do I look stoned?"

As his younger sibling studied him, a pain wrenched deep in Devin's chest. He was telling the truth. For once, he had done the right thing. But did it matter? Would Travis ever fully trust him again?

Their eyes remained fixed on each other.

Travis shook his head. "What about Mika? You gonna screw her over like you did to Lea?"

Devin felt the burn and let it go. "No Trav, I'm not."

"Seems like everything is riding on you staying clean. If you mess up again you're going to hurt a lot of people."

"I know, brah. I already hurt a lot of people, but how am I gonna fill my own shoes if you don't gimme a chance?"

Travis felt the pressure. Devin, his father, Shayla—they all stood watching, waiting to see what he was going to do. And what should his decision be? Travis didn't even know. His whole body hurt, but he ignored the pain and forced himself to think.

Over the last few months, he'd been getting along fine without his brother. With Shayla by his side and his relationship with his father closer than ever, he had been happy enough. But *happy enough* just wasn't what he wanted.

He thought about the surf school, the opportunity for a fresh start and a purpose. He needed to find his own way, his own destiny, yet he couldn't imagine doing so without Devin by his side. At least not without trying.

Feeling as if he was going to collapse, he leaned against the side of the car. Shayla pulled on his hand, insisting they needed to go. It was all too much. He just wanted the fighting to end. "Kay den." He gave his brother a nod. "I'll give you another chance, but if you screw up again, that's it. I got my own life to live."

Relief flooded Devin's eyes. He pulled Travis forward, embracing him. "No regrets, bro. I promise."

Travis pulled away weakly. "Yeah, we'll see."

~Beating the Odds~

As soon as they left the beach, Shayla insisted Travis go to the emergency room. "Is it really necessary?" he moaned. But he went to make her happy. After what he'd put her through, he owed her that much.

It was dark by the time they got back to his house. He had never felt so exhausted, but his mind was much too keyed up for sleep, so he and Shayla relaxed on a lounger out by the rocky beach at the edge of his father's property. He slid his arm around her. A strip of gauze covered his forehead, and he had bandages wrapped around his elbow and leg.

She smiled at him. "You look silly."

He shrugged. "That's what happens when you make me go to the doctor. Do you feel better now that you know I'm okay?"

She smiled again, and then frowned. "Promise you'll never scare me like that again, okay?"

He kissed her cheek and said with a wink, "We'll see."

She gave him a disapproving look. "You almost died out there!"

He stopped joking and took her hand. "I can't promise I'll never go surfing, but I won't go out if I'm not in the right frame of mind, okay?"

She nodded. "Never again when you're angry?"

"Never," he vowed.

Devin came out of the house and joined them. His arm was tied up in a sling. Shayla looked at the wrapping curiously but didn't say anything. "I'll let you guys talk," she said, and headed back to the house.

Travis pointed. "What's up with that?"

Devin shrugged. "Yesterday at Chun's, you told me to live without an arm for a day. So that's what I'm gonna do."

It thoughtful, and Travis almost laughed, but he held back. He had given Devin another chance, but he wasn't ready to be buddies with him yet. For that to happen, Devin needed to prove himself more.

Travis pressed the small bundle of cocaine into his brother's hands.

"What are you doin'?" Devin looked puzzled.

"I want you to get rid of it," Travis explained. "That way I'll know for sure."

Devin grinned, and with an indifferent shrug, he tossed the tiny bundle into the sea. "Fishies are getting high tonight. Better them than me."

As the drugs disappeared into the murky water, Travis felt a smile on his lips. Four months ago, there was no way his brother would have thrown away his coke. "I'm proud of you, Dev."

Devin wrapped an arm around his shoulders. "Right back atcha, lil' braddah."

Stretching out on the chair, Travis shook his head and let out a chuckle. He pointed at the sling again. "You're really gonna wear that thing for a day?"

"Heck yeah," Devin replied, "but it's frickin' annoying already. I can hardly do anything."

Travis laughed and waved his hand toward the ocean. "You should go try surfing."

"Tha's nuts, bro! I ain't goin' out there like this!"

Smiling widely, Travis peeled off his own bandages and tossed them on the ground. Six stitches held the wound above his eye shut, and his arm and leg were covered in scrapes and bruises, but it didn't bother him.

He stared out at the shadowy waves. He could barely see them from where he sat, but he could hear them pounding the shores. Soon the North Shore would die out completely for the summer, but there was still some juice left in the sets.

His brother sat on the chair beside him. "Shayla still pissed at you?" he asked.

"Nah. She was just worried," Travis answered.

Devin gave him a sideways glance and a knowing

smirk. "You're already thinkin' 'bout surfing Pipe again, aren't you?"

Travis couldn't help but laugh. His brother had him pegged. Although he had nothing left to prove, he was still a surfer, and surfing was all about challenging nature—beating the odds against something so gnarly it could crush the life right out of you if it chose to.

Plus it was fun.

"I almost got up out there, ya know."

Devin snickered and stuck out his hand. "Well, next time take me with you, okay? And maybe try when the waves ain't so big."

Travis shook on it. "Deal."

As the two brothers smiled at each other, Devin pulled something out of his pocket and held it up. Moonlight flickered off the keys to the surf school. "Tomorrow mornin' bright and early, you wanna go open up shop, get this business goin'?"

Travis almost burst with excitement. "Yeah, bro. I can't wait."

~Grand Opening~

Two weeks after the doors opened, Kelly Bros' Surf School held its official grand opening celebration. At the beach at Ali'i, just a few blocks from their building, people lined up by the cooking tents, eager to enjoy the tasty hamburgers and ice cold drinks. The high noon sun shone brightly above, baking the beachgoers, providing perfect weather for a fun afternoon.

Travis couldn't believe how many people had shown up for the barbeque lunch. Almost everyone he knew had come to show their support, including some of his old surfing buddies. He smiled when he saw them and greeted them with high fives and welcoming embraces.

Out in the water, children splashed in the shallows with boogie boards, while others tried their hand at surfing the small beginner waves. It was well into spring now, so the swells on the North Shore had died down, and a day like today was the perfect time for learning.

"I goin' be your bestest student," Makani boasted.

Travis ruffled his hair. "For sure, Mak, although you may have some competition." He glanced over at his niece.

Taking a huge bite out of her burger, Allisa smiled and tugged her father's hand. "You'll teach me, right, Daddy?"

Devin grinned and pointed to a big foam board. "Wanna go now?"

Travis laughed as Allisa tried her best to help drag the longboard down to the water. He watched Devin coax her into the soup, and in no time at all, she was standing and riding toward shore.

"Uncle Travis!" she called out. He waved back.

Beside him, Mika sat under a pink umbrella, running her hand over her rounded belly as she sipped her iced tea. "I heard about Shayla's dad," she said. "Is he really going to rehab?"

Travis smiled. "Yeah. He checked himself in last night. We're pretty stoked about it."

"Sweet." She smiled back. "I hope it works as good for him as it did for Dev. Shayla deserves to have her father back. He used to be such a nice man."

With a happy nod, Travis looked out at the surf again. Allisa had already given up surfing and was running back up the beach, leaving her dad to carry in the board.

Shayla slid up next to him and slipped her arm around his waist. He gave her a squeeze as she nuzzled into him.

He looked around at his friends. To the right, Kimo was telling Brady all about his latest surfing disaster. From the sounds of it, Kimo had taken a beating out at Bowls and had broken his favorite board.

"Man, that sucks," Travis commented.

Kimo nodded. "Yeah, brah. I got pounded. Try look." Turning around, he showed Travis his back, which was all cut up from the jagged coral.

Brady rolled up a towel and whipped him across the exposed skin. Hollering, Kimo whirled around and punched him in the arm. "Ow, you jerk! Sore you know!" He rubbed his back, and everybody laughed.

Suddenly, Travis froze. Kane headed toward them. He didn't say anything, nor did he stop, but as he passed, he glanced at Travis and nodded slightly.

Surprised, Travis nodded back.

"Wha's that all about?" Devin asked, plopping down on the blanket beside him.

Travis shrugged and watched his old rival join some friends at the other end of the beach. "Guess he knows he don't bug me no more. Maybe he's given up trying. Besides, he's your problem now." Travis jabbed Devin in the ribs. "You better start practicing if you're going to beat that guy this season."

Travis smiled proudly. The world tour was starting up again in a couple weeks, and Devin had been granted a wild card—a guaranteed spot on the tour.

"Kane's nothing," Shayla piped up. "You better watch out for my cousin."

"Das right, brah!" Kimo gave his future competitor a slap upside the head.

Devin jumped to his feet and lunged at the surfer, wrestling him onto the ground. Travis laughed at them both, and when the friendly brawl ended, he pulled his brother aside. "I feel like catching some waves. After the party, you wanna cruise to Bowls?"

Devin grinned. "Fo' shua, lil' braddah!"

Later that evening, Carl stood with Iva and Shayla on the rocks at Ala Maona Beach Park, watching his two boys surf. In the distance, Diamond Head jutted out to sea, and a huge yacht crossed the golden-red horizon. The sound of steel guitars occasionally drifted in from the hotel patios on Waikiki Beach, as the first of the tiki lights came on.

Carl wrapped an arm around Iva's shoulder. Beside them, Shayla held her binoculars to her eyes, a smile crossing her lips as Travis leapt off a wave and into the air. Devin followed with a similar move.

A man with a large camera walked up, a local surf photographer. He stopped and peered through his lens. "Is that the Kelly brothers out there?" He snapped some pictures. "Never thought I'd see that again."

Carl smiled. "Me neither," he said, as he hugged Iva tightly.

~

408

A Note on Pro Surfer, Bethany Hamilton:

In publishing Liquid Comfort, it is a concern that some people will think I'm trying to capitalize on the recent popularity of Bethany Hamilton's story/autobiography, *Soul Surfer*. However, this simply isn't the case. When I started Liquid Comfort in 2001, I had no idea that a real surfer living in Hawaii would actually live Travis's fate.

In 2003, Bethany Hamilton, an American professional surfer, lost her arm in a shark attack on the island of Kaua'i. Originally, I had my main character, Travis, never surfing again. However, when Bethany overcame her injury and returned to professional surfing, it astonished the world and I knew I had to revise my story.

Since recovering from her shark attack, Bethany has participated in numerous ASP and World Tour Events with her major highlight being a second place finish in the ASP 2009 World Junior Championships. She is a true inspiration to people everywhere, including me and my writing.

- Cheryl Petro

Watch for Other Books by Cheryl Lee Petro:

Damn You

&

The Home Heart Series

COMING SOON!!!!

www.cherylleepetro.com

Email: cherylleepetro@gmail.com

Made in the USA
Lexington, KY
10 November 2013